Yashin was KGB. Yashin wasn't just a target: he was an adversary to be reckoned with.

Soon, perhaps dawn tomorrow, they would call on Anatoly. Question him, harass him. 'You knew your father was going to defect, didn't you.' And then: 'He's sick, mentally disturbed, but you can help him – plead with him to come back.'

Yashin, having been a KGB officer for ten years, knew exactly what form the interrogation would take. But they wouldn't hurt him, not yet: they didn't know what he had taken with him. Despite the heat Yashin shivered.

DEREK LAMBERT

Chase

SPHERE BOOKS LIMITED

SPHERE BOOKS LTD

Published by the Penguin Group
27 Wrights Lane, London W8 5TZ, England
Viking Penguin Inc., 40 West 23rd Street, New York, New York 10010, USA
Penguin Books Australia Ltd, Ringwood, Victoria, Australia
Penguin Books Canada Ltd, 2801 John Street, Markham, Ontario, Canada L3R 1B4
Penguin Books (NZ) Ltd, 182–190 Wairau Road, Auckland 10, New Zealand

Penguin Books Ltd, Registered Offices: Harmondsworth, Middlesex, England

First published in Great Britain by Hamish Hamilton Ltd 1987
Published by Sphere Books Ltd 1988

Copyright © 1987 by Derek Lambert

Printed and bound in Great Britain by
Richard Clay Ltd, Bungay, Suffolk

For Gunar and Vari in Florida

ACKNOWLEDGEMENTS

My thanks to Charles and Julia Bolton for providing me with a beautiful and tranquil haven in Florida from which to research this book.

CHAPTER 1

To begin with an ending.

The end of normality for Mikhail Yashin sitting in the back of a black Buick bearing diplomatic plates taking him from New York's Kennedy Airport to Manhattan.

Such was the mass and momentum of the traffic, such was the nonchalant venom of the drivers juggling their vehicles, that Yashin, on his first visit to the USA, should have been awed. But the traffic scarcely registered; nor did the first glimpse of clustered skyscrapers.

Yashin's focus was escape.

He concentrated on red traffic lights. On the spaces between trucks and taxis and limousines waiting for the green. On the demeanour of the man sitting beside him behind the driver.

Dobykin, who looked like a sturdy Russian general fattened by a desk job, pointed at the distant high-rise, serene beneath a blue summer sky. "The gates to the Land of Opportunity. You don't seem very impressed, comrade."

"'Fungi spawned on the rotten bed of capitalism' according to my last lecturer."

"Ah, those warnings about the fleshpots of the West. A little over-stated. Envy perhaps. What do you think, comrade?"

Less than an hour in America and he was being tested. "I prefer the domes of the Kremlin," unclenching his fists so that Dobykin wouldn't notice the polish on his knuckles.

"A somewhat premature judgement, comrade. In any case

it wasn't what I asked."

A bruised yellow taxi swung in front of them. The muscular shoulders of the driver of the Buick stiffened beneath his jacket.

Yashin, lean and contained, said: "I didn't understand the question."

"The advice we get drummed into us before we come here . . . I asked if you thought it was exaggerated."

Dobykin, chief of the KGB operation in the United States, masquerading as a diplomat with the Soviet Union's Mission to the United Nations, would be expected to report on his initial reactions to America.

The driver leaned back, ears tuned.

"Exaggerated?" Two hundred metres ahead a traffic light shone green; by the time they got there it would be red. "Flamboyant perhaps." The whine of tyres on the road surface was elastic pulled through his brain. "But dulled by repetition."

"Really?" Dobykin was intrigued: newcomers didn't doubt. He popped a peppermint into his mouth and crunched it.

Fifty metres ahead the light was still green. Neighbouring drivers on the broad highway strained to reach it in time. Thirty metres.

" . . . the envy."

"I'm sorry?"

"I asked," grinding the peppermint, "whether you thought the advisers might be motivated by envy."

"It depends," as the lights changed to red, "whether the adviser," as the driver of the Buick braked, "has been to the West before."

"He wouldn't be lecturing if he hadn't."

Yashin placed his left hand lightly on the door handle. "I suppose you're right."

The Buick stopped between a taxi and a long black limousine that looked like a hearse.

Yashin pulled the handle gently but firmly. Nothing. He pointed with his right hand.

"What?" Dobykin followed the arrow of Yashin's finger. "I can't see anything," a blade of suspicion forged by a working life of distrust already in his voice.

"There!" Yashin's other hand was a talon on the handle. "In the sky."

The driver's head moved fractionally.

Dobykin turned his blunt profile towards Yashin. "Did you have a lot to drink on the plane?" he asked as the lights turned green, as the traffic began to advance, as, still pulling the handle, Yashin shouldered open the door and fell on the highway beside the wheel of the black limousine.

Then he was on his feet, dodging vehicles, pushing at their hoods with his hands. Horns blared, faces gaped. As he crossed the central divider in front of the oncoming traffic Yashin waited for the first shot. He glanced behind. The driver, gun in hand, was weaving his way through the accelerating traffic; the lane behind the stationary Buick was congested and the drivers were leaning on their horns, anxious to get away from trouble.

Beside the divider the driver paused, aiming the pistol in a two-fisted grip. Yashin dived into the traffic; he thought he heard the shot but he couldn't be sure: his priority was avoiding vehicles – they came at him like punches.

One sedan was only trundling though. It was big and green and battered with a rusty wound round the base of its bodywork and it was filled with blacks. He ran with it, pulled a blistered door handle and piled in.

The grey-haired black at the wheel said: "Hey, who the fuck are you?" but he wasn't outraged; nor were his passengers.

"Hi honky," one of them said. "You coming on vacation with us?" He inhaled smoke greedily from a cigarette and passed it to his neighbour. The sedan was a canister of pot fumes.

"Gotta pay your way," another said; they all laughed.

Yashin said: "You've got to help me. They're trying to kill me." He pointed through the window towards the barrier where the driver was aiming the pistol again.

"Gotta die some time, honky."

The bullet hit the rear window showering them with nuggets of shatter-proof glass.

"Holy shit!" The driver trod on the gas pedal.

3

The second bullet hit the bodywork low down.

"Going for the tyres," one of them said.

The sedan jerked forward, stalled. The driver turned the key. "Told you we should have dumped this mother and gotten ourselves a couple of cabs." The engine fired. He pressed the gas pedal, more gently this time. The sedan moved forward majestically.

As it picked up speed, changing lanes, taking on all-comers, Yashin saw the Buick driver's hand drop to his side.

They dumped him outside the Pan-Am complex at Kennedy. "Going for a little peace and quiet," the driver told him, "so maybe it's no great idea for you to come with us." He leaned out of the window and punched Yashin on the shoulder. "Good luck, honky. By the way, where you from?"

"Home," Yashin said.

*   *   *

On his second journey into Manhattan, Yashin relaxed fractionally for the first time since he had left Moscow that morning on the new direct flight to New York.

He observed the marauding cars and ruthless trucks, small villas proclaiming their independence, the famous collection of high-rise looking vulnerable in the afternoon sunlight. And it wasn't until the taxi, driven by a young Fidel Castro, stopped in Queens Tunnel under the East River that he stiffened because, to a claustrophobic, a tunnel is a gun-barrel with a bullet in it.

Yashin who hadn't been affected by confined spaces until three years ago – "A neurosis reflecting the conflicts of your job," according to a psychiatrist – fought the bird inside him struggling to escape.

Its wings touched the sides of the tunnel.

The driver shouted: "Roadworks. Been like this for months." He pulled irritably at his beard.

The line of traffic inched forward, stopped. Yashin tried not to consider the weight of water above the tunnel and reassured himself like an understanding nurse. His chest ached with confinement.

The driver said: "Look at those guys."

4

Yashin gazed down the gun-barrel and saw two men, stocky and unremarkable, hurrying past the panting traffic, peering into the windows of cabs and limousines. Dobykin surely couldn't have covered all the entries into Manhattan so quickly. Could he?

The traffic moved funereally. Most of the drivers, insular inside their capsules, remained impassive; a few spoke angrily with their hands. A tunnel overseer read a magazine in his cabin. Yashin noticed that one of the two men, now only six vehicles away, had a pistol bulge in his jacket.

He said to the driver: "Who are they?" The driver shrugged theatrically. *Who knows, who cares?* He combed his sideburns into his beard with his fingers.

The traffic picked up speed when the two men were separated from the taxi by two cars. Yashin felt their scrutiny as the cab swept towards the widening mouth of light ahead.

The driver said: "Cops. Guess they know who they're looking for and it wasn't me or you."

He dropped Yashin on 42nd Street outside Bryant Park. Normally when he left an enclosed area the bird flew away but alone in an alien sweating city, hunted by his own kind, the claustrophobia took on a new dimension and the bird stayed in its ribbed cage.

Concentrate on a single phenomenon, the psychiatrist had advised him. He concentrated on the park because it was small and ordinary, thin plane trees and beds of dusty ivy edging the paths, a policeman at every corner, each wearing a moustache.

In common with most Russians, Yashin had seen New York in movies and he felt conspicuous as though, labelled Russian by the Slavic angles of his features and the cut of his blue suit and the cheap shine of his Czech-made shoes, he had wandered into a film in the Metropole cinema on Sverdlov Square.

He walked past a stall blooming with cut flowers; he could smell their perfume above the fumes of the traffic. Carnations. In the short frenzy of the Russian summer his apartment in the Arbat had smelled of carnations. And of Galina's perfume before she left him.

A white van stood at the kerb. A counter had been

5

unfolded from one side and an earnest young man was leaning on it offering advice on how to stop drinking. In front of the van two men, one black, one white with hopeless features, were arguing. The white man handed the black some dollar bills and pocketed a small packet. A drug deal?

An elegant woman walked past leading a poodle on a chain; the poodle was wearing sunglasses. A fat man corked his mouth with a hot dog. Two sunny girls on roller-skates waltzed by. A silver balloon shaped like a heart escaped from a child's hand and sailed towards the distant channel of sky.

Yashin stopped at a row of chess tables. "Fifty cents a game, three bucks if you win," said a man with tousled hair and tired eyes. Yashin had beaten many an old-stager in Gorky Park. He handed over a dollar bill, pocketed the change and began to play.

Where was Galina now? As if it mattered. Where was his son? Yashin glanced at his watch – even that small motion was time enough for his opponent, an automaton, to make a move and punch his clock. It was night in Moscow. Anatoly would probably be in bed. With a girl? He *was* 18. What would happen to him when news of his father's defection reached Moscow?

Yashin pushed a pawn forward. His opponent swept a bishop across the board, punched his clock, stared at the buttocks of a girl in tight jeans. Yashin castled.

In Gorky Park the old-stagers, fuelled on vodka, played deep into winter only abandoning the rows of worn tables when their breath crystallised and their mittened fingers froze in mid-gambit. Long ago he and Galina had travelled to the sky together on the ferris wheel in Gorky Park.

His opponent moved a knight. "Your move," he said when Yashin, still in Moscow, failed to respond.

Pedestrians strode purposefully past. The resolve, that was what was different to Muscovite crowds: these people weren't just going home: each had a project.

Yashin moved a bishop purposefully. "Don't forget your clock, buddy," his opponent said.

And I will miss the song of skates on ice and the numbed silence of the forest and the babushka crocheting a shawl in a corner of a room as hot as an oven . . .

"Sure you want to play?"

Yashin moved his king's rook one square.

"You know something?" his opponent said. "Maybe once a day I meet brain muscle. And I thought maybe you had it but I was wrong. And you know something else? That makes me unhappy because I'm just a computer." He moved his queen. "Want to quit?"

Yashin resigned and, crossing 42nd, made his way down Fifth Avenue. Past emporiums of elegance and opulence that perversely beckoned images of half-empty stores in Moscow. Warm images. Galina's cheeks had been bright and bunched with excitement when she had found a store selling a new consignment of clothes from Hungary or Yugoslavia.

On this side of the avenue St. Patrick's Cathedral, on the other Rockefeller Center. Outside Tiffany's a begger with a dog holding a placard: I'M BLIND. PLEASE HELP. HAVE A GOOD DAY.

At 59th Yashin crossed Plaza Square and entered Central Park. He had read that poor families raising pigs and goats had been evicted from the site so that the park could be laid out to accommodate the carriages of the rich; according to a newspaper article it was now a hunting ground for degenerates.

This evening it was populated with the joggers and cyclists and lovers. He walked down the Mall and sat on a bench overlooking the lake. A young man rowed past, a small boy in the stern of the boat trailing his fingers in the mossy water; he and Anatoly ten years ago.

Soon, perhaps dawn tomorrow, they would call on Anatoly. Question him, harass him. "You knew your father was going to defect, didn't you." And then: "He's sick, mentally disturbed, but you can help him – plead with him to come back."

Yashin, having been a KGB officer for 10 years, knew exactly what form the interrogation would take. But they wouldn't hurt him, not yet: they didn't know what he had taken with him. Despite the heat Yashin shivered.

CHAPTER 2

He recognised Hamilton at once. Athlete's muscles beginning to wander, fair hair thinning, handsome head slightly
bowed as though he were looking for answers that had eluded
him all his life.

He stood on the iron bridge across the lake peering into the
dusk. My partner, Yashin thought. My adversary. He walked
half way across the bridge and stood in front of Hamilton.

Hamilton offered his hand. His grasp invited trust. He said:
"You pick the darndest places to meet. Muggers' paradise at
this time of day."

"If I can't cope with muggers I shouldn't be in the KGB."

"I doubt if you are anymore."

At Bethesda Fountain they turned down the Mall. The
evening had brought a trace of cruelty with it; good citizens
walked with care and the battlements of residential Fifth
Avenue were inky with menace.

"I guessed it would be you," Yashin said.

"You have a file on me?"

"Of course. They say you're the best." Sympathetic,
according to the computer. "You got here quickly: I only
called Washington an hour ago."

"I happened to be in New York."

Yashin stopped walking. "Listen," he said, "I've done my
homework. I know a little about New York. Michelin, Fodor,
the KGB guide. I know Central Park . . ."

"So?"

"There's a statue of Hans Christian Andersen in the park.

8

Right?"

"You probably know more about New York than me, Comrade Yashin. Isn't that often the way with strangers?"

"Leave the fairy stories to Mr. Andersen," Yashin said. "You flew to New York from Washington when you heard that I had jumped out of the car picking me up at Kennedy."

Hamilton smiled wryly. "This is going to be an interesting relationship."

"You heard from an informant inside the Soviet Mission?"

"I caught the shuttle," Hamilton said. "I called Washington when I landed. They said you had 'phoned."

An old woman wearing sneakers and eating bread from a paper-bag wandered past staring at them incuriously. In Moscow she would have been in the corner of an overcrowded room sharing the past with children.

"I hope we can continue like this," Yashin said. He started to walk again.

"You've created one hell of a stir," Hamilton said. "But I guess you realise that."

"You wouldn't be here otherwise."

"We're taking you to a safe house."

"How safe?"

"Fort Knox is open house by comparison." Hamilton glanced behind him and Yashin said: "He's a hundred metres behind us, wearing a fawn raincoat and an FBI hat. It isn't their shoes that betray American policemen, it's their hats."

"It's in Vermont," Hamilton said. "Very pretty, very historic." His eyes searched the ground ahead of him. "You see you're something special Gaspadeen Yashin."

Americans in Russia introduced first names after the first handshake; Yashin cringed from such precocity; he hoped Hamilton wouldn't offer his just yet.

Hamilton said: "The car's parked on Central Park South. This is your first visit to New York?"

"You know it is."

"I was in Moscow once, briefly."

"Second secretary, commercial section. Did you enjoy Moscow, Mr Hamilton?"

"It was weird, I seemed to see it from a distance. Now I see it more clearly."

9

"You left after three months. Did your people think that was enough time to see the other side?"

"It wasn't long enough," Hamilton said. "Not nearly long enough."

They skirted the pond at the south-east tip of the park. A bird squawked in the sanctuary across the water. Nocturnal life began to awake around them.

"Couldn't you have parked the car closer?" Yashin asked.

"It's easier to get the introductions over walking. Sitting in the back of a limousine, it's like being in a confessional."

"And now I must warn you—"

"Don't," Hamilton interrupted. "Whatever you were going to say, leave it for now. We'll start tomorrow."

"Do you know why I defected?"

"I'm not sure that you have defected yet."

"You have an indirect approach, Mr. Hamilton. You answer questions and yet you don't answer them. I don't think such an approach comes naturally to you."

"I'm in intelligence like you. Is anything natural in our profession?"

They left the park, dark pastures of conspiracy and degeneracy, by the Artist's Gate. In front of them New York, wearing her jewels, reached for the stars.

"What were your first impressions?" Hamilton asked as they walked towards a limousine parked by the kerb.

"New York? As I expected it," Yashin lied. New York intimidated him.

Hamilton swept his arm in an arc. "They're out there in the jungle stalking you," he said.

Directed by Kiselev. Nominally Dobykin would be in charge of the manhunt but the assassins of Executive Action took little heed of bureau chiefs.

"And tomorrow," Hamilton remarked, "the Soviet protests will start."

"Maybe not so soon. The Mission will first want to be sure that I have defected. They won't want to make fools of themselves."

"Like we did with Yurchenko?"

"I hope," Yashin said as they climbed into the back of the limousine, "that your questions are going to be more subtle

10

than that. Please don't disappoint me, Mr. Hamilton.''

The driver turned his head. Hamilton nodded. The limousine took off. Followed by another.

* * *

He awoke to the smell of coffee and frying bacon; his imagination cut loose and embraced orange juice, toast, butter and honey. His last breakfast in Moscow had been lemon tea, black bread and cheese. He felt ashamed of his appetite.

He swung his legs out of the bed and sat naked on the edge. The house was built of wood and the room smelled of clean dust. There were a few books on the bed-side table; he had opened one last night but left it unread, a Saul Bellow. The light reaching him through cornflower-blue drapes made his body very pale.

He drew the curtains and saw green hills webbed with trails, thistledown clouds in a serene sky, lawns sparkling with dew and beds of petunias and snapdragons. Beside a tall laurel hedge stood a man in a black raincoat.

Yashin stood up. He wished he had a change of clothes; his suit and shirt hung in the closet creased and soiled with yesterday's deceit. He padded into the bathroom; a white robe hung from the door; he put it on to hide his nakedness and his scars.

He picked up the electric razor on the shelf above the washbasin and began to shave. Slanting grey eyes above high, cheekbones looked at him conspiratorially. Four days had transformed his expression. It had been steadfast, complacent perhaps; now it was a secret.

He showered and ran a comb, still bearing a stick-on price tab, through his dark crewcut, blew the bristles, lightly salted with grey, from the head of the razor. He wondered if anyone was watching him.

When he returned to the bedroom he found a change of clothes on the bed. Navy V-neck sweater, white shirt, grey slacks, brown tweed jacket. His own clothes had gone.

Hamilton was sitting at the table in the kitchen drinking black coffee. He wore a clerical grey suit and he looked tired, as though he had slept with his questions. He pointed at a

11

hotplate. "Help yourself, Mikhail."

"No devilled kidneys?"

"Should there be?"

"In the stately homes in old American films there were always devilled kidneys on a silver dish on the sideboard. Ronald Colman loved them."

"This isn't a stately home." Hamilton dropped a sweetener into a fresh cup of coffee. "Are you a film buff?"

"Only old black-and-white movies. You can see them in the Soviet Union if they portray western decadence." Yashin sat down with a plateful of scrambled eggs and bacon. "I've been in love with Paulette Goddard since I was a boy."

Hamilton said: "You speak very good English. Where did you learn?"

"Moscow University. I'm sure you know that."

"And then the Gagarin Air Force Academy?"

"Has the interrogation begun?"

"I want to be able to talk to my superiors about you with familiarity."

"Have a word with your computer."

"You're forty-two?"

"Forty-three," Yashin said.

"And you really left the Academy speaking English . . . like a native?"

"After the accident," Yashin told him, "I took an intensive course at Higher Intelligence School 101 on the outskirts of Moscow. I'm sure you know that as well. I thought we agreed last night that we would be honest with each other."

Yashin surveyed the kitchen. It was an electric show-room, from toaster to dishwasher. When a washing-machine had been installed in their apartment in the Arbat he and Galina had declared a day of rejoicing.

"I know what you're thinking," Hamilton said. "It's decadent."

"Only if such luxuries are confined to a privileged few."

"Nothing unusual about this kitchen."

"They have them in Harlem?"

Hamilton said: "Help yourself to more coffee. Or would you have preferred tea? I should have thought of that," he reproved himself.

"A difficult decision. Would tea with lemon help me to relax or make me homesick?"

"You can have anything you want. Do anything you like within reason."

"But only here." Yashin looked out of the window; they were on the opposite side of the house to the bedroom. A gravel drive led to wrought-iron gates tipped with gold-painted spikes. A muscular gardener was trimming the grass round a bed of petunias. "One of yours?"

"A crack shot," Hamilton said. His hands moved restlessly, the hands of a reformed smoker looking for employment. "Letz is coming here at ten. You know who he is, I presume?"

"Your boss. A hard liner."

"He'll want to know whether you're going to co-operate."

"So what are you going to tell him?"

"That you seem reasonable."

"You don't even know why I defected."

"You're here, that's all that matters at the moment."

Yashin studied his own hands. He had always been particular about them but this morning the nails were chipped – together with excess loose change in your pockets, a reminder of a heavy night.

He said: "Tell him I must be able to telephone Moscow whenever I want and I must have an assurance that the calls won't be monitored."

A helicopter clattered overhead. Hamilton consulted his wristwatch, stood up and swallowed the last mouthful of coffee. They drink coffee like we drink vodka, Yashin thought.

"And then you'll co-operate?"

"Just tell them about the telephone."

"He's very anxious to meet you. You're the first one from the Eighth Directorate."

"But he won't do the dirty work. That's your department. You have quite a reputation, Mr. Hamilton."

"John," Hamilton said. "Most people call me Jack." He smiled and was ten years younger. He stood up. "If you want anything, tell the gardener."

"About my suit," Yashin said. "You won't have much

13

trouble, it's Russian stitching. But take my advice, don't bother, there's nothing there."

* * *

The gardener brought him *The New York Times* rolled up in transparent plastic. "All the News That's Fit to Print." You couldn't say that about *Pravda* or *Izvestia*.

But Yashin didn't believe that a free press, sanctified in the West, was necessarily in the interests of the people. Dissent, violence, promiscuity: they were all infectious and an unfettered press was a carrier.

He scanned the front page. Nicaragua and the rebels. When is a rebel a terrorist? When he's on the other side, that's when. Star Wars. Charges of police brutality in New York's police force . . . Why did they publicly undermine trust in the law? In the CIA even. In the Soviet Union neither allegations nor punishments were published; it was better that way.

And the by-lines. The American family tree, inverted branches fingering the world. Fuerbringer, Weinraub, Sciolino, Roberts, Lubasch, Raab, Hedrick Smith . . . Didn't he write a book about Russia?

Yashin turned the pages, pausing at the sports section. He liked the bold ring of baseball. Pirates, Cardinals, Giants, Red Sox . . . He balanced the paper in one hand: it weighed more than a week's *Pravda*s.

He patrolled the living-quarters. Stripped pine, casually distributed rugs, antique furniture – some of it genuine – the memory of winter log fires lingering on the imprisoned air. He had visited dachas like this in the woods girdling Moscow where the *nachalstvo* spent their weekends.

He tried to assess where the bugs and cameras were installed. They would be difficult to locate because this house, not as old as it seemed, would have been designed with surveillance in mind. And the ears and eyes would be listening and watching now; even when he was talking to Hamilton they would be activated to pick up stress, lies and evasions.

Security, too, would be clenched after the Yurchenko fiasco. No chance of this prize catch changing his mind and bolting to the Soviet Mission on East 67th Street. The walls of the living room closed in upon Yashin; wings fluttered in his chest. He opened a window.

The gardener was cutting the laurel hedge with an electric trimmer; polished leaves fell like manicured fingers. The helicopter passed low overhead; plants cowered beneath its blades.

It would be late afternoon in Moscow. In the gloomy chambers of KGB headquarters on Dzerzhinsky Square the consternation of the morning would have been inflamed by vodka lunches at the Aragvi or the Ararat. And no one would be more inflamed than Vasily Lozak, head of the Eighth Directorate, who had tried to frame him.

Who had tipped off Yashin? Where was he? What did he intend to do? How much does he know?

Yashin joined Lozak, sleekly heavy, family man and black-mailer, as he stood at the window of his office facing Dietsky Mir, the biggest toy shop in the world, and shared his frustration: poised to accuse a dupe of planning to defect, beaten to the draw! But what would be worrying Lozak most was how Yashin intended to hit back.

He had two weapons: his insurance policy and Tuslov in the Eighth Directorate. The first might protect Anatoly physically; the second might be able to nail Lozak. *Might.* Is that the best you can do, Yashin? Even now they were probably questioning Anatoly. What would an 18-year-old boy know about the guiles of trained interrogators?

Come to that, how intransigent will I be, faced by a professional? Hamilton *was* good: his name had materialised first in green quivering letters when Yashin had consulted a computer before flying to New York. He pretended to see the other side of the coin, the electronic brain had sneered.

Should I call Moscow now regardless of the inevitable telephone tap? Alert Tuslov? Tell him to warn the Chairman of State Security and the interrogators of Special Investigations that if Anatoly comes to any harm I will talk?

Yashin picked up a cream telephone. The line was dead.

He switched on the television. A voice: "Spiderman and his friends will return after this message," followed by a man wearing a wig selling cars at prices no one else could match.

Yashin returned to the kitchen. He switched on the electric

15

kettle, found some teabags and a dessicated lemon in the refrigerator and made himself a glass of tea. To the invisible microphones he said: "Please send loose tea, fresh lemons and a samovar."

He sipped the sharp beverage; it comforted him. If Dzerzhinsky Square was alarmed then East 67th Street would be in shock. Dobykin's men would be shaking down New York and Washington, contacting every informant inside American intelligence, while Kiselev from Executive Action waited. Some defectors were allowed to escape unmolested: not one from the Eighth Directorate.

A car drew up at the gates. The limousine that had picked him up outside Central Park. Behind the driver sat Hamilton and a companion, Letz.

Letz was a nerve-ending, razored instincts disguised by languor. The languor was accompanied by occasional affectations of speech, elaborate manoeuvres, that Yashin, his own speech sensor, detected rather than identified. Letz was in his mid-forties with brittle blue eyes, soft silver-blond hair and a keep-fit sheen about him.

In the living room where they sat in a triangle, deep in American history, Letz took a file from his briefcase, extracted a clip of computer print-outs, and said: "So, to what do we owe this pleasure, Comrade Yashin?"

"I'm here, that's all that matters at the moment."

"I wish that were so." Letz smiled politely. "But more is at stake than just your physical presence, Comrade Yashin."

"Mister," Yashin said. "We're in America. And you're not a communist." He smiled for the first time since he had landed at Kennedy. "Or are you Comrade Letz?"

"You operated in a very sensitive area in the Soviet Union. You must possess knowledge that can further the interests of mutual understanding." Letz turned to Hamilton. "Isn't that so, Jack?"

"He was Eighth Directorate, sure."

"Communications, extremely sensitive. Not just codes. Space, satellites . . ." Letz consulted the file. "Have you fully recovered from the accident, *Mr*. Yashin?"

"That was a long time ago."

"Your injuries were horrific. We had a similar accident

16

over here. There should be more co-operation . . ."

Yashin said: "I told Hamilton that I must be able to call Moscow whenever I want. I have a son there."

"I have three sons, Mr. Yashin. I understand. Of course you can call Moscow."

"No bugs?"

"No bugs."

Yashin noted the disbelief on Hamilton's face.

Letz said: "And your wife, do you want to talk to her?"

"We were divorced five years ago," Yashin said. "We hardly ever see each other."

"Your reasons for defecting must have been acute. You know, leaving a son behind . . . You must be very confident that no harm will come to him."

"I have to make that call."

"And then you will co-operate?"

"Then we can talk."

"You must understand that we have to be absolutely sure of your intentions. We've had some unfortunate experiences recently. We used to be much more tolerant."

Yashin wished Letz would be conducting the interrogation: it would be very easy not to tell him anything. Or was this a technique? One hostile, one sympathetic. Surely they wouldn't be so amateurish; there was too much at stake.

" . . . when this is all over," Letz was saying, "you will be able to settle down quite safely. On the West Coast, maybe. A house, an apartment, money, a new identity, maybe a little plastic surgery."

Yashin picked up a pewter mug and examined it without interest. In Chimki-Chovrino in the north of Moscow there was a factory where they manufactured antiques, icons, Tsarist candle-sticks, chandeliers to sell to tourists from the West in the commission shops.

"Are you fond of sport, Mikhail?" Hamilton asked.

"I follow football. Soccer."

"Spartak?"

"Dynamo," Yashin said, hearing the whistling of the spectators – when Dynamo were playing badly the stadium in Petrovsky Park was an aviary.

"I'll introduce you to baseball," Hamilton said. "A

17

beautiful game."

"Yankees?"

"Mets."

Letz said: "In six weeks the president will be in Russia." He wrestled his hands together. "We wouldn't want you to change your mind on the eve of such an historic occasion, Mr. Yashin."

"Don't worry," Yashin said, "I won't. I hope it's more successful than Iceland," he added.

"But I do worry. Yurchenko's timing was immaculate. He redefected on the eve of Geneva."

"You shouldn't have allowed him to escape." Yurchenko's about-turn had devastated the CIA.

"I don't think there's anything phoney about Mikhail's defection" Hamilton said. "The Soviet Mission is in an uproar."

"Then why won't you tell us why you've come over?" Letz leaned towards Yashin, as eager as he would ever allow himself to be.

"Disillusionment?"

Letz consulted the print-outs. "Nothing here to suggest such a frame of mind."

"There wouldn't be, would there?"

"You emerge as the complete patriot."

"If you were going to defect to Russia would you advertise your intentions?"

"After the accident, were you happy in your new job?"

Before it he had sometimes been exultant. When Anatoly had been proud of him and word of that pride disseminated at Work-Polytechnic Middle School No. 18 off Leningradsky, had reached him. When he had overhead Galina telling a film director: "*My* husband's a cosmonaut."

"It wasn't written in the stars that I should work for State Security."

"In the stars . . . I like that, apposite. I think you've answered my question."

Letz stood up, shorter than you expected, but compact, graceful even. The gods had been good to Letz, a little heavy on obduracy, perhaps, light on compassion.

He extended his hand. "I hope you don't think I've been

18

too harsh but you must understand that defection is a delicate area right now. We have to be very analytical. Especially when a Hero of the Soviet Union comes across, for no apparent reason, shortly before Gorbachev plays host to the president."

Yashin stood up, shook his hand. It was warm and dry, tensile. Hands were giveaways. Eloquent, brutal, entreating, calloused, soap-soft . . . Eyes told you nothing.

"Another possibility we have to consider," Letz said making for the door, "is that you could be a plant. Either to penetrate the CIA or, after a period of reticence, to undermine it by falsely naming KGB sleepers."

"Don't give me ideas," Yashin said.

Letz opened the door. "Anyway, you're in good hands. Look after him Jack."

"Jesus," said Hamilton as the door closed. "Let's have a drink." He went into the kitchen and returned with a bottle of vodka.

*   *   *

Later Yashin telephoned Tuslov in Moscow. As far as Tuslov knew Anatoly hadn't yet been approached. But, yes, the shit had hit the fan in Dzerzhinsky Square and the Chairman had been summoned to the Kremlin.

Then Tuslov dictated from a one-time pad which even the most Machiavellian cipher expert on the other end of a wiretap would be unable to break.

The decode told Yashin that Tuslov had made some progress in his efforts to incriminate Lozak. Nothing brilliant, it implied. How long will the Americans allow me? Yashin wondered. Three weeks? Optimistic. He burned the decode and powdered the charred paper.

He went to bed at 10.30.

Asleep, he was sitting beside the commander of the Soyuz spacecraft, Col. Andrei Korolev. They exchanged bored smiles: ground tests were tedious.

The oxygen-rich atmosphere ignited with a soft, phlegmy explosion. As he tried to beat out the flames on his spacesuit the walls of the cabin began to close in.

19

His hands twitched beneath the bedclothes, his scream was no louder than the cry of a dying rodent. He switched on the light and shielded his face with his hands as the walls of the bedroom continued to advance.

CHAPTER 3

The best disguise is removal not addition.

The man with the pale hair and eyes snipped his moustache with nail scissors, then shaved the stubble with an Army issue razor. He elevated his sideburns, took off his plain glass spectacles and placed them carefully in the bathroom cabinet.

In the bedroom he checked his forged passport, exit visa and travel documents, picked up his shabby suitcase and walked down the stairs of the functional apartment block into the sunshine on Moscow's Mir Prospect.

The avenue, shouldered with high-rise, bloomed with women in print dresses. A thirsty queue had formed in front of a kvas van. Even two grey-uniformed militiamen were smiling as they fined the driver of a Zhighli for failing to keep his car clean.

Tal, surveying the jaunty promise of the day from the entrance to his block, wasn't stimulated. He preferred the anonymity of winter; veiling snow, heads tucked into 30 degrees of frost.

Not that his features were memorable. Undistinguished, in fact; coldly glazed and inward-looking. Long ago, at school, they had been responsive but in every class there is a nervous child who attracts hostility or ridicule, and he had been the one. Worse, he had stammered.

After a while he had accepted his isolation, nursed it, sculpted his life around it, conquered the cause of the ridicule.

Apology for a suitcase in his hand, Tal climbed into the

waiting taxi, a black Volga, one of the fleet used by the Seventh Directorate to monitor the movements of foreigners, and told the driver to take him to Sheremetyevo airport. The cab took off, passing the Ostankino television tower, 537 metres high, with the Seventh Heaven restaurant revolving half way up like an all-seeing, automated eye.

As the cab driver traversed the north-west of the city Tal, an actor with a new script, studied his passport. Nikolai Lvov, Ukrainian, from Nikitovka, city of mercury, secretary with the Soviet Union's 28-strong team at the United Nations Secretariat in New York. Aged 34, bachelor. Recreation: fishing.

Lvov had been assembled two years ago with finesse. *United Nations* – daily contact with diplomats and agents from many countries. *Fishing* – hunting and shooting closely allied. *Ukrainian* – if he wanted to penetrate the CIA or FBI they would be intrigued by the dissident possibilities. And he *was* from Kiev. *Bachelor* – vulnerable to advances by either sex if he wanted to fake treachery.

"But why me?" Tal asked when Simenov briefed him in a cramped but exclusive restaurant near the Church of the Nativity of Putniki in Chekhov Street.

Simenov smeared red caviar on a finger of toast. Where did all the calories go? Tal wondered as he watched Simenov's bony jaws chomping. The head of Executive Action's suit hung loosely on his frame, his skin was grey.

"Who else?" Simenov reached for the dish of glistening orange roe. "You're the best."

"What's wrong with Kiselev? Why station an operative in New York if you don't use him when he's needed?"

Tal drank Borzhomi mineral water, nibbled gherkins and black bread. He didn't eat gourmet food and he didn't touch alcohol; the latter heresy compounded his isolation from his fellows. He didn't like the restaurant, either, with its bubbling fish tank, lattice screens and fawning waiters. Outside he had noticed two Chaikas with MOC and MO11 registrations; so Central Committee members were here stuffing themselves behind discreet lattice.

"I should have thought that was obvious," Simenov said. "Yashin will seek political asylum. Can you imagine the

22

uproar if a member of our mission in New York was caught sniffing round a safe house? Diplomatic immunity abused, all that shit. And supposing the FBI know Kiselev is Executive Action? They'll keep him under round-the-clock surveillance and he'll have as much chance of killing Yashin as dining at the White House."

It made sense but Simenov was assembling his words with too much care. An undertaker addressing the bereaved. When Simenov was nervous he cracked his knuckles.

"Tell me one thing," Tal said. "Why did Yashin defect?"

"Ask him. Before you kill him," the crack of his knuckles a dry twig snapping.

"He was patriotic, a good communist. A Hero of the Soviet Union. A colonel in State Security. He had everything going for him. Why give it all up?"

"The accident? Maybe his brain was scarred as well as his body."

"Not according to the medical board."

A waiter with tired lapels on his black jacket served them chicken satsivi and poured a mouthful of Tsinandali for Simenov to taste. Simenov seemed relieved at the diversion. Tal removed the walnuts from his chicken while Simenov mimed a close acquaintanceship with Georgian white.

Tal said: "And he left his son here."

"Everyone posted abroad has to leave someone behind. You know that, the magnet to draw them back."

Tal did know it. Nevertheless it struck him as curious that a devoted father should jeopardise his son. It was out of character and Tal, who had trained himself to observe behavioural habits, was on the alert when patterns lost their symmetry.

"It would appear," he said, watching Simenov, "that Yashin acted precipitately. As though he learned something just before he left Moscow. Since when does a defector who has planned his escape jump out of a car?" It was a dropped stitch in the pattern that was Yashin.

"I still think the flames got to his brain." Simenov aimed a forkful of green vegetable at his mouth. "A variety of Georgian grass I believe."

"Crazy? Lozak didn't think so. He promoted him three

23

months ago."

Lozak. The name of the fat-cat chief of the Eighth Directorate lingered on his tongue. Could he be the cause of the hesitancies in Simenov's reasoning? If he wanted Yashin good and dead for his own motives he might have blackmailed Simenov.

A tall man with a cloud of snow-white hair wearing a western suit walked past the table on his way to the restroom. Central Committee. The waiter almost curtsied.

Tal chewed a mouthful of chicken: it was too tender: he preferred the tougher fare of the restaurant among the wooden theatres in Hermitage park which, like the service, put up a fight.

He cleansed his mouth with Borzhomi and said: "Are you sure, Comrade Simenov, that there is no other reason why Yashin has got to be killed so urgently?"

"Other than what?" Simenov laid his knife and fork beside the stripped bones of his chicken. Every move a distraction. He lit a cigarette packed with tobacco as black as mourning.

"Other than the obvious, that he's defected."

"From the Eighth Directorate."

"But without access to Red Classifications."

"Dangerous just the same."

"Shouldn't we have waited? Followed normal procedure? Worked on his son?"

Simenov inhaled deeply. The black leaf burned malignantly. If everyone smoked like that I'd be out of a job, Tal thought. He sometimes made jokes with himself. Not often, not to anyone else.

"I would remind you," Simenov said in a shredded voice, "that this is a briefing by me not an interrogation by you." He cracked his knuckles.

"If you're going to kill someone it helps to know why."

"Suluguni," Simenov said to the waiter. "You?"

"Just coffee. Black."

"You have to kill a traitor. Isn't that enough?"

"It has to be," Tal said. "It doesn't really matter. I carry out orders, like a soldier. Like everyone in the Soviet Union."

"Like everyone in the world," Simenov said. "But you're

lucky, you like your job."

Did he? Its consummate finality gave him a certain satisfaction, he supposed, after the mess of his childhood. Why should a stammer attract derision? Sometimes, when cleaning a gun, he shot one of the grinning faces in the playground.

"I'm a perfectionist," he told Simenov who was swallowing Georgian cheese and smoke. *Perfectionist* – he couldn't have tackled that as a kid.

"Perfectionists don't question orders. Not in your profession."

"No more questions." But don't be surprised if I find out the answers, Tal thought. He stood up abruptly. "I have things to do, I'll call you from New York."

The alcohol flushes on Simenov's cheeks looked like mortician's cosmetic on a cadaver.

On the Ilyushin taking him to Charles de Gaulle airport to connect with Air France 077 to New York, Tal, with two empty seats beside him, opened a maroon file and peered into the life of Mikhail Yashin.

His father had been director of the Likhachev Works in Lenin Suburb which produced the Zavod Imeni Likhatcheva limousine and so Yashin had been privileged. Who in the Kremlin hierarchy wanted an old Zil when his father could supply one still smelling of factory paint and leather?

He had lived with his two sisters in an apartment by the Hill of Farewells and a dacha at Nikolina Gora; his goodies would have been bought in beryozka stores, his nose wiped by a doctor from the Kremlin Clinic.

Young Pioneer, Komsomol, acceptance at Moscow University, no problems. Tal who had grown up in a workers' flat in the shadow of a ball-bearing factory bled for him. Then Yashin had reached for space, attended the Gagarin Air Force Academy and graduated to Tyuratum cosmodrome.

In between these achievements he had found time for a marriage arranged in heaven, or whatever utopia awaits good communists, to the daughter of a tame columnist on *Izvestia*. She was aloofly photogenic, as shallow as a colour-print, part-time actress at the Mosfilm studios, member of the Dom Kino club etcetera; he was handsome in a tight, contained sort of way, a man seeking release. To the firmament?

A blonde stewardess, her blue skirt shiny around the buttocks, bent over him. "A drink?" She smiled. Stewardesses' smiles were regarded cynically, toothpaste, plastic . . . He found them warm, a glimpse of friendship others enjoyed.

He ordered a cherry-flavoured cordial, observed the smile fray with disbelief and returned to Mikhail Yashin.

The fire had been similar to the accident at Cape Kennedy in 1967 when an electrical arc in a spacecraft on a ground test had ignited in a 100 per cent oxygen atmosphere and burned to death astronauts Grissom, White and Chaffee.

Yashin's commander had been roasted alive. Yashin had escaped with appalling burns to his torso and lower abdomen. His wife, Galina, had left when, because of his knowledge of space communications, he had been enlisted by the Eighth Directorate of the KGB.

Why she had left him Tal had no means of knowing. KGB stigma? Humiliation of a marriage to a cosmonaut who had never left the ground?

Careful, you're sympathising with the poor bastard.

The stewardess served him his pink beverage, her smile now irredeemably lost in the complexities of who was drinking what.

Beneath the aircraft grey clouds like brains.

Tal put Yashin on rewind. A boy in a school near the Kremlin. Athletically vigorous, one of the gang.

A face in a playground.

Tal shot him.

* * *

Dobykin who met him at Kennedy exuded hostility.

Tal, distancing himself from the KGB bureau chief's meaty presence in the back of the Buick, said: "Is this the car Yashin travelled in?"

"Does it matter?"

"It matters."

"The same."

"And the driver?"

"The same."

"I'm Yashin now," Tal said.

"So?"

26

"I want you to take me through the whole thing."

"Is it necessary? Your job is to kill him, nothing else."

"The whole thing. Starting now."

"Let's get one thing straight I am——"

"My superior officer. Take me through it."

"I was surprised he wasn't more impressed by his introduction to the United States. You don't seem——"

"I've been here before. So what happened? What did you talk about? When did he jump?"

"We didn't talk about anything much."

I have just arrived in America. I have never been here before. But I am not impressed. Why? Because I don't give a shit about the scenery. I am geared to escape.

Tal's shoulder muscles tensed. "You must have talked about something."

"I sounded him out."

"With a stethoscope?"

"I asked if he was impressed by the lectures we get before we're posted here."

"Was he?"

"He prevaricated."

"Did you just swallow a dictionary?"

"You know the penalty for insubordination?"

"The only penalty I know is a bullet."

But why do I have to escape before I reach the Mission? Plenty of time, surely, to make a leisurely break afterwards.

"He pointed," Dobykin said.

"Pointed?"

"At nothing. That's when I knew something was wrong."

"When?"

"A kilometre or so ahead."

"Red light?"

"Just turning green."

Traffic hummed around the Buick. *But I'm not interested in sleek tin-cans. Or the nest of skyscrapers. I have to jump before I get to 67th. Why?*

"You should have shot him," Tal said.

The driver turned his head fractionally. "I took a couple of shots but I couldn't risk killing Americans."

"You could," Tal said, "if you knew how to shoot

27

straight."

We're getting near to that light. I have to get out now. Why, why, why?

"Is that everything?" Tal asked.

"That's it."

And now we're stopping. Squeezed between a silver coach and a truck.

Tal spread his hands, fingers pointed outwards. "Who were your neighbours?"

"I can't remember. A stretch Lincoln, I think . . ."

Why now? Come on tell me Yashin, you sonofabitch. *Why do I have to jump?* He grasped the handle of the door, pointed with his right hand.

"What? I can't see anything. You're not going to—"

"No," Tal said, "because we, Yashin and I, have just realised why we had to jump before we reached the mission."

CHAPTER 4

The processing started with a girl, Hannah Martin, introduced by Hamilton as "adviser and interpreter of the scene." He added: "She also speaks Russian."

In the KGB they were known as swallows. Although their techniques, farmyard sex mostly, were probably cruder than anything contemplated by Hannah Martin.

She was tall and pale with short dark hair that should have been longer; her greenish eyes X-rayed pretence and there was a spider-web crease on one side of her mouth, a question mark that threatened to smile. Her long legs invested blue jeans and boots with elegance; a moulting fur jacket contradicted them. She was half fashion model, half farmer's daughter.

"And I suppose you play chess," he said as Hamilton left them on the lawn where scattered jewels of dew were losing their brilliance in the sun.

"Badly."

"By what standards?"

"Mine."

Yashin began to walk. Sunday. On the other side of the laurel hedge America dozed complacently. In black and white Yashin saw two-car families relaxing in detached homes planted in open-plan gardens, mailboxes at the end of the drives. He even smelled brunch in black and white. He wanted to peer over the hedge.

"If there's anything I can do," she said, "please let me know. Within reason, that is." The spiked heels of her boots left a trail of puncture wounds on the lawn.

"You *are* employed by the CIA?"

"Of course." He admired the honesty of her dishonest designs. "But only to make you feel at home." Honesty permitted only the briefest of airings. "Do you want to talk Russian or English?"

"English," knowing that one day, when she sensed that his defences were in disarray, spring would become *vyesna*, summer *lyeto*.

He paused beside a pile of logs. The guard in the black raincoat watched him. He scraped lichen from a log. The morning was as quiet as prayer. Until the helicopter returned.

She asked: "Are you thinking about Russia?"

"I think about it all the time."

"Your son, does he know what's happened?"

Yashin was aware that pertinent queries often came in bland packaging, poison inside gellatine capsules. He offered a quarter-truth. "He was aware of my feelings."

"Your reasons for leaving must have been very strong . . ."

"I wish," Yashin said, "that you, Hamilton, Letz, would find another tape."

"It's my job, Mr. Yashin, to put you at your ease. You aren't helping."

"Why did you learn Russian?" Yashin started to walk again.

"Everyone should learn it. Every Russian should learn English. Then we might begin to understand each other."

"I think you and I understand each other very well," Yashin said.

"If you feel that way . . . Sorry, I'll change the tape." She stopped to watch a ginger cat walking across the grass as though it were a minefield, pausing every so often to shake dew from its paws. "Russia has always fascinated me," she said. "I have Polish blood." That was an explanation?

"Hannah Martin?"

"On my mother's side."

Yashin stooped to pull a weed from a bed of petunias. It had two parsnip-shaped roots, a tooth pulled in a nightmare. "Are you going to show me America, Miss Martin? The *real*

30

America?"

"Wherever that is . . . Do visitors see the *real* Russia?"

"They never see her soul," Yashin said. "You see they never look for it. GUM, the Bolshoi, Gastronom No 1 in Gorky Street, the Kremlin Armoury, no bath plugs in the hotels, deplorable service in the restaurants . . ."

"Why did you learn English?" she asked.

"In case they spoke it on Mars."

"I'm sorry—"

"Forget it," he said, hand straying towards the scars.

They passed an old sun-dial eroded by time, an ornamental pond with diseased goldfish resting in thick water – props for a Russian garden emerging from winter. Then America once more, a tree clotted with blossom.

From this side of the garden, beneath his bedroom window, he could see the green mountains snaring white clouds.

"One of them is called Magic Mountain," Hannah Martin said, following his gaze. "Good skiing, very Swiss. Russian maybe?"

"We don't ski down mountains," Yashin said. "We slog it through the countryside." There was a pair of ancient cross-country skis in his apartment, old limbs with curled toes.

"Lincoln's son, Robert Todd, built a house here. Hildene. You can take a tour. There's a 1,000 pipe organ there and they'd play it for you."

"I'd prefer to see an old movie. Is there a cinema?"

"At the Center at Manchester. And a twin movie house at Londonderry."

"You live here?"

"New Jersey. And yes I do know the area. You see you're not the first, Mr. Yashin." She reminded Yashin of a girl in an old-fashioned scenario summoning the courage to tell her fiancee that she isn't a virgin.

* * *

Q: When did you start to feel disillusioned?

A: A long time ago.

Q: Before the accident?

A: Forget the accident, it's got nothing to do with anything.

Q: Indirectly maybe?

A: I don't understand.

Q: Your wife left you after the accident . . .

A: That was the best thing that ever happened to me.

Q: You don't mean that, do you?

A: *No reply*

Q: When she left did you feel a sense of betrayal?

A: A sense of relief.

Q: Mikhail, you say you defected because you were disillusioned. You must know when you became . . . disenchanted. 'A long time ago' isn't good enough. When?

A: Disillusion isn't a road accident. There isn't a time, a place, a specific wound . . . Five years ago maybe.

Q: Afghanistan?

A: About then, yes.

Q: Did you start making plans then?

A: To defect? Subconsciously perhaps. Nothing more.

Q: What suddenly made you decide to act?

A: I was posted to New York.

Listener 1: First positive answer so far.

Listener 2: Too pat. Stress on the meter. Hamilton gave him the opportunity to snap. He snapped.

Q: When was that?

A: A couple of months ago. A little more, a little less.

Q: So you had plenty of time to make plans?

A: I had time.

Listener 1: Steady, boy, push him too hard and he'll bounce back.

Q: You're a Hero of the Soviet Union?

Listener 1: Good boy.

A: You know I am.

Q: For your contribution to the exploration of space?

A: Except that I never got there.

Q: You're a Party member?

A: Is all this relevant?

Q: I'm trying to establish why someone with impeccable credentials should want to defect. You understand that?

A: Back to square one.

Listener 2: Stress nil. Smug. Hamilton's a pro.

Q: I have to ask myself why a potential defector who has had two months to orchestrate his escape should jump out of a car within an hour of arriving in New York . . .

A: I suggest you do that, ask yourself.

Q: Why didn't you wait until later, Mikhail? Until you'd been booked into the Mission? Until, maybe, you'd adjourned to the Soviet residence at Glen Cove.

Listener 1: *Mikhail*, nice.

A: Because that was the way I had planned it.

Listener 2: The meter nearly bust a gut.

Q: You know something? Your command of the English language is remarkable.

A: For a Russian?

Q: Were you taught English for a specific purpose?

A: Such as?

Q: To enable you to travel outside the restricted zone in the United States? To enable you to mix?

A: To spy?

Q: Well?

A: It would be stupid to deny that many diplomats are engaged in intelligence. Your military attachés in Moscow aren't merely counting rockets on Red Square.

Q: I was asking about you. You *are* a member of the KGB.

A: Communications. That doesn't make me a spy.

Q: Espionage is confined to the First Chief Directorate?

A: I only know about the Eighth.

Q: You've never heard of Directorate T formed in 1963 to penetrate Western missile and space research?

A: I've heard of it.

Listener 2: The half truth. Every subject's escape route.

Q: Isn't it a fact that Directorate T and the Eighth work closely together?

A: You would have to ask the Chairman of State Security.

Letz to Listeners 1 and 2: How's it going?

Listener 1: It's going to be a long haul.

Letz: We don't have time for long hauls.

Listener 2: Hamilton's doing a good job.

Letz: Let me have the tapes as soon as he's through.

Q: Where did you work in the Soviet Union?

A: Baikonur – Tyuratam if you prefer it – Plesetsk, Kapustin Yar, Moscow . . .

Q: Dzerzhinsky Square?

A: Occasionally.

Noted that when the interrogation centred on Moscow the roles of inquisitor and subject lost some of their definition.

Hamilton: Where Lubianka Jail used to be?

Yashin: Years ago, yes.

Hamilton: I went to the toy store there, Dietsky Mir. Wonderful. Twice the size of F.A.O. Schwarz, maybe more.

Yashin: What part of Moscow did you like best?

Hamilton: The Garden Boulevards . . . Sverdlov Square . . . the Lenin Hills – Sparrow Hills once? . . . a little street lined with lime trees . . .

Yashin: Bolshaya Ordinka Street?

Listener 1: Shit, what the hell—

Listener 2: Lulling him into a false sense of security, I guess.

Hamilton: I used to walk a lot – against Embassy advice. The bird market . . . Sokolniki Park . . . the wooden houses between Arbat and Vorovsky Street . . .

Yashin: I lived near there.

Hamilton: So did the United States Ambassador.

Yashin: Did you go to any football matches?

Listener 1: Jesus!

Hamilton: Ice-hockey. It was winter.

Yashin: The cold can take your ears off in Red Square at night with the wind coming in from Siberia.

Hamilton: And ice crystals sparkling in the lamplight. I like cold.

Yashin: You should have been a Russian.

Hamilton: Why did you defect, Mikhail?

Yashin: I forget Jack.

*   *   *

In his bedroom Yashin took off his shirt, sweat-soaked from the first interrogation even though it had been more foreplay than inquisition. His hand went to the scar stretched across his chest and half way round his back; if the burns, charred and blistered, had ringed his body he would probably have died. The tissue, pink and shiny, felt like someone else's; his own, in fact, transplanted from unscathed portions of his body by a plastic surgeon who had even contrived a

34

semblance of a nipple. Tiny suture scars were discernible around a square of tissue between the fifth and seventh ribs.

Yashin put on a yellow T-shirt, compliments of the United States Government, lay down on the bed and opened his wallet. Anatoly wearing a red Young Pioneer scarf smiled back. The smile had the shape of trust. But that had been a long time before Yashin had been conscripted into the KGB; before Anatoly had discovered human rights and samizdat literature; before his father had become the enemy.

Yashin placed the wallet on the Saul Bellow paperback and considered the possibilities of regaining his son's respect and returning to Russia. In illogical order but that was the way they presented themselves. He concentrated and the fragile possibilities became one.

The obstacles also synthesised. Into Lozak. What would the head of the Eighth Directorate be doing to stop him hitting back? Trying to kill me?

Yashin swung his legs off the bed and, from behind one of the cornflower-blue drapes, peered through the window. Green mountains to the right, a white church with a spire embedded in the foothills. A quilt of maple that in the autumn would be embroidered red and gold. A couple of red roof-tops like playing cards over the top of the hedge. A rise, evergreen with pine, affording a text-book view of the bedroom window . . .

Yashin took a mirror from the dressing table and placed it on a chest of drawers to one side of the window. Then he drew the curtains, showered and dressed for dinner. Hannah Martin was cooking it. Chicken Kiev?

Even if they forcibly fed him vodka or shot him full of drugs they wouldn't find what they were looking for. He doubted if anyone would.

As he walked into the living room Hannah Martin called out from the kitchen: "Guess what we've got for dinner."

He guessed Chicken Kiev.

"Beef Strogonov," she called back.

*　　　*　　　*

A hundred and fifty miles away in the referentura of the Soviet Mission in New York, Tal considered the addresses of

35

four safe houses provided by the KGB sleeper in the Domestic Operations Division of the CIA. Bethel, Connecticut; Carlisle, Pennsylvania; Manchester, Vermont; Albany, New York. The sleeper had promised to deliver Yashin's exact location by midnight. It was now 8 pm.

CHAPTER 5

Letz said: "You should work out. It tones up your brain." He dropped neatly from the steel bars clamped to the wall of the gymnasium in Georgetown. "That Yashin interrogation: it wasn't up to your normal standard."

"Early days," Hamilton said, leaning against the wall bars, exhausted by Letz's exertions.

Letz moved to a gleaming weight machine and began to pull the bar, leisurely exertion disguising application.

In the CIA such application had projected him to Director of Domestic Operations. In Washington society, although he frequented the right restaurants, bars and parties and cultivated the chosen of Capitol Hill, he hadn't risen beyond minor league. Letz's problem was his job which invited suspicion; even when he strolled past the museums and memorials of L'Enfant's vision he was a visitor.

Letz professed patriotism verging on chauvinism but Hamilton suspected that he also fantasised about revenge from a position of clandestine power on those who had rejected him.

Currently he had one obsession – to rise from the ashes of Yurchenko. Even now Domestic Operations winced collectively when the name of the prize defector who had redefected cropped up. Letz had survived the blood-letting because he had only just been appointed director when Yurchenko slipped surveillance and scurried back to Moscow. But Yurchenko hadn't enhanced his future: he needed Yashin.

"Early days?" The weights rose and fell on their rods with

oiled rhythms. "You make it sound like a presidential campaign."

Hamilton folded his arms. Beneath his jacket his biceps felt flabby. "It's not going to be easy. Yashin's tricky."

In the background an overweight Congressman savaged a punchbag.

Letz, muscles pulsing, said: "You know what I think?"

Hamilton didn't.

Letz let go of the bar. "I think he's going to stall until the President is about to fly to Moscow. Then he'll do a Yurchenko."

"I can't rush him," Hamilton said.

Letz towelled sweat from his chest. "That was apparent from the tape. Moscow. Did I hear violins in the background?"

"Sharing a common interest. Routine."

"Making him so goddam homesick that he wants to go back?"

"Establishing sympathy," Hamilton said. "He can't go back."

"I got the impression," Letz said, heading for the locker-room, "that you would like to return to Moscow. Was it cosy?"

"You've heard Russian choirs?" And without waiting for a reply: "It was like that."

"Maybe you should go back to Russia. Provided Yashin stays." Letz offered a white, frank smile. "I was only kidding. Why don't we meet in Clydes in say thirty minutes?"

Behind them the Congressman, a Democrat, hammered a last right-hook into the punchbag, a Republican, and, shaking a limp fist, followed Letz.

Hamilton wandered through the backstreets of Georgetown, past boutiques and health-food stores, emerging on M Street.

Powdered rain was blowing in from the Potomac, cleansing the sweat from the air. Everyone seemed to be eating, ice-creams, hot-dogs, furtive secrets from tall paperbags. He passed Junior League, Earl Allen, Laura Ashley and entered Clydes.

He would have expected Letz, peering into middle-age, to

have been more comfortable at F. Scott's. Wrong. Letz extended his hand to youth and hung on.

Hamilton, finding a space between brass fittings and a group of preppy hustlers feeding off Capitol Hill, ordered a beer. These people were his wife's people. And Letz's. He remembered drinking dark brown beer from a fluted bottle in a Moscow pub off the Intourist route, nibbling tiny crabs and treading on the shells. One foot moved involuntarily, squashing nothing.

Letz materialised freshly showered, studiously casual in grey slacks and an open-neck white shirt that might have been silk. He ordered a Bloody Mary and guided Hamilton to an uncrowded corner.

"I hope," he said, sipping blood, "that you didn't think I was being gratuitously offensive back there."

"You're the boss."

"And you're the best interrogator in the business bar none." Letz dwelt on his words. "The fact of the matter is that we can't fuck up with Yashin. You understand that?"

"You haven't understated the position," Hamilton said.

"It's just that I figure you're being too sympathetic. If Yashin *really* can't go back to the Soviet Union then you can start to get tough."

"A hostile collaborator? No thanks. If Yashin is as important as you think he is then we've got to win his trust. Lose that and you've lost the game."

"I wouldn't have thought Yashin had much choice."

"He can tell us as many lies as he wants to. Just like Yurchenko."

Hamilton sipped his beer waiting for the stress indicator. Everybody displayed one; the most common, theatrical indifference. "Yurchenko? It hasn't been proved conclusively that everything he told us was fabricated." With Letz it was grammatical embroidery; when he was distressed, or lying, he stitched a tapestry of words.

The only indicator that had so far eluded Hamilton was his own. Because I no longer know when I'm lying to myself?

He said: "Some of the stuff Yurchenko told us was genuine; a few agents were sacrificed. The rest of it? Dangerous bullshit."

39

"You should have interrogated him."

"You should have called me back from vacation." Knowing that Letz had briefed his own man.

"I should. But I didn't want to spoil things with you and Catherine." The lie was so transparent that it didn't affect Letz's speech pattern. He swirled ice in his Bloody Mary with a cocktail stick and went on: "Anyway that's past, lost. How is the girl making out?"

"Hannah? They're sparring."

"Sparring? Jesus! Are you sure you know what you're doing? She should be sympathetic, you should be tough."

"She sure as hell shouldn't be obvious," Hamilton said.

"Do we know what he said when he called Moscow?"

"He used a one-time pad."

"Get it."

"He destroyed it."

"Why would he want to call Moscow?"

"To get a message to his son, I guess."

"And some more." Letz put down his glass and pressed Hamilton's arm. "Let's take a walk."

They turned into Wisconsin Avenue and headed in the general direction of Letz's Federal-period house. Past Britches, Francis Reilly, Peter's Flowers. The rain had stopped but it had coaxed wet scents from the street; Georgetown had once been a tobacco port and Hamilton fancied he could smell snuff.

Letz, walking urgently through the trend-conscious crowds, asked after Catherine. "My wife was only saying this morning that she was looking great."

"Take your wife's word for it."

"They've known each other a long time now."

"Friendships forged at Radcliffe," Hamilton said, "last forever. Or so I've heard. Is the same true of Harvard?"

"She said she was looking great. She didn't say she was happy."

"Is Betty happy?"

"She doesn't complain. She enjoys her charity work. Maybe Catherine should espouse some good cause."

"Husbands of the Company?"

"Just one," Letz said, slowing his stride to allow a

40

Japanese loaded with parcels to pass him. "How are things with you and Catherine?"

"Fine," Hamilton lied.

"Not the way I heard it." Letz paused outside The Phoenix and contemplated the Mexican exports; a tin mask stared back. "If you pull this one off you'll get promotion. Paris or London. Catherine would like that."

"You mean I'll really get to be somebody?"

"A watching brief for the Company at European interrogations. More time at home. More cash. You and Catherine could get it together again."

"Wow," Hamilton said.

"You might even start to get yourself together again," Letz said, a flint in his voice. He tapped the window and pointed at the mask. "Do you think Betty would like that?"

"I didn't know she was Mexican."

"If you blow it . . ." Let smiled tightly. "I believe there's a vacancy in archives."

"The morgue? Great place for a Q and A – no one answers back."

"I think I will buy it for her." Letz fished a wallet from inside his blazer and checked his credit cards. "Do you see anything Catherine might like?"

"I'll wait till we get to Paris," Hamilton said.

"I hope I've got through to you," Letz said. "You see speed is of the essence." *Stress*!

"Supposing Yashin redefects after we've cleaned him out?"

"No way. Didn't you just refer to archives as the morgue?"

Letz walked briskly into The Phoenix. Dismissed, Hamilton waited outside until the tin mask was removed from the window.

*   *   *

The stewardess on the Washington-New York shuttle pushed a trolly bearing credit-card stamping apparatus. Had the plastic revolution reached Moscow and, like computers, spawned a new breed of criminals?

Hamilton closed his eyes and tried to see America through Yashin's eyes. What would impress him most? Hamilton

41

dealt himself a hand of possibilities and discarded *freedom*, the worn trump card of the West. Freedom was a canvas for generalisation. Most Muscovites he had met weren't even aware that they were oppressed. Cheap holidays on the Black Sea, full employment, drunk as a skunk every Friday night . . . Who cared if you couldn't move house from Kazan to Kirovograd without permission? Oppression only clenched its fist if you were stupid enough to buck the system.

In any case, would Yashin recognise liberty when he saw it? Americans viewed it complacently unaware that it harboured distorting mirrors. *Two men look out through the same bars: One sees mud, and one the stars.* Which would Yashin see? Hamilton hoped he never travelled on the New York subway.

What would impress him, Hamilton guessed, were the contrasts. The choices. The colours. The intensity of endeavour. The ingenuity.

He handed the stewardess a card and signed the voucher. She reminded him of Catherine. As though she had been assembled from Harper's. It still amazed him that he had married someone whose views were trends; astonished him that he was still crazy about her.

As Yashin had been about his wife? We have too much in common, he cautioned himself. He hoped he never began to respect him.

*   *   *

As Hamilton alighted from the shuttle at New York's La Guardia airport William Spivak, driving north in a red Ford Tempo, was joining the Hutchinson River Parkway three miles away.

He drove carefully like a man with a new car which hasn't yet succumbed to dents and upholstery stains. Not because this car was in mint condition – there was a cigarette burn enlarged by inquisitive fingers on the passenger seat and a deep, curved scar on the hood; not because the Tempo, hired from a shabby garage in the Bronx, even belonged to him; he drove cautiously because that was the way he was. How many criminals had been caught because of a misdemeanour? Five kilometres an hour over the speed limit, a forbidden U–turn . . .

As he drove, gloved hands light on the wheel, he got to know the car, the surge generated by the slightest pressure on the gas pedal from an engine far more powerful than anything envisaged by the manufacturers. And he renewed his acquaintanceship with American highways.

He wore a tweed hat sporting a green feather and from time to time he glanced into the back seat at the canvas sheath containing his fishing rods and a Mannlicher-Carcano 6.5 mm rifle, the same weapon used to assassinate President Kennedy. The telescopic sight, wrapped in chamois leather, lay at the bottom of a fish-smelling bag containing tackle.

Like Lvov, from Nikotovka, city of mercury, Spivak was a keen fisherman. Tal, making a left onto US 7, fifteen miles into Connecticut, congratulated the creators of Spivak because their ingenuity took him logically to Manchester: the Battenkill River was said to be stuffed with brown trout, Emerald Lake with bass, pike and perch and there was a fly fishing school nearby. And if anyone questioned his presence he was, unlike Lvov/Tal, an American citizen unhampered by travel restrictions.

He stopped at a diner near the Massachusetts-Vermont stateline for lunch. Cheeseburger and French fries shouted into a stainless-steel kitchen by a dark-rooted blonde searching the horizon for lost love. He daubed the hamburger with relish, ketchup and mustard. Delicious. Hot rolls with silver-wrapped cubes of butter and, unsolicited, coffee because no one had ever refused it. It was all over in eight minutes; in Moscow he would still be waiting for service.

He consulted a road map and guide book. Manchester – "Don't confuse it with the city in New Hampshire," the informant in the CIA's Domestic Operations had warned him – was thirty miles to the north in the Valley of Vermont, subsidised by winter sports and history. The white clapboard house in which Yashin had been installed was a couple of miles east of Manchester on a botany trail which, according to the guide, supported 67 varieties of birches and wild-flowers. It was protected by 12 guards on shifts, electronic alarms and helicopter surveillance. No one in the vicinity knew it was CIA property, or so Domestic Operations believed. It was overlooked by a rise which would be patrolled by guards;

43

guards could be distracted.

"Will there be anything else?" The waitress's eyes searched the parking lot for a man on a white charger.

Tal said there wouldn't and thanked her.

"You're welcome. Have a good day."

The fat-thighed motorcycle cop said: "Is that your car?" His crash-helmet reminded Tal of an eggshell that could be cracked with one blow.

"It's rented."

"Where you fishing?" The policeman pointed at the rods in the back of the Tempo. An aggressive moustache was stuck on the pink moon beneath his helmet.

"Up north," Tal told him. "Near Stowe."

"Ah, *The Sound of Music?* Did you know the original Trapp family had a house there?"

Tal who had no idea what he was talking about shook his head.

"Great spin and fly fishing on the Lamoille. Mind if I take a look at your rods?"

"They're just rods," Tal said.

"I always reckon you can tell the man by his rods. Me, I don't like anything too fancy."

"Just ordinary rods," Tal said. "Nothing fancy."

"Do you mind if I take a look?"

"Ordinarily not but I'm in a hurry."

"So you stopped to eat?"

"I made a call from the diner. My host has been taken ill."

"Anything I can do?" The policeman made a slight adjustment to his helmet.

"Nothing, the doctor's there."

"Well, I sure hope—"

"Thank you," Tal said, opening the door of the Tempo. "Perhaps another time . . ."

"Do you know why I stopped you?"

Tal turned the ignition switch and, as the engine fired, spread his hands. "No idea, officer."

"I was going to recommend some great trout fishing. Gale Meadows Pond. Near Manchester where I live."

Five minutes later Tal was in Vermont. The hillsides were covered with pine and maple and the fields were stitched

44

neatly together.

Indian country. An independent state, so Tal had read, for 14 years after independence from the British. Some Vermonters apparently still fantasised about secession so they had something in common with Ukrainians.

Tal looked beyond the Green Mountains and saw white villages with warm-smelling stores and churches with needle-point spires. And schools and playgrounds. The Tempo accelerated.

He parked it among the cars belonging to tourists visiting Hildene where Lincoln's son, Robert Todd, died in 1926. Organ music reached him faintly from the manor.

Carrying the canvas sheath containing rods and rifle over his shoulder and swinging the tackle bag, he made his way downhill to the Battenkill Valley.

The sun was warm on his back, insects buzzed industriously. Fishing licence to hand in case he was challenged, Tal sat on the bank of the stream, a frustrated fisherman taking a rest, an assassin waiting for dusk. To his right he could see the rise overlooking the safe house. From the tackle bag he took a pair of field-glasses and made a casual survey of the terrain, focussing finally on the gentle hill.

When his time came he walked with the fatigued tread of a city dweller exhausted by sun and fresh air towards the rise. Mist was clothing the stream for the night, bird-song was fading. A single star, a diamond stud, was pinned in the cooling sky.

How many guards would there be on the rise? Not many, probably only one; a safe house was a secret. At the foot of the incline a couple of children were still playing. Tal took a firecracker from his pocket, lit it with a match and threw it.

As it jumped and exploded, as the children yelped, as the guard came boring through the undergrowth, Tal slipped between the trees and began to climb. Behind him he heard the guard bawling out the children.

He froze behind a tree. From time to time he heard the guard patrolling the base of the hill. When it was as dark as it would ever be beneath the stars he fitted the 'scope to the Mannlicher-Carcano and rested the barrel of the rifle on a branch.

45

Through the 'scope, over the rim of a laurel hedge, he could see the upstairs windows of the house. There were no lights in the rooms but a faint radiance reached them from below.

Tal waited. His life was a waiting.

The trees rustled and breathed. Somewhere a fiddler played discordant snatches of a jig. A woman laughed. A star moved, a satellite.

Who would have thought that a boy in Kiev who had only wanted to join in the fun would one day be keeping a pine tree company in America waiting to kill a fellow Russian?

Suddenly Yashin's room was a square of cosy light. Tal stopped breathing, pulled the butt of the rifle into his shoulder, touched the trigger, squeezed it gently as the 'scope found Yashin's face.

The explosion was a shock even though it was he who had pulled the trigger. It always was. Yashin disappeared, a fallen glove puppet.

Tal, lifting the rifle from the branch, continued to wait until the guard, looking for another firework, presented himself in silhouette. He shot him in the chest, returned the gun to the rods and made his way back to the parking lot where the Tempo was waiting for him alone in the starlight.

CHAPTER 6

For a long time no one spoke as the Thunderbird, the girl at the wheel, sped south; as though the impact of the bullet had projected each of them into a private crisis. Headlights swooped at them baring their fears; trees stuttered past, black and silver, giving the fears a saw-edge.

Hannah spoke first. "So who taught you that ingenious idea?" she asked Yashin.

"A friend in the Seventh Directorate. Surveillance," he explained. "It only works if you figure out the angles in the daylight and line yourself up with the mirror in the dark. You switch on the light, you're hidden by a drape and, if the angles are right, all the marksman can see is your reflection. His reactions are so swift that he doesn't give himself time for questions. He squeezes the trigger and, bang, you're dead, your skull a shower of broken glass. But he doesn't see the glass, he doesn't see anything, you're gone."

Hamilton, sitting beside Hannah, said: "So safe houses aren't safe anymore." He turned to Yashin in the back seat. "I'm sorry."

"Makes Fort Knox open house by comparison?"

"You've got a sleeper in Domestic Operations?"

"It's possible. I don't know. If we have he's doing a good job."

Secondary shock waves pulsed. The shards of glass were splinters in his skull. He saw his face disappear, his body decapitated. If Executive Action could get to him so quickly what chance did he stand? Wherever Hamilton takes me

47

Kiselev will follow.

He said: "Maybe you should take me to Fort Knox. Or would our sleeper get in there?"

"This is very embarrassing."

"Understatement of the year," Hannah said braking as red lights loomed.

If I had known it was going to be like this, Yashin asked himself, would I have jumped? But what other option did I have? What do I have now? Wait to be shot, knifed, bombed by my own people while the Americans reach for my soul? Enemies both.

As the lights beckoned green he said: "This time it has to be somewhere not on your list."

"There will be an investigation," Hamilton said. "It isn't necessarily DO; it could be another department. It could be FBI or Secret Service."

"The Secret Service! They even put their phone number in the directory. Some secret." A thin moon hanging like a scimitar over a black range of hills had joined the stars. "Don't deceive yourself, Hamilton. The address was only known to Domestic Operations – you don't share information like that – and that's where the leak is."

The shock waves were razoring into a single blade of pain; the pain was also reason, simplicity. He only had one immediate option: string along with the CIA until Tuslov could expose Lozak. If Tuslov failed then he had three options: betray Russia, return to Moscow or kill himself.

"Where are you taking me?"

"A motel near Baltimore," Hamilton told him.

"On the list?"

"I don't even know which motel."

"Any motel," the girl said. "The third one we see within ten miles of the city limits. How about that?"

"If he knew the safe house he'll know your car."

"We'll rent one," she said.

"In any case," Hamilton said, "we have some time on our side. Whoever took a shot at you thinks you're dead."

"*Thought*, if the sleeper's doing his job."

"Thinks. We haven't told Langley yet." Hamilton rubbed condensation from the side window and peered into the night

48

as though searching for truth. "You came here to penetrate the American space programme. Right?"

"The Center wouldn't have been adverse to any information."

"Russians speaking English like a native—"

"A Red Indian?"

"–aren't that common. When they do show they've been briefed to infiltrate a particular field . . ." Yashin heard Hamilton searching his pockets for non-existent cigarettes. Before this was over he would be smoking again. "What I'm getting at is that an agent like you would know the identities of other agents."

"There are so many," Yashin said.

"Don't bullshit me, Yashin."

"Mikhail," Yashin said. "But I promise you I don't know the identities of any sleepers in Domestic Operations," oddly pleased that he had been able to tell the truth. "Why should I?"

"Agents in other departments?"

"You don't expect me to tell you?"

"One could lead us to the leak. Save your life."

"I thought you were going to do that," Yashin said.

"One thing baffles me," Hamilton said with weary patience. "And Hannah. And Letz."

"And the President?"

"Maybe him too . . . Why did you defect if you were determined to be hostile? You act more like a captured POW, name, rank and serial number, just like the movies – vintage black and white – than a deserter."

"Why Baltimore?" Yashin asked.

"Why not? Good communications. Near Washington, not too far from New York."

The bullet had punched a hole as big as a fist in the bedroom wall. It would have blown the back of his head off. He saw himself dead in a life-after-death vision.

They retreated into silence again until light flowed thickly past the windows and Hamilton announced: "The Bronx."

With the lights came rain spattering the windshield, channelling into upstream rivulets. Traffic hissed past on the black canal of the highway. The rain and the water-noise made

Yashin feel helpless, afloat.

"Interstate 95," Hamilton told him. "All the way to . . ."

"Baltimore?"

"Beyond," and Yashin sensed that Hamilton had almost committed an indiscretion. Did the girl know?

She was driving with more composure now. There weren't many women drivers in Moscow; Galina had driven his black Volga but she hadn't been blessed with road sense and when he sold it in the second-hand market in a field near Somonovskaya Quay on the Moscow River before he left it had still born the scars; it had been at least 10 years old – there was no such thing as an old car in Russia.

Where was Kiselev now? Reporting contract completed to Dobykin? Yashin frowned. There was a discrepancy there somewhere.

Kiselev. If Lozak wanted a job carried out efficiently, speedily and unofficially he wouldn't employ the established assassin in New York. Wouldn't have the authority to do so. So what would he do? He would, Yashin supposed, open his black file on Simenov, head of Executive Action, and *persuade* him to dispatch the best contract killer in the business to New York. But Yashin didn't want Hamilton to suspect the real reason why he had escaped with the implication that if he was cleared, he would return to the Soviet Union. Not yet anyway. Buy time!

He said: "Who do you think tried to kill me?"

Hamilton said: "You would know better than me"

"Kiselev?"

"Who—"

"Don't *you* bullshit *me*," Yashin said. "We both know Kiselev is Executive Action in the United States."

"Kiselev then. If you insist."

"Haven't you had him under surveillance?"

"Surveillance can be slipped."

"You lost him? You know something? I'd feel safer in Disneyworld."

Irritation rasped Hamilton's voice. "You would have to have big ears or a beak," he said.

* * *

The walls of the room in the motel off John F. Kennedy Highway to the east of Baltimore were on the move. Closing, a four-sided vise.

They were papered in faded autumnal tones, worn and brown-greased round the light switches. A stain shaped like Australia had been splashed long ago beneath a mottled print of tall ships in Chesapeake Bay at the turn of the century.

Yashin, standing between the two beds, the bird fluttering inside his chest, concentrated on the door connecting with Hannah Martin's room. One hand searched inside his jacket for the scar tissue slippery beneath his shirt.

Pushing at the walls with his free hand, he made his way to the door. It was painted with sticky varnish and buttoned with a thumb-tack. He raised his hand to it, paused; they had been there two hours; she would be in bed. He looked at his watch. 1 am. He retreated. The bird spread its wings. He knocked and called: "Can I speak to you for a moment?"

She was still dressed in a white blouse with a tall collar and a blue, rustling skirt. The question mark beside her mouth bent into a smile. "Your place or mine?"

"Yours." He sat on a chair beside a dressing-table, its edge serrated by cigarette burns. She sat on one of the beds. She had washed her face and it was night-pale and vulnerable. She said: "You look terrible."

"I felt trapped."

"The accident?"

"Maybe. It started a couple of years later. The psychiatrist thought it was connected with my job. *A free spirit suddenly contained by conspiracy*," Yashin quoted.

"But you're not a conspirator. Are you?"

"They made me one," Yashin said. "Did they make you one?"

"I volunteered. Disappointed?"

"Should I be?"

"My husband was in intelligence."

"Was?"

"He was killed on a mission in Berlin. By the KGB," she added. Dilated pupils had pushed the green from her eyes.

"I'm sorry."

"I carried on where he left off. He didn't have much time

51

for people who betrayed their country."

"I'm beginning to wish I hadn't knocked on that door," Yashin said. He bounced his finger over the cigarette burns. "Betrayed?" He dissected it. "What about the German generals who tried to kill Hitler during World War II? They were heroes, weren't they? Martyrs."

The bird, diverted, stopped beating its wings.

"Hitler was a monster."

"And Stalin was a good guy?"

"Hitler attacked Stalin."

"Stalin was a monster too," Yashin said. "Stop putting values in pigeon-holes. You think to escape is to betray? I don't agree," wondering if sincerity had trapped him into an admission – that he had no intention of divulging any information.

But she didn't seem aware of any nuance, her theme too strong for such subtleties. "To escape from East to West . . . Surely that's a form of betrayal. It will be used as anti-Soviet propaganda. Unless . . ." She leaned against the headboard, hands clasped behind her neck and stared at him. Lies would burn in such a gaze. "Unless you're planning to redefect."

He stood up. "I knocked on the door because I felt as though I was being crushed. I don't need any of this."

She relaxed, crossed her long legs. Lies could survive now. "You should feel at home here," she said. "Communications . . . Morse's first telegraph message was received here at Fort McHenry."

"Where's Hamilton?"

"Gone to find a safe, safe house."

"Here?"

"I wish it was. Baltimore is a graceful city. But it has a complex – Washington, 40 miles away."

"Somewhere at the other end of Interstate 95?"

"You don't miss much," she said.

"Where?"

"Nothing's certain yet." She spun the conversation around. "Why were you such a good Communist?"

He told her that he had never been given the opportunity to be a bad one. That from kindergarten, as an Octobrist, he had been set on course. Young Pioneer, Komsomol . . . That from the nursery he had been taught collective responsibility. *Zvenovoi* . . . "Do you know what they are?" and when she shook her head: "Kids who have to report other kids for bad behaviour . . . Do you know what we did to them?" and even though she nodded: "We kicked their asses."

"But you believe in the system?"

"Like everyone else I criticised it but I accepted it. We lost 20 million lives defending it." How many times had he heard that explanation, 40 years old, trotted out? "Do you accept your system?"

"I don't accept anything."

"An anarchist?"

"I don't believe and I don't disbelieve. Was your wife a good Communist?"

"She was the wife of a good Communist; that was all that mattered."

"A chattel?"

"She was never that," Yashin said. "Liberated? As much as any Russian woman is. The Party pretends that women are equal. More women in the Supreme Soviet than all the parliaments in capitalist countries put together. But where it really counts, in the Politburo, there isn't one. And, sure, a husband and wife both go to work but you take a look at them in the evening: he's swigging vodka in front of the television while she's washing the dishes."

Galina was a whore, he thought.

"Are you feeling better?"

He saw the fatigue on her face. He stood up. "I'm sorry—"

"Stop feeling sorry," she said.

A KGB swallow, he reflected as he lay in bed, eyes level with Australia, would give it five minutes before barging through the connecting door naked. He closed his eyes; when he opened them it was light and he was still alone.

* * *

The Victorian mansion, russet-walled and blank-eyed, stood on the east shoreline of Chesapeake Bay, 20 miles from the motel; in the sunlight it was a benign anachronism preserved in the memory of gentility. It had been built on the proceeds of shipping coal, a source rarely mentioned in latterday family conversation, although spice, a subsidiary cargo, was occasionally given an airing.

Hamilton parked the Thunderbird at the end of the gravel drive and walked round the mansion saluting the black who was driving an old-fashioned, gasoline-powered mower in parallel swathes across the lawns leading to the water.

"Hi there, Mr. Hamilton," he said. "How you doin'?"

"Fine," Hamilton said. "Just fine."

"Okay. You take it easy now."

He found her half way to the landing-stage snipping flowers with a pair of scissors. On one arm she carried a willow basket. Hamilton sometimes felt that she saw herself in impressionist paintings. Her harvest-coloured hair was loose, the smile on her tranquil features indulgent.

Snip. She consigned a pink daisy to the basket and offered her cheek. He kissed it lightly. She wore a yellow dress; Hamilton saw her in a field of blood-red poppies.

"What brings you here?" as though he were a remote relative who had suddenly materialised from the West Coast instead of her husband who lived in Washington.

"I wanted to see you about the house in Florida," he said.

"As a matter of fact I wanted to see you. I was going to call you. Everyone else is in Newport."

"That's why you were going to call me? Because they wouldn't be upset by me?"

"Don't be ridiculous. Leave your complexes in Langley."

"It's overcrowded with them," Hamilton said.

Ten years ago Langley had been a citadel, but no one had warned him that you must not doubt; that doubt is failure.

A breeze coming in from the water flirted with her hair. She pushed it back from her forehead with the tips of her fingers. An actress's gesture. Paulette Goddard for Yashin, Joan Fontaine for me.

If I had been an outrageous success would we still be together? If I hadn't suspected that happiness is a filament that glows outside ideologies would we be in bed by now?

But you are a success, Hamilton. The best interrogator in the business. Why? Because you're a failure.

She said: "I want to talk about the future." The present had once been the future.

54

She dropped the scissors in with the flowers and walked towards the broad inlet of Chesapeake Bay. Sailboats had settled there like butterflies; motor yachts bulldozed avenues in the water. She leaned against the bronze bust of a man with a patrician profile gazing towards Baltimore. One word had been weathered from the inscription. Coal?

She said: "I know what you think, that we could have made out and kept ideals." One finger found the parting in her hair. "If they had been our ideals maybe, but they weren't, they were yours. I have to respect someone . . ."

"About the house . . ."

"You're so goddam self-righteous," she said. "Okay, so you don't believe life behind the Iron Curtain is as bad as they make out. That's your privilege. I happen to enjoy the lifestyle here. That's my fault: I was born here. And I want to enjoy—"

"The respect?"

"Sure, the respect that a man who believes in our values commands."

"Perhaps those values aren't so different."

"Don't say *relatively speaking*. For God's sake don't say that."

Hamilton shrugged at the bust. "It's just that I sometimes wonder why two countries can't just leave each other alone."

"You sound as if you're still at college. I happen to believe that we have to fight Communism. You thought that once." She stroked the back of the bronze head. "I could still be happy with a rising star in intelligence. I'm not like the others—"

"Your parents?"

"I'm not like them. Or their kind. I don't want to be married to a senator. I believe in the work you're doing. I just wish you did."

"I haven't said I don't. I just question."

"Everyone questions but they don't make a big thing about it." She walked towards the landing stage; waves thrust aside by a motor launch slapped it. "Most people are doing a job they don't like; you aren't so special. But they make something of it. And they expand outside it." She stopped by the landing stage. "We could start again in Europe."

"Letz?"

"He called me. Apparently you've been given a very important job."

"Did he tell you what it is?"

"No. But obviously it's an interrogation. He said it was so important that if you brought it off you would be promoted. He said we could go to Paris," she said. "Or London."

"Which would you prefer?"

"I want you to succeed."

"If I don't?" He followed her onto the landing stage; tiny fish darted ahead of their creaking footsteps and the air smelled of mud.

"It would be sad."

"An ultimatum?"

"We're half way to being separated now," she said.

"You should have married someone like Letz."

"At least he has pride."

"And ambition," Hamilton said.

"That too. Is that so terrible?"

"Values are what he's short on."

Hamilton tossed a splinter of wood into the water; the little fish arrowed in upon it, then swam away in disgust. A yellow biplane buzzed past; the pilot waved and Catherine waved back.

She was standing with her back to him and, remembering, he placed his hands on either side of her waist. He kissed her neck and she leaned against him. "The house," he said. "If I'm going to succeed I must have the house."

"We'll talk about it later," she said. "Let's go inside now." She took his hand and led him past the bronze bust, across the parallel swathes of the lawn, across the hallway and up the magisterial stairs to her bedroom.

* * *

As they bowled south in a rented Buick, Hamilton, at the wheel, told Yashin about the house in Florida.

"It belongs to my wife's family. An old mansion between the Atlantic and the intracoastal waterway just outside Palm Beach. It will be deserted at this time of the year."

"Why?" Yashin asked. He was sitting in the back of the

56

blue Buick beside Hannah. "The weather should be good. Shouldn't it?" he asked Hannah.

"Palm Beach is for winter," Hannah said. "And Thanksgiving. People who own property wouldn't be seen dead there out of season. The Kennedys, for instance."

"People go all the year round to Yalta," Yashin said. "The road leading from the port to the centre of the town is called Franklin D. Roosevelt Street," he told them for no reason that he could think of.

"It's going to be very hot," Hamilton said. "Do you mind the heat?"

He crept past a fast-moving silver truck on the US 1 approaching Richmond. He had taken the old route to confuse, although pursuit was surely impossible. He intended to rejoin Interstate 95 at Petersburg.

"I prefer the cold," Yashin said. "The real cold when a wet cigar butt becomes a bullet when you take it out of your mouth."

"Are all Russians as defensive about their country as you?" Hannah asked.

"Defensive, proud – there isn't much to choose between them." He pointed out of the window. "That truck, it's a wall. *God bless America*. Isn't that a little defensive? As though he forgot to bless it in the first place."

"What else have you noticed about Americans?" Hannah asked.

"I haven't met many but I've noticed that you say shit a lot." He turned to look at the retreating truck; from his throne in the cabin the driver looked down at small vehicles with disdain. "Why didn't you tell me about the mansion in Florida yesterday?"

"I wasn't sure I could get it," Hamilton told him.

"Why not if it belongs to your wife's family?"

"I'm not exactly their golden-haired boy."

"Hans Christian Andersen," Yashin said. "Remember him?"

"No fairy tale," Hamilton said. "I had to ask my wife to ask her parents."

"In Baltimore?"

"Nearby."

57

"Why didn't you tell me?"

"I didn't have to," Hamilton said. "Did I?"

"You should write a thesis on half-truths," Yashin said. "An interesting theme. How to tell the truth and not tell the truth. It could become a standard work on interrogation."

"This time it should be perfectly safe."

"You wife knows . . ."

"She doesn't know about you."

"Not by name. But she's not stupid, is she?"

"She married me," Hamilton said, as three motorcyclists, faces whipped lean by speed, stormed past. THINGS GO BETTER WITH COCAINE was emblazoned across the back of one of their leather jackets.

Yashin said: "You didn't tell because you thought I might tell the Mission."

"Why would you do that? You don't have suicidal tendencies, do you?"

"Maybe you thought I had given them the address in Vermont. That the attempt on my life was rigged to make my defection seem more genuine. After all, you don't want KGB camped around the mansion in Florida. You don't want me rescued. You don't want another Yurchenko . . ."

"'O what a tangled web we weave'," Hamilton said.

"'When first we practice to deceive'," Hannah said. "Shakespeare."

"Scott," Yashin said.

"We have to examine every possibility," Hamilton said. "We nearly blew it in Vermont. That one-time pad you used to communicate with Moscow . . . That wasn't exactly laying your cards on the table . . ."

"What makes you think I have any cards?"

"Why use a one-time pad?"

"If you want it forget it – I burned it."

"You have cards all right," Hamilton said.

Hannah said: "I'm hungry, let's have lunch."

They bought sandwich boxes at the New York Delicatessen in Richmond and took them onto the lawns of the Capitol. Afterwards they walked round the tree-lined avenues and copper and bronze monuments and plaques commemorating battles of the Civil War.

"I thought the Unionists won," Yashin said.

"Not here," Hannah said. "This is Robert E. Lee's city."

"We have that in common," Yashin said. "A civil war. Both fought for freedom. 'A government of the people, by the people, and for the people.' 'The workers have nothing to lose but their chains ...' although Marx was a little premature."

"If we both fought for freedom," Hamilton asked, "then why are we fighting each other now?"

"Perhaps neither of us won it," Hannah said and to Yashin: "Adviser and interpreter of the scene, wasn't that what I was described as? Someone to make you feel at home?"

"Isn't there an American saying, 'You could have fooled me'?"

Hannah pointed at an art gallery. "Take a look in there – it contains Fabergé's Easter Eggs made for the Czars."

* * *

The weekend retreat of the Soviet Mission in New York is located at Glen Cove on the north shoreline of Long Island, 20 miles from Manhattan. The shabby mansion is shielded by thick woods and sealed by a high fence that satisfies the Russian instinct for secrecy and confirms the American conviction that all Soviet activity is subversive.

On this warm, burgeoning morning the most sinister activity in progress inside the mansion was a one-handed game of pool. Tal v. Tal. The pockets were targets and he potted the balls with such drilled precision that an onlooker would not have suspected that he was consumed by impatience.

Where the hell was Dobykin? He was supposed to have checked into the mansion at nine with confirmation of Yashin's death. He looked at the old-fashioned wall clock. 9.35. He set up the balls again, broke them and watched them scatter across the balding surface of the table. If Dobykin didn't arrive soon he would miss the Pan-Am flight to Moscow.

Dobykin walked in as he was poised to pocket the first ball. His sturdy figure seemed to be possessed by conflicting emotions. Anger and satisfaction?

Tal, still crouched over his cue, said: "What took you so long?"

Dobykin said: "Yashin's still alive." That was the anger. "You fucked up." That was the satisfaction.

Tal took his shot and missed.

CHAPTER 7

America was a motel room.

America was a TV screen. Religion, weather, cartoons and *messages* – jeans, tampons, stains.

America was an endless highway.

America was breakfast in a diner. Iced water and coffee and grits and robots serving.

America was a dark bar containing lonely statues, hands cupped round friendly drinks.

America was the fit and the fat.

America was uniformity.

America was a church across the street from a topless bar.

America was murder – two paragraphs in a fat newspaper.

America was drugs.

America was black versus white.

America was a motel room.

*   *   *

And I have to get out of it, Yashin decided.

It was 11 pm. According to Hamilton there were no guards. If you believed that you believed the earth was flat.

He slid the bolt on the door leading onto a long balcony. Beneath, cars waited in ranks for their owners. The parking lot was silvered with moonlight but the air smelled brown, swampy.

A mile away headlights on the highway burrowed into the night; the yellow glow in the sky to his right was Savannah, the South.

Yashin, wearing sports jacket and blue shirt and carrying the fire-extinguisher he had taken from the wall of his room, walked along the balcony; it reminded him of the balconies in American prison movies. Tipsy voices issued from a lighted room, a woman's laugh abruptly gasping, sighing, crooning. The whole building breathed.

He reached the end of the balcony. Stone steps led to more cars. The first guard was seated at the wheel of an automobile three spaces from the foot of the steps. As Yashin descended them he got out of the car.

He stared uncertainly at Yashin. "Excuse me, sir, could I ask where you're going?"

"For a walk," Yashin said. To the guard the truth would be a lie: no one walked in America.

"Better stay put, sir. It can be dangerous alone at night."

"You'd better come with me then."

The guard, young and bulky, said: "Those aren't my—"

"Your instructions are to protect me, aren't they?"

"Sure. But—" Yashin came down the last two steps. "Hey!"

The guard's hand slid inside his jacket as Yashin produced the extinguisher from behind his back. The foam hit the guard in the face. His shout was clogged with it.

Yashin ran.

The second guard was in a pool of darkness near the Buick. In case I've stolen the keys or know how to start a car by joining wires.

He was a silhouette, long and square shouldered, and part of the silhouette was the gun in his hand. "Hold it right there."

"You're supposed to be protecting me," Yashin said, "not shooting me. God help you if you shoot me."

"God help me if you escape. Where's Chuck?"

"Fire-fighting," Yashin said. "Here, catch this," and threw the fire-extinguisher at the second guard and, hearing the gun fall to the ground, ran.

The wail of the train was loneliness, Yashin thought as he ran across the track into another America.

Small wooden houses leaned against each other for support; arthritic automobiles knelt in their yards. A rat scuttled for cover. But the lighted rooms inside the shacks looked neat and scrub-clean.

In a yard a group of blacks, lit by a naked bulb hanging from a tree, were drinking from bottles and playing cards. Laughter and thick whispers hung on the moist air.

The two guards, guns in hands, approached with more caution, Yashin thought, than an unarmed, disorientated Russian merited. He ran down an alley and crouched behind a shack that smelled of chemical fertiliser.

He heard the guards blaming each other.

Two children ran past him. An indignant cat arched its back. An aircraft drifted across the sky winking its lights.

One guard said: "The asshole could be anywhere." Yashin saw foam on his face.

One of the blacks slapped down his cards and swept up a litter of dollar bills. A train whooshed past shaking the buildings.

"You take left, I'll take right," the second guard said.

The first guard came down the alley wiping foam from his cheek with his unarmed hand. Yashin shrank inside the shack. The smell of chemicals pleaded with him to cough. He peered through a gap in the slats. The guard had stopped outside.

Cough, said his throat.

The guard said to himself: "Sonofabitch."

The train hooted farewell.

The cough gathered strength.

The guard coughed. Yashin coughed with him.

The guard moved away.

Yashin gave him a couple of minutes before emerging and returning the way he had come. So where do I go? he asked himself. Deeper into this other America which in the moonlight had acquired fragile graces? He could imagine what it looked like in daylight.

*   *   *

Hannah Martin, standing on the balcony above the parked cars, hammered on Hamilton's door.

"What is it?" Hamilton's voice was lazy with sleep.

"He's gone," she shouted. "Yashin's gone."

He had no money, no ID, no chance of communicating with Moscow. Without the CIA he had nothing. So why escape? To prove I can do it? he answered himself. No, more. To prove I am not a tame rabbit, that a motel room is not my hutch. No, more. To prove I am not just another gutless escapee fleeing from a system that offends me. What he couldn't understand was why he wanted to prove these things and, shaking his head slightly the way Hamilton did when he perceived unanswered questions ahead, turned down the path leading to the railroad track.

The arm that grabbed him from behind, locked round his throat, felt boneless, all sinew. The blade of a knife pricked the flesh beneath his ear. He could smell the man's sweat, feel his breath.

"Okay," the man said. "You just tell me where that wallet is. Don't you go for it. If you ain't got a wallet your shoe maybe. That where you keeping the bread to pay for black pussy?"

"I haven't got any money," Yashin said.

"Don't give me shit, man." One hand rifled the pockets of his jacket. "Tell me where the bread is and you won't get cut and don't give me any of that ten bucks in your shirt pocket crap."

If you're attacked from behind by an assailant with a knife don't resist. "That way you lose your head," the instructor had told them.

"In the inside pocket of my jacket."

"I just tried—"

"You missed one. To the left. A roll of bills."

As the hand reached inside the jacket from behind Yashin kicked back with one foot and, ducking his head down and away from the knife, plunged forward executing a wrestling throw; except that his opponent didn't want to be thrown and his feet were embedded in concrete. So this was the climax of one man's fight against injustice, death at the hands of a Sokolniki thief, a mugger. This, the final injustice, fed his strength. He rolled forward, pulling. A bone or a tendon snapped within the entity that was the two of them; his assailant, screaming, came over his head like a sack of flour thrown by a miller.

Yashin went in with his feet, kicking. The knife sprang away, a silver fish leaping in the moonlight, a minute distraction, enough for the wounded man to grab his ankle and bring him down. "Now I'm going to kill you, motherfucker." He wore only a singlet and shorts and his limbs were oiled pistons. A knee slammed into Yashin's crotch; the pain was a charge of electricity. Powered by it, he threw himself to one side and found the knife under his hand. His fingers tightened round the handle.

As a foot stamped on his wrist. "Okay," the guard with the foam on his face said. "Hold it right there. Both of you." The gun barrel embraced the two of them. "Now get up, nice and easy, hands behind your heads," and, as the other guard arrived, "go over to that wall. Now move it."

The black waited till they were close to the wall, then dived through a hole in an adjoining fence punching the hole in the rotting wood bigger in his trajectory; the guards let him go as Yashin had guessed they would. "You're the one," the second guard said, prodding the pistol at Yashin.

*   *   *

"Why?" Hamilton asked.

The motel room again. Except that it was no longer a hutch and he was no longer rabbit with timid pink eyes.

"Something I had to do."

"B movies."

"I saw a lot of those."

Hannah Martin said: "I think I'll hit the sack. Proving yourself isn't that clever. Too many guys think they have to do it."

"Too many have to," Yashin said. The pain in his crotch came in lances. "Do you understand?" to Hamilton.

"All it got you was a knee in the balls."

Hamilton paced the room. Hannah got to her feet and nodded goodnight.

Yashin lay on his bed; the stain on the wall this time was . . . where? Sakhalin?

He said: "I heard frogs croaking."

"And cicadas?"

"I heard the outside. Have you ever listened to it, Hamilton?"

Hamilton stopped pacing and stared at Sakhalin. Finally he said : "We all try to hear it, Mikhail. We all try to hear it."

"This cage, it isn't necessary."

"For your own protection. And you *were* protected."

"From a thief."

"He could have been Kiselev."

"Not if only Letz and you and your wife know where we're going. But that can't be, can it Jack? The two guards know where we're going . . ."

"They're following, that's all."

"Andersen?"

"You claim you were coming back when you were hit. Is that a fairy story?"

"I was coming back," Yashin said. "*To the other side of the tracks.* What is it about tracks?"

"A natural dividing line. Cross it and you can get hit by a train. Do you want a doctor?"

Yashin shook his head slowly; it was becoming a habit. He said: "Sometimes you look at a middle-aged man and you can see him when he was young. You aren't even middle-aged and yet I can't see you when you were young. What were you like, Jack?"

"Promising," Hamilton told him.

Another train cried plaintively. Yashin thought about the highway beaded with lights travelling in opposite directions. The constant, 24-hour movement astonished him and he had developed a theory about it. A sophisticated computer into which you fed all the travellers' reasons for making a trip; at least half would cancel out each other; a plumber going north, a plumber going south – stay where you are and do each other's jobs.

Yashin yawned. Hamilton had given him a pain-killer but it may have had other properties.

He said sleepily: "We were all promising. The sad thing is we didn't know it."

"They got me on the campus," Hamilton said. "At the age when promising can lead you almost anywhere. They beat big

66

patriotic drums. The war against Communism which never ceases, just goes underground. Me with my way with languages, sport . . . Did you know I beat the college record for home runs?" And when Yashin spread his hands uncomprehendingly: "The all American boy but without that touch of class to distinguish values."

"Sounds like character defect to me."

"More common than the common cold." Hamilton sat on the edge of the other bed and ran one big hand through his thinning hair. "Chauvinism – the processing starts when you're a kid. The glory of war. The crusades. I wonder what Islamic history books have to say about them."

"*'War is hell'*. General Sherman?"

"Fifteen years after he had devastated 60 miles of homeland between Atlanta and the ocean."

"Is it so wrong to be a patriot?" Yashin heard his words dragging after each other.

"Patriotism fine. Professional patriotism? Dubious."

"Aren't you a professional?"

"They made me one; that's the point. We should have a choice."

"I had a choice," Yashin said. The pain in his groin was a gentle ache, not unpleasant; sleep was muslin enfolding him, making gauzy folds of his vision. "I wanted to help establish Russia in space."

"To start with you had a choice. Not after the accident."

"I still . . . had . . . a choice. Communications . . . nothing wrong . . . with that."

"Unless you were concerned with hostile intent in space." The softer his own voice became the more Hamilton's boomed; as it boomed his face expanded. "Did you want to be a spy? Was that your choice?"

The drug. Was it to stop him trying to escape again or to make him vulnerable to interrogation? Maybe his words weren't as fuzzy as they sounded. Maybe they were as crisp as snapping crackers. Yashin smiled, handled his delivery with care. "Stop putting words in my mouth, Jack. Stop making me come out in sympathy with your own complexes."

The words sailed away in red balloons. Just before the last of them exploded gently against the ceiling Yashin noticed that, beneath his jacket, Hamilton was carrying a gun.

*   *   *

The house stood on a stretched finger of land about 20 miles long separating Florida's intracoastal waterway – Lake Worth at its broader reaches – from the Atlantic Ocean.

This strip, fed by the A1A, is shouldered at decent intervals by condominiums and mansions each of which comes complete with moss-smooth lawns, sprinklers and brawny young gardeners. At the northern tip of the finger lies Palm Beach where, from the road, from the yachts that challenge each other on the sea and the intracoastal waterway, from the small planes that buzz the yachts, the residences look like papier-maché film sets awaiting a clapper board.

The pile owned by the parents of Catherine Hamilton lay to the south of Palm Beach, between Gloria Vanderbilt's old shack and a majestically discreet dwelling occupied at different times by the Duke and Duchess of Windsor and Winston Churchill.

Yashin saw a Grecian portico, benign brick, arrows of water through Australian pine and sea-grape, a deep and leisurely pool, leaning palms and a tennis court. A reclusive aristocrat kept alive by the breathing rollers of the Atlantic.

And a tunnel from the house, under the A1A. An extravagant convenience, according to Hamilton, to give access to the ocean beach.

To Yashin a gun-barrel.

CHAPTER 8

On his second day in the mansion Yashin called Tuslov in Moscow. It sounded as though they were throwing their voices into a tunnel, each response overlapped by an echo.

"How's Anatoly, Anatoly . . .?"

"Fine, fine . . ."

"Have they approached him, approached him . . .?"

A resonant pause after the last echo; Yashin bit into the inside of his lip. "Nothing more, nothing more . . . He's okay, okay . . ."

The taste of blood in his mouth was sweet.

In echoes he asked Tuslov if there had been any progress. Even if the eavesdroppers understood it didn't matter: they could not have understood the first call when one-time pads had been used.

Tuslov said yes there had been progress. Not dramatic but significant. How much longer? Impossible to say. "Trust me, trust me . . ."

And the overall picture? Acute anxiety at Politburo level. Because – here Yashin mentally congratulated Tuslov – no one knew what Yashin had taken with him. A beautiful ambiguity that would force Letz to prolong the interrogation.

Time, my only currency. And when it runs out . . . Yashin thrust aside the possibilities and said to Tuslov: "Thank you my friend, friend, take care, take care . . ."

"And you, Misha." Tuslov cut the last echo.

*   *   *

Q: So, Mikhail, tell me about your first impressions of America.

A: I already have.

Q: Tell me again. I'm interested, I really am.

A: The extremes, they disgust me.

Q: It isn't typical here.

A: It never is.

Q: You know why we're here. Now if we were in say the Mid-west, in a small town, you'd find equality.

A: You mean they're Communists?

Q: Don't be a Holy Joe, Mikhail. Don't forget I've been to the fount of Communism. How about those dachas at Peredelkino? How about the mud huts in Kazakhstan?

Listener 1: Here we go again. Some interrogation.

Listener 2: Hamilton's intimidating him. Hoping to trap him into an admission.

A: Peredelkino and Kazakhstan aren't separated by a railway track.

Q: You know, Mikhail, you worry me. If you feel so strongly about the way of life here why did you defect?

A: Maybe I didn't believe it was like this. Maybe I didn't believe the Soviet propagandists.

Q: So what are you going to do?

A: I'm thinking about it.

Q: Thinking about it! Sweet Jesus! I thought the British had the copyright on understatement. Look, Mikhail, don't be a smart-ass – you can't go back.

A: Yurchenko did.

Listener 1: Ouch.

Q: That was a set-up.

A: A fuck-up. Good American parlance?

Q: You're different to Yurchenko. You left under a cloud.

A: I did? I was under a cloud and I was given a top job in the Soviet Mission in New York?

Q: Dzerzhinsky Square's in an uproar not to mention the Kremlin. Why are you so important, Mikhail?

A: I'm KGB.

Q: The KGB is constructed so that no single operative has access to material that can seriously endanger the Soviet Union. Why are you so different?

70

A: I wasn't aware that I was.

Q: Bullshit. We know you've brought a bagful of secrets with you.

Listener 1: Attaboy. The meter just went into shock.

A: You know more than me, Jack.

Q: Hans Christian Andersen?

Listener 1: What the hell . . .

A: Did you know there's also a statue of Alice in Wonderland in Central Park? That's where you are right now, wonderland.

Q: A defector must co-operate. That's part of the deal.

A: I am co-operating.

Q: Have you considered the alternative? If you don't co-operate?

A: You wouldn't do that.

Q: Think about it, Mikhail. Think about it.

*   *   *

The beach near the jetty was mined with empty beer cans, razored in places with broken glass. But the sand near the laced waves of the Atlantic was flat and clean, the water turquoise. White sails made a paper-chase of the ocean while motor yachts and power boats commuted between sea and intracoastal on the inlet on the other side of the quay. Families had staked claims to roasting spits of sand and the air smelled faintly of tanning oil. Behind Yashin and Hannah Martin strode a dogged guard wearing Bermuda shorts and a Hawaiian shirt; his partner, balding without his fedora, holding a cream jacket over his arm, watched from the jetty.

On the beach two green-uniformed policemen wearing Stetsons were arguing with a young couple flushed with heat and slurred with beer. The couple were indignant; the police, beefy and languid, indulgent. The girl had been topless, her partner bottomless. Someone had called the cops.

"Just as God made me," the young man said. His long hair had been sea-washed lifelessly over his ears and his pale skin was singed pink by the sun.

"Yeah?" One of the policemen watched a power-boat cutting a swathe through the water. In his green uniform, gun at his hip, he looked like a gardener poised to shoot aphids.

"Jealousy," the girl said. "Who called you? Some fat old cow with tits down to her kneecaps?" The girl, freckled and small-breasted, glared at her audience.

"I don't know, lady." The second policeman yawned. "All I know is no more skinny-dipping otherwise you get busted. Okay?"

Hannah said: "Do you have topless in Russia?"

"All the time," Yashin said. "You should see them on the river beaches outside Moscow."

"You surprise me."

"But the women have to wear tops."

"Why are you a spy? You should have been a comedian."

Her short hair was polished by the sun. She wore a white blouse and a knee-length skirt; beneath its hem her legs were firm-muscled and efficient.

The girl said to the policemen: "What is it with you guys? You want to make out with me at the police station?"

"Over my dead body," said the young man.

"Okay," said one of the policemen. "If that's the way you want it." He fingered the butt of his pistol.

The second cop shook his head. "I don't see anything I want over his dead body."

"You mentioned river beaches," Hannah said. "What are they like?"

"Narrow. Flat. Fresh water coasting past, deep and fast. A cafeteria, wooden benches . . ."

And matrons with hard faces that weren't hard at all and big soft bodies and white-skinned men muscled according to their trade paddling in the shallows and children drinking from bottles of cherry cordial stuck in the sand and white steamers swooning with lovers . . .

He said: "Why did Hamilton suddenly get tough?"

"Letz, I guess."

"Hamilton isn't a lackey."

"He'll satisfy Letz. Then he'll talk to you the way he wants to."

Hannah and Hamilton trying to catch me on the rebound from Letz?

The girl said: "I know what you guys want."

The two policemen yawned in unison.

72

The young man said: "If I had a uniform, a gun . . ."

One of the policemen: "Okay, pal, just keep your shorts above the Mason Dixon Line."

The girl said "You macho bastards are all the same."

Coins of light danced in the troughs of small waves.

"Tell me about Galina," Hannah said.

He couldn't stop.

*   *   *

She was born in Leningrad, the daughter of a flamboyant actor at the Musical Comedy Theatre on Rakov Street. When Yashin met her she was 17, Siberian-blonde and self-possessed, already taking bit parts, but without any discernible talent, at the Komsomol Theatre in Lenin Park.

When she was 18 Yashin, who had met her when the Komsomol performed at the Gagarin Space Institute, made love to her during the 40 minutes of dusk that divide the White Nights in Leningrad in the old Astoria Hotel. The following morning she asked him if, as he was *nachalstvo* – privileged he might be, but hardly élite – he could help her to obtain a permit to move to Moscow where life began. When she made it to Moscow she never ceased to remind him of the cultural superiority of Leningrad.

"Like a Bostonian in New York," Hannah said.

They were married in a Palace of Weddings six months later and Galina diligently applied herself to being the wife of a prospective cosmonaut and establishing herself in Muscovite society. She got a job with Mosfilm; she was little more than an extra but she brought directors and writers back to their apartment in the Arbat – Yevtushenko read one of his poems there – she shopped at the hard-currency beryozka shops, she ate at the Aragvi and drank whisky in the bar of the National and, her coup, gave birth to Anatoly in the Kremlin Clinic.

Because fledglings don't fly into space Yashin remained firmly on the ground until Anatoly was eight, the year of the accident.

Yashin slid his hand inside his shirt.

"How long after that did you split?" Hannah asked.

They had retraced their footsteps printed beside the waves

and they were approaching the tunnel leading from the beach to the house. Pink shells like baby's fingernails crunched under their feet. The beach, apart from globules of congealed oil, was cleaner here, its occupants far apart and subdued.

"She left me two years later."

"Were you a martyr?"

Her contempt surprised him. He searched her face for clues. Her eyes, even greener in the sunlight, were flecked with gold. But her face was a shadow, a dark glade wooded with her thoughts.

He said: "You remind me of Zontik, the little umbrella. One of the 129 fountains in the Grand Palace at Petrodvorets, 35 kilometres from Leningrad. A sad jet compared with Samson or the Chessboard Cascade. I wish you were more like Dubok, the little oak."

"I didn't know you were so fanciful, Comrade Yashin."

"Zontik is full of surprises. Go near him and he showers you. Maybe he even smiles."

"Okay, so why did she leave you?"

"A film director took her away. He was going to make her a star."

"And your son?"

"He absorbed it all, the way kids do without letting you know. The rebellion came much later. It shocked me, God knows why. Student protests, samizdat periodicals, the usual scene. He's 18 now, almost a full-time dissident. Next stop a labour camp or a psychiatric clinic. It's marvellous what they can do with drugs."

"I thought you were a good Communist."

"I'm a good Russian. There is a difference. That's what no one outside the Soviet Union understands."

"It didn't matter that other dissidents were victimised? It only matters now that your son is threatened?"

"I regard them as enemies of the State. And yes, you're right, it didn't matter until it was my son."

"Is he close to your wife?"

"My ex-wife. They meet a couple of times a week. She's worried about his attitudes."

"Your reactions, surely."

"Why do you think he's still at university. Divine intervention? I've saved him half a dozen times."

"Was he grateful?"

"He spat in my eye."

"But he accepted your help?"

"Oh yes," Yashin said, "he accepted it all right. But now I can't help."

Yashin turned away from her and stared at the ocean.

"Your wife, is she a star?"

"She's the ex-wife of a cosmonaut who never made it to the cosmos. The film director kicked her out."

"But she makes a living?"

"I support her," Yashin said.

"It's a pity Marxist-Leninism doesn't canonize saints." She found the question mark beside her mouth with the tip of her finger. "So your answer to everything, after you had been burned, when you couldn't make it to the *cosmos*, was to join the KGB?"

"I didn't kill your husband," Yashin said.

*　　　*　　　*

The mansion was full of lives trapped before death. Photographs quick with long-ago life observed him. Children called down the years with autumn voices. Cupboards redolent of Christmases past opened and voices said: "There is no time, come . . ." And on the beach the ageless waves agreed.

Yashin, listening one night to the fronds of the palm trees riffling the years, gazed into a deep sky and saw a shooting star. A death. Whose? And when?

75

CHAPTER 9

A week had passed and there had been no word from the sleeper in Domestic Operations. To maintain credibility Tal reported to the Secretary General of the United Nations in his office behind the dais of the General Assembly hall.

Afterwards he paused outside the 39-floor mirrored monolith of the Secretariat and considered his options. There was no point in returning to the Mission until Dobykin had re-awoken the sleeper; in any case the atmosphere, crackling with recrimination, didn't beckon.

The flags of the world snapped in a warm breeze. Clouds floated in the marble pool, roses bowed their heads in the mannered gardens, pleasure boats creamed past on the East River.

The breeze stirred Tal's appetite. He followed a group who looked like UN staff along the Plaza, down 45th Street and finally into a steamy diner.

The waiters were stage Irish, carroty hair, green aprons, humourless blarney. The tables were grey marble and the brasswork behind the bar had been polished wafer thin.

Tal sat at a table where one of the group, a girl, was already sipping iced water. She wore glasses, her dark hair was combed dutifully, her body beneath a grey skirt and white, tutorial blouse was plump, a lemon-shaped birth-mark burned on one cheek.

She took a book from a net bag and opened it. He glanced at it incuriously. It was in Russian cyrillics!

He said: "*Zdravstvuytye*," and was instantly angry with

himself because one of his professional strengths was isolation.

She looked up from the book. "A lot of people speak Russian at the United Nations," she said, and returned to the book, a novel by Aitmatov.

Tal's irritation increased. She was acting as though he were trying to pick her up. He never tried to pick anyone up and, in any case, she wasn't exactly a catch.

He said: "He writes better in Kirghiz."

This time she didn't look up. "I speak six languages but Kirghiz isn't one of them." She turned a page.

A waiter told them his name was Liam O'Donovan and took their orders smiling mirthlessly at each item.

"I read that," Tal said, pointing at the book, "in *Novy Mir*." Stupid to be inveigled into conversation by a patronising bitch.

"That must have been a long time ago." The girl put down the book as the soup arrived. "Seven years?" She took off her glasses; without them she was vulnerable.

"Something like that." He dipped a dented spoon into the khaki soup; it was lukewarm.

She broke pieces of bread into her bowl. Silence separated them. Why was he aware of it? They were strangers. The silence was a fog.

She said: "Are you Russian?"

The fog cleared. "Ukrainian."

"Ah." She pushed her bread scraps around the soup with her spoon. "You make it sound as though there's a difference."

"What do you do at the United Nations?" he asked.

"Instant translation," she told him.

During the Irish stew he learned that she was Jewish, Deborah Klein, and she lived with her parents in Brooklyn. He also discovered that her initial hostility was shyness wearing fancy dress.

In return he offered Nikolai Lvov, Soviet Mission at the UN, from Nikitovka, founded on quicksilver.

Over the dessert, apple pie, she told him that her intelligence was zilch, but instead she had been born with a magnet that attracted languages; her hobby was New York.

77

He responded with only two weeks in New York, a two-year tour of duty, and fishing.

"You should try Vermont for fishing," she told him over coffee. "My parents have a place there."

He almost told her that he already had. Stupid. That had been William Spivak.

"Do you like hunting?" She put on her glasses.

"Just fishing."

They drank more coffee.

"Why New York?" he asked.

She peered into her coffee; steam misted her glasses. "Because it's the world."

"That was a rehearsed answer," he said in Russian.

"Okay, so it's the world exaggerated. You don't feel lonely in New York." She took off her glasses again and wiped the steam with a tissue. "Except on Sundays. Except at Christmas."

"*More* coffee?" The waiter's blarney was gritted now. "You folks guzzle coffee like an old Caddy."

Deborah Klein said: "I really must go."

"I'll walk back with you," Tal said and to the waiter: "But we will have more coffee."

"Je-sus!" said the waiter.

Tal paid both their bills and left no tip.

The rest of the group had left and she walked quickly on flat-heeled shoes. Watching her, Tal glimpsed a hidden possession, grace.

Feeling his gaze, she touched the birthmark.

As they turned into the United Nations Plaza she said: "Turtle Bay. Forty years ago it was a slum. Breweries, flop houses, sweat shops . . ."

Tal thought: What vantage point would you choose if you were going to assassinate a delegate? A fast boat? By the time the shock had registered you could be on the far bank of the river.

A group of tanned, silver-haired visitors wearing badges identifying them as attorneys from San Diego wandered past conspicuously trying not to crane their heads at the shining package of civil servants that was the Secretariat.

"I'm sorry," she said, "I can get very boring on the subject of the Big Apple."

"A rotten apple?"

"Just ripe," she said. "You should see it on a Sunday."

"I'd like that," he said, astonishing himself.

*   *   *

Sunday morning. Manhattan abandoned by the weekdays; roads cracked, steam escaping from its lungs; shop windows blind; heat settling in concrete and glass canyons; a few cops, tourists and Saturday night leftovers on the prowl; Gotham wide open for an invasion.

Tal left the Pickwick Arms Hotel on East 51st Street at 8.30 am and turned into Madison. Yellow cabs drove past aimlessly, water dripped from air conditioners outside delicatessens, antique shops, art galleries.

He would not be surprised if she wasn't there and he wouldn't be disappointed. She was a diversion on another yawning day.

He called first at the Mission on East 67th and went up to the referentura, the stronghold on the 7th floor where communications were located. Dobykin was reading a cable. His sturdy frame slumped before its impact. He handed it to Tal.

Cipher. Yashin's code-name came at him in salvos. There had been many such cables from Moscow because *if* Yashin had robbed the computers at Plesetsk, the military cosmodrome south of Archangel, he could establish the West in space.

Normally classified material was rationed. Operatives possessed a piece of a jig-saw but not the picture. Yashin was different: Yashin was communications: he could complete the picture. Satellites, lasers, CPB's . . .

The rouble had been deftly passed from the Kremlin to Dzerzhinsky Square; from there it had been bounced across the Atlantic to the Mission to be reluctantly fielded by Dobykin.

Dobykin beckoned Tal through the steel door and down two flights of stairs to his office. They sat on opposite sides of a shabby desk watched by an urbane Mikhail Gorbachev and an avuncular Lenin.

Dobykin produced a bottle of Stolichnaya and two glasses.

Tal shook his head. Nine-thirty, shit. Dobykin threw a measure down his throat and munched a peppermint with blunt yellow teeth.

"I don't understand," he said. "Why would a good source suddenly dry up?" Tal didn't ask who the contact was: Dobykin would enjoy refusing to tell him.

"Blown?"

"And turned?" Dobykin celebrated the faint hope that he couldn't be blamed for such a possibility with another slug of firewater.

He said: "If only you hadn't missed."

"If only you hadn't let him escape."

Tal's original theory that Yashin had jumped from the Buick because he knew he was going to be arrested on arrival at the Mission had since been confirmed: the order to detain him had been received after he had landed at Kennedy.

And Yashin had somehow anticipated this. Curious. There were cross-currents to his defection that puzzled Tal.

Tal returned Lenin's gaze and said: "The normal procedure is being followed in the Soviet Union?"

"With the informant's relatives? Of course."

"What about Yashin's son?"

"He hasn't co-operated. So far. He's more loyal than his father thinks he is."

"What are you doing here?"

"That needn't concern you."

"But it does," Tal said. "I have to kill him."

Dobykin sniffed the bottle, placed it to one side and bit through the remaining wafer of peppermint. "We're checking out Hamilton's friends and relatives."

"His wife's?"

"Today. Every day we've been expecting a lead from Domestic Operation."

"You should have done it earlier."

"Fuck you," Dobykin said.

Tal glanced at the wall-clock perched on Lenin's head. 9.45. He had to be outside the Temple Emanu-el Synagogue at ten even if she wasn't there. He stood up. "I have an appointment."

"May I ask who with?"

"You can ask," Tal said.

"Your attitude will be reported to the Center."

"To Simenov?"

"Kiselev wouldn't have missed," Dobykin said, hand crawling towards the bottle.

"As a matter of fact," Tal said, "I didn't either."

*   *   *

I shot a mirror, Tal thought as he strode towards the biggest synagogue in the United States. Kennedy's head just didn't disappear when it was hit by a medium velocity supersonic bullet fired from a Mannlicher-Carcano. It blew the top of his skull off on exit but his head didn't disintegrate instantaneously.

Yashin was KGB. Yashin wasn't just a target: he was an adversary to be reckoned with.

Tal turned into Fifth Avenue opposite Central Park. The city was busier here, families heading for the Metropolitan Museum or the Frick Collection or the park itself. The park, according to the KGB manual, was popular on Sundays and relatively safe.

Gorky Park was also one big picnic in the summer. A beer hall, cafés, an open-air theatre, a ferris wheel, row-boats, chess tables, strolling players, a shooting gallery. When he was 17 Tal had arranged to meet a girl beside the stone portals of the park; he had planned to demonstrate his prowess at the shooting gallery, escort her along the banks of the Moskva and take her for a trip on a ferry boat.

He couldn't believe his luck because she was one of the most sought-after dates in his Komsomol. He had drawn his savings, bought a new shirt in Tsum department store and waited. By 11.30 he realised he had made a mistake: the appointment must have been for midday not 11. Ten minutes past twelve, a girl's privilege to be late; he smiled but his hands inside his freshly-pressed trousers were fists. 12.30. Lovers everywhere, ice in his soul.

Two Komsomol stalwarts strolled by, ice-hockey jocks who were irresistible to women if you believed their morning-after claims. "Hallo, Sergei," one of them called out. "Waiting for someone?"

81

He heard their laughter escaping from their gagging hands and he knew.

He didn't doubt that Deborah Klein would not be outside Temple Emanu-el. He slowed his pace because punctuality in such circumstances was degrading.

10.14.

"You're late," she said.

She wore a dark blue skirt and a yellow blouse and court shoes with small heels and her hair shone as though it had been brushed many times. She held her head at a slight angle, tilting the birthmark away from inspection.

"I had to call at the Mission."

"So you don't have to apologise."

"I'm sorry," he said.

"You don't have to come if you don't want to."

"Come where."

"Are you a good Communist?"

"Average," he said.

"Then you've got to see the heart of capitalism, the financial district. Wall Street." She began to walk towards the Plaza. "Would you like that?"

"Why not?"

"On a Sunday New York can belong to you."

"You said you felt lonely on a Sunday."

"That's right, but you feel as if you're in charge."

"Aren't you always?"

"Me?" She looked surprised.

"You seem very self-assured," he lied.

She pointed down 65th. "Franklin and Eleanor Roosevelt lived down there. My hobby. Do you have a thing about Moscow?"

"I don't have a thing about anything."

She walked quicker. "Then you have to invent things." The tap-tap of her stumpy heels was brisk. "You have to invent things that are missing." She marched in front of him. "But you wouldn't understand."

"I wouldn't?" It was the most ridiculous statement he had heard: he had invented killing.

"You're too self-possessed."

Was he? "We all wear masks," he said.

82

They took the subway. It was just as the Soviet newspapers described it. Aerosol graffiti and embalmed squalor. In Moscow the stations were chapels and galleries and beefy women harangued you if you dropped litter.

She showed him Trinity Church praying beneath shining high-rise and the Bowling Green where Peter Minuit bought Manhattan from the Algonquin Indians for a song and the US Custom House and Fraunces Tavern where the British evacuation of New York was celebrated in 1783 and the Stock Exchange in Wall Street where Peter Stuyvesant built a wall in 1653 to keep out the Indians.

"You should be a guide," Tal told her.

"I couldn't do that."

"Why?"

"Isn't it obvious?"

It wasn't immediately. He no longer saw the birthmark; she saw it all the time. He didn't know how to reply.

There were only a few intruders in the tall streets and he felt oppressed by dormant power. A breeze seeking the sea rustled with dollar bills; the sunlight was gold-leaf.

"I bought some stuff at a deli," she said. "I thought maybe you'd like a picnic in Battery Park. I bought wine too," she said. "Californian white. You don't have to—"

"A picnic would be fine," Tal said. He hated picnics.

They spread themselves on the grass facing Castle Clinton. Couples taking an old-fashioned Sunday promenade navigated whooping children; the breeze channelled through high finance accelerated as it made for the convergence of the Hudson and East Rivers rustling the picnic wrappings.

She poured wine in plastic cups. "Everyone thinks of Ellis Island when they're talking about immigration. But seven million passed through the castle."

"New York. Some hobby," Tal said, sipping the sweet wine.

"Jenny Lind sang there," she said. "Have you been to the Bolshoi?"

"I'm not interested in ballet."

"What are you interested in?"

"Just fishing," he said. "Russians like to fish," bracketing 15 republics and more than 130 ethnic identities the way

Westerners did.

"I would never have guessed. Chess maybe. Reading. You know, you look studious. You don't mind me saying that?"

"Why should I?"

She opened the packages. French bread and brie, salami and ham and tomatoes and caviar in a small glass jar.

"You like caviar?" Her voice was shy.

"Love it." He loathed it. He spooned some into his mouth and washed it down quickly with wine. "It must have cost a lot of money."

"I don't spend much on myself," she said. "Buses, trains, cabs, meals . . . What else is there?"

She stared across the water occupied by a few busy boats. Her skirt blossomed on the grass; when she was middle-aged she would be stout, like a Russian woman.

When she asked him what he did at the United Nations he juggled the answer. Nothing so far, this was his first week. Married? He shook his head. How could she think of such a thing? he wondered.

"Two cycles touching," she said. "What are the odds against it?"

He bit into a tomato; juice spurted. He broke a roll; the bread was foam light.

She drank more wine, then lay back with her head resting in her hands staring at the serene clouds. "So it's not true that you're prisoners of your mission?"

He wanted to say: "Not me," but that would have been a dangerous boast so he said: "It's exaggerated." He glanced at his watch. "I must call them."

"And then I thought we might take a boat to the Statue of Liberty. They leave every hour."

He spoke to Dobykin from a booth on the promenade.

"Where the hell have you been?" Dobykin demanded.

"Does it matter?"

"It matters. We've got a lead on Yashin."

Tal told Deborah Klein that the Statue of Liberty would have to wait.

CHAPTER 10

Mikhail Gorbachev was to blame. He had decided to smoke out corruption and too many trails had led to the Communications Directorate of the KGB. Codes, computers, satellites . . . You could rule the Soviet Union from the Eighth.

Lozak did his best. Every day he milked messages flowing into Moscow from Russian embassies and regional Soviets, inter-departmental communications inside the Kremlin and KGB. Every day he filed his intelligence in his computers.

He lived in an apartment in Kutuzovsky, he spent his weekends in a dacha at Nukolina Gora complete with sauna, tennis courts and stables. His possessions included a Chaika, two Volgas and a Lincoln Continental – a gift from a departing American diplomat whose name had been stored in his electronic memories – a gallery of ikons and two mistresses. But what Lozak extorted mostly was the invisible currency of Russia, *blat*, influence. Armed with this, Lozak practised bribery and corruption throughout the 22.4 million square kilometres of the Soviet Union. It was rumoured inside the Eighth Directorate that he operated on the same scale as Otari Lazishvili, the Godfather of Georgia, who had been accused of defrauding the State of 1.7 million roubles.

When Gorbachev started his crusade Lozak promptly laundered all his assets. But if the investigators wanted a scapegoat they could have one. Yashin.

*   *   *

"Well," Hannah Martin said. "Why *did* you leave Russia? Is

85

it such a big secret?"

She poured herself a cranberry juice at the bar at the deep end of the pool. Yashin watched drops of water chasing each other down her body that had begun to glow with Florida sunshine. A line of fluff, barely visible, ran from her navel to her bikini bottom.

Yashin wore a grey cotton shirt to hide his scars.

* * *

"It's time," Lozak had said, piloting his cross-country skis across a white field, "that you were rewarded."

Yashin glanced at Lozak's face framed in the hood of a black ski suit. Cold aged some people: it polished and rejuvenated Lozak.

The cries of the children skating on the tennis court, hosed with instant ice, had faded. Although it was March snow was peeling hesitantly from a warship-grey sky. Ahead lay a forest of pine, dark and winter-secret beneath its white roof.

Yashin and Lozak were united by their isolation.

"The cold," Lozak exclaimed. "Where would we be without it? It has taught us survival." He leaned on his ski-sticks, a compact bullet of a man.

"What do you mean, rewarded?" Yashin asked. The candour of Lozak's gaze disturbed him.

"You suffered. God, how you suffered. You had your purpose in life taken away from you. No man deserves that. And what was your reward? A gong! Hero of the Soviet Union. And a decent job. Do you like working for the Eighth Directorate, comrade?"

"Have I ever complained?"

"I have often wondered about you. How can a man who sought the freedom of space be happy working for the secret police?"

"I had no choice," Yashin said.

"You're not a sycophant. I like that."

Lozak thrust forward, skis hissing softly. Yashin followed, snowflakes dabbing his cheeks. If you liked cold you liked pain. Are we truly masochists, we Russians?

In the distance the falling snow was blending sky with land. They were skiing into oblivion.

When they reached the forest it was stiff with quiet. Lozak sat on a log and took a bottle of Zveroboy vodka and an automatic pistol, a 6.35 mm TK, once the darling of the KGB, from inside his parka.

He offered the bottle to Yashin. "Part of your reward." He smiled sleekly.

Yashin tilted the bottle. The vodka – this one was known as animal killer – lit a fire in his stomach. He swallowed snow to douse the flames.

Lozak wiped the neck of the bottle with a black-mittened hand and drank from it, still holding the small pistol with CCCP on the butt in his other hand.

Lozak planted the bottle between them. "It's always better to escape to talk," he said. "Not just bugs, space." A ledge of snow fell from a branch with a muffled thud. "I've been studying you on the computer. Not a lot on the debit side except a marriage to a bitch which does indicate emotional weakness."

"I wasn't in the KGB then," Yashin said.

"I'm surprised we took you: you were a risk."

"Perhaps the computers decided I had learned my lesson."

"You still support her?"

"We have to pay for our mistakes."

"No one ever becomes destitute in the Soviet Union. This isn't the United States, comrade."

Lozak pointed the gun at Yashin.

"So, what's my reward, a bullet in the head?"

Lozak lowered the pistol. "I have to carry this, I'm vulnerable." He aimed at the bottle of vodka. "Would you like to visit the United States?"

"To see the other side of the coin? Of course."

"There will be a vacancy in the Mission in New York soon. Would you like to fill it?"

Uninvited, Yashin drank from the bottle. The spirit inflated visions of understanding. "When?"

"Three months. A little more, a little less. You won't get much warning." Lozak reached for the bottle.

The afternoon was frosting into evening, the time between dog and wolf.

Lozak stood up. "Well?"

"Anatoly?"

"He'll be all right. You have my word on it."

"Then you must know the answer."

"I wanted to hear it from you. Out here, in the open, away from hidden ears. Suspicion, you know, is an infection. Well?"

"Of course," Yashin said.

"And no one must know about this. Understood?"

"You have my word on it," Yashin said.

"Until everything is settled. Otherwise I'll have the whole directorate on my back. Favouritism, Hero of the Soviet Union, all that shit."

At the edge of the pine forest Lozak turned, raised the pistol and shot the vodka bottle.

* * *

Three months. A little more, a little less. The vagueness, Tuslov told Yashin much later, was deliberate: the waiting period was however long it took Lozak to concoct a case against him.

Yashin hadn't voluntarily broken his pledge of secrecy: Tuslov had come to him. Tuslov the comedian who would have been performing at the Variety Theatre on Bersenevskaya Naberezhnaya if he hadn't been born with a computer instead of a brain.

Tuslov called at Yashin's department one evening in late June when, playing white, he was giving black a hard time on a chess computer. A greasy plate and a glass collared with dry beer foam stood beside the board.

Tuslov, unasked, fetched two bottles of beer from the kitchen where the washing-machine, once a sensation, stood abandoned in the corner. The whole apartment was numb, as though it had been beaten with rubber hammers. As a single man living in a family flat he would have been thrown out years ago if he hadn't been KGB.

Tuslov, grey curls bobbing, patrolled the room, touching the plastic-skinned furniture and flowerless vases, memorabilia of a family. The smiling slant of his eyes might have deceived a stranger – he had been twice disciplined for dumb insolence in the army – but Yashin who had known him for a long time sensed that he was worried.

Finally he slumped into an easy chair opposite Yashin, crossed his legs, drank from the brown bottle and said: "It's a beautiful evening Misha, shall we take a walk?"

On the chess board black beeped for attention. Yashin moved a rook and swore. "You spoiled my concentration."

Tuslov surveyed the board. "You had lost anyway." He put one finger to his lips, pointed at the door.

Yashin shrugged incomprehension but he stood up. "Perhaps the house spirit will take over my game."

"Misha you are a peasant."

Tuslov's dobermann, Kolya, was waiting for them on a chain in the yard.

They walked past the world, Vorovsky Street, occupied by Germany, Hungary, Norway, Sweden . . . Tuslov pointed at the embassies somnolent in the June sunshine. "I've been inside all of them at one time or another. Through their computers, of course."

"What do you want with me, Sasha?" It could be that he had a tip: Tuslov would gamble on who could piss the highest.

"Is there something *you* want to tell *me*?"

"Some thoughts never make words."

Tuslov said: "I've always admired American slang. Cut the crap."

They passed the Film-Makers' Union at No. 31. Galina had been a frequent visitor; in the evenings she had pestered him for advice on the political implications of Soviet movies.

"I've been sworn to secrecy," Yashin said.

"Don't be so fucking pompous."

Tuslov walked carefully, making sure he didn't scuff his new shoes. He was a snappy dresser – grey mohair suit, bought at a closed store – which made a surprise out of the unruliness of his hair.

His sermon began outside the horseshoe structure of the Writers' Union, the Rostov house in *War and Peace*. "You're probably aware, Mikhail Mikhailovitch, that bribery and corruption, not to mention bureaucratic bumbling, are to be banished from the land."

"Who's pompous now?"

"What you may not know is that I am one of the investigating officers." He brushed dust from one shoe. "Every ministerial department, every section of State Security, has one. Frightening, isn't it? In a way it's just like the purges of the 30s. With a difference. Stalin purged anyone he thought might be enemies of Stalin: Gorbachev is purging the enemies of Russia. A good man, Gorbachev, an enlightened man. Let us hope he can overcome his greatest obstacle, bureaucracy. Vault over it and ferret out the corruption. What people we are, eh, Misha? We overthrow tyranny and replace it with hypocrisy. *Blat* rules instead of the rouble. Kiss-my-ass instead of a curtsey. *Na levo* a way of life. And yet we still try to tell the world that we're enlightened."

Yashin said: "Get to the point, Sasha." He led Tuslov into Vosstanya Square skewered by a gilt-spired skyscraper.

"Don't think I'm anti-Soviet. Quite the opposite. I think the same way as Gorbachev."

"He will be delighted to hear it."

Tuslov walked quicker, grey curls following behind. "I suppose I was picked because I was an unlikely investigator. All the best ones are. True?"

Yashin said it was true.

"But I took on more than I had anticipated: I took on Lozak."

"You must have known that. Everyone knows about Lozak."

"Ah." Tuslov sighed. "There you're wrong. Everyone knew; now no one knows. Everyone knew when *blat* was a way of life. All of a sudden it's immoral and no one knows anything. Overnight a custom has become a crime. And Lozak's pickings have disappeared."

"So?"

"He was such a fat cat that we pursued him."

"We?"

"The KGB within the KGB."

Led by Kolya, they turned into the great avenue of the Sadovaya, the ring containing the centre of Moscow.

"And you've nailed him?"

Tuslov shook his curls. "He's nailed you. You've been framed as beautifully as the Mona Lisa."

Bribery, fraud, moral turpitude, you name it, Tuslov said.

Press any button on Lozak's computers and up popped Yashin on the screens. And, anticipating the layman's distrust of electronics, Lozak had briefed witnesses from as far away as Vladivostock to implicate him.

They passed the Planetarium where every day Soviet achievements in space were recounted.

"You haven't heard the coup de grace yet," Tuslov said. His voice was scratched with irritation, an actor without a responsive audience.

Kolya cocked his leg against the wheel of a kvas van; the vendor raised a foot to kick him but recoiled from the dobermann's malevolent black-and-tan glare.

Tuslov said: "You're going to America, correct?" and in exasperation: "There's no point in denying it. Your brief is to penetrate the American space programme and your code name is Cipher."

"Why ask me if you know?"

"I was merely establishing a platform of truth. A stage on which we can plan your escape. You see as soon as you arrive in New York you are going to be accused of planning to defect."

They swung into a bar, steely bright and clinically appointed, across the street from the zoo, where Tuslov ordered cucumber salad, vodka and Narzan mineral water.

Yashin, reeling at last, poured himself a measure of vodka and a glass of Narzan. "Why wait till I get to New York? Why doesn't Lozak throw the book at me now?"

Tuslov, watched keenly by the dog, bit crisply into a slice of cucumber dripping with sour cream. "Because Lozak wants a five-star traitor. What better proof of treachery on the grand scale – giving the Americans the Soviet military blueprint for space, for instance – than by defection? Foiled at the last moment by the astute, the illustrious, the patriotic Vasily Lozak."

Yashin ate some cucumber; it tasted of summer. So what did Tuslov propose that he should do? he asked. Drive to Dzerzhinsky Square and denounce Lozak?

"Not a chance. No proof." The manager of the bar came up to the table and told Tuslov to remove his werewolf; Tuslov showed him his red ID; Kolya stayed. "You've only got one hope. You're going to be arrested as soon as you set foot in the mission in New York, no risk of you escaping then. The order will be telexed from Moscow when you're on your way from the airport to Manhattan so not even the resident KGB gorilla will know about it."

"And that's when I have to make a break for it?" A piece of cucumber stuck in his throat; he hosed it on its way with vodka and mineral water.

"Then give yourself up to the Americans. Pre-empt Lozak. That way you'll be safe. Or safer. Protected by the CIA: I like that."

"For how long?"

"As long as it takes me to sign Lozak's death warrant. I don't have to tell you how."

"Lozak's computers?"

"The electronic files containing his dossiers on every *apparatchik* from here to the Pacific." Tuslov gave the dog a slice of cucumber; it licked off the cream and left it on the floor.

"Hasn't he erased everything?"

"Only evidence of his own criminal activities. He's got to keep his dossiers: without them he's a toothless tiger and the guys he's screwed would screw him tomorrow. If I can penetrate them Lozak might as well slit his throat. Why would he store such evidence? Blackmail, extortion, no other possible reason. And in any case why hasn't he handed over the evidence against other *apparatchiki* to the chairman of State Security? After all we do have a purge. Furthermore" – Tuslov fuelled his excitement with a generous slug of firewater – "we'll have enough proof to nail every other fat cat in the Soviet Union. A Volga and one of these new apartments overlooking Frounze Park for me, a triumphant return to Moscow for Mikhail Yashin, reinstated Hero of the Soviet Union." Tuslov wiped sour cream from the dish with black bread. "All I need is Lozak's terminal identification number, key code and data code."

"All?" The excitement generated by Tuslov's enthusiasm faded; he heard the voices of caged animals in the zoo. "He'll change the codes every day."

"If someone can transfer non-existent funds to the Soviet

Union Bank and then withdraw them then anything is possible." Tuslov tapped his curls. "You forget I have a computer up here. And I will have time – Lozak can't change the codes every five mintues."

"I won't have much time," Yashin said. "Not when the Americans realise I'm stalling."

Tuslov stared at Yashin with his wise, clown's eyes. "Then perhaps you should take an insurance policy with you." He stood up abruptly; even so the dog was on its feet first. "Now I've got to take Kolya home because today's Saturday and the Hippodrome opens at four and this computer," tapping his head again, "has come up with a couple of winners."

Yashin said: "What odds would you give on me?"

"Evens. A little more, a little less . . ."

"How did you find all this out?" Yashin asked.

"A clue here, a clue there. A witness there, a witness here . . . Your wife, a clever woman."

Yashin stared at Tuslov uncomprehendingly.

"If you come back a hero she'll say she helped to clear you. Bask in your reflected glory. Remarry you?"

"Is she helping?"

Tuslov ignored him. "And if you're executed for treason she'll say she helped to incriminate you."

"How could she do that?" Yashin asked.

"She's one of Lozak's prime witnesses. And he's had ample time to brief her. You see," Tuslov said, "he's screwing her."

The following day Yashin flew to Plesetsk. It was while he was there that he was told to get ready to fly to New York within 48 hours. Abruptly as Lozak had forecast.

*   *   *

"It doesn't make sense," Hannah Martin repeated. "You've defected: there's no reason for secrecy."

She dived tidily into the pool. From the bar Yashin watched her blurred figure swimming under water. No reason. Except that if the CIA realised he had defected to avoid arrest they would also realise that he was an imposter.

CHAPTER 11

Darryl Strawberry was a threat. When he was batting well Yashin relaxed; when, in the third game he watched on television, Strawberry hit a home-run he was euphoric. And vulnerable.

Baseball, he decided, was more dangerous than interrogation. Sharing the Mets' fortunes with Hamilton, he was liable to be indiscreet.

What he didn't know was whether Hamilton was single-minded enough to capitalise on any mistakes. What he did know was that he was hooked on baseball. Its lore, its skills, its muscle, its mysteries which Hamilton tried to explain. Strikes, hits, fastballs, knucklers . . .

Hamilton, handing Yashin a can of beer, pointed at the screen, Mets v. Pittsburgh Pirates. "See that? Backman bunted for an infield single to score Christensen from third."

"It's another language," Yashin said.

"It's American."

"You know what I like best about baseball? The uniform. It's old-fashioned."

"Goes back to the New York Knickerbockers, the Knicks. But the Cincinnati Red Stockings were the first to adopt it. They were the first pros, too, in 1869."

"Were you always a batsman?" Yashin asked.

"I started as a pitcher, then I concentrated on being a batter. Just like Babe Ruth." Hamilton folded a grin at Yashin.

"And then what happened?"

"I joined the CIA."

Outside the air-conditioned lounge beside the pool it was steamy. Palm fronds moved lazily, thunder grumbled over the ocean.

Later, when Gooden was pitching for the Mets, Yashin ventured: "Are negroes better than whites?"

"No black really played major league until 1947. Jack Roosevelt Robinson, compliments of Branch Rickey, part-owner of the Brooklyn Dodgers. After that Bob Gibson, Hank Aaron, Roberto Clemente, Roy Campanella . . ." Hamilton waved his beer can at the TV. "Strawberry, Gooden . . ."

"Are you boasting or apologising?"

"Neither," Hamilton said. "A buddy of mine, a diplomat, had an apartment on Kutosovsky. They had a plague of cockroaches in the apartment. The Russians blamed the Africans for importing them."

"We don't have a racist problem," Yashin said.

"You don't have that many blacks," Hamilton said. "And to answer your question there's no difference between colours out there on the diamond."

On the screen Gooden struck out a Pirate.

Yashin, clapping, said: "Do you know where baseball started?"

"Sure. England. A derivative of cricket and rounders. Eighteenth century."

"Sorry," Yashin said. "Read *Nedelya*, the supplement to *Izvestia*. *Beizbol* was played centuries ago in Russia."

Strawberry was back on the screen. Another home run. Yashin rose in his seat and Hamilton said: "Maybe you should re-introduce it when you get back to the Soviet Union," and Yashin, shaking his head, said: "You never give up, do you."

* * *

That evening they watched a movie on a silk screen in the tunnel beneath the A1A. Black and white. Bergman in *Casablanca*. To make him feel at home . . . or homesick? Lull him into a false state of security or accentuate his insecurity?

After the film Hamilton said: "I thought maybe you'd like

95

to take a trip tomorrow. You know, a guided tour of the locality. On one condition – you give me your word you won't try to escape."

My word? We're enemies, you stupid bastard. "My word," Yashin said.

*   *   *

Pink lemonade, cheeses – Monterey Jack with Jalapeno peppers, pita, cold meats – turkey, salami, bologna – cranberry apple juice, root beer, a confusion of Cokes, Seven Seas Green Goddess dressing, Bumble Bee solid white tuna, Perrier with a twist of lime or orange, Coors beer brewed with pure rocky mountain spring water, selected Californian sun-dried Calimyrna figs naturally good for snacking and baking, heavenly-hash ice cream, Aunt Jemima's original waffles, an avenue of tissue rolls . . .

In an ordinary food store! Spill the contents of every such shop in Moscow into one outlet and you wouldn't have that choice. The varieties and enticements gorged Yashin. Take a pack of toothpicks, just tiny slates of wood to dislodge garbage from your teeth, you might think. Not these. They were fancy, strong, sure-grip, square center, round-tapered ends, polished white birch. They were stronger, more uniform, easier to handle and wouldn't roll. And in case there was lingering doubt: THE NEW WORLDS FAIR round tooth-pick is square in the center and is easier to use and handle. How could you soil such precision-tooled blades with teeth?

Outside the store Yashin noticed a man with a ruined face delving into the trash cans.

After they had toured the shopping precinct – three rows of stores, stagnant in the morning yawn, embracing a parking lot occupied by a few forlorn cars – Hamilton led him back to the white, newly-rented Mustang where Hannah sat reading the *Miami Herald.* Yashin watched the guards moving casually to their cars. If the assassin had traced him this would be as good a place as any to pull the trigger.

"By the way," Hamilton said, turning the Mustang onto the Dixie Highway, "three thousand five hundred Finns live here in Lantana. If anyone asks you're Finnish; it gives you a

96

reason for being here."

Hamilton drove south past the entrance to the *National Enquirer*. More shopping precincts, gas stations, burger joints, motels . . . Water towers introduced new towns but this was a fiction: there were no identities here, the highway was a conveyor belt.

Hamilton, overtaking a rusty limousine driven majestically by a black matron, said: "You've left us. Where are you?"

"In a small town in the Urals. A couple of stores, a church, unused, with an onion dome, wooden houses, children coming out of school. It's snowing."

"We have towns like that. Are the apartment blocks on Novy Cheriomushky so beautiful?"

At Boca Raton they took a left onto the A1A and headed north again, over the tunnel towards Palm Beach.

In the backseat Hannah persevered with her newspaper without speaking. Time fed her dislike of him. Why? Simply because no one loves a traitor?

Approaching Palm Beach they drove past the mansions of the very rich, brick corpses in the out-of-season summer.

Worth Avenue. An FBI hat ahead, another behind, as they walked its undistinguished length. One of the most exclusive shopping parades in the world, it reminded Yashin of an abandoned film set. Gucci, Saks, Bonwit Teller, Ralph Lauren etcetera with squat boutiques in attendance. Mid-afternoon Mexican without the dust.

"If you brought me here to impress me," Yashin said, "you're wasting your time."

Hannah said: "I got the impression it's you who's been wasting time." It was the first time she had spoken since they left the foodstore.

Yashin entered Cartiers. An elegant saleswoman said: "Can I help you, sir?"

Yashin tapped the side of his nose. "I'd like to see the most expensive rock" – George Raft, 1938 – "you've got."

Her eyes flicked towards the uniformed guard at the door. Yashin felt closed circuit TV cameras staring at him, heard locks freeze electronically.

"What sort of price were you thinking about, sir?"

"I told you, the best."

"May I ask how you intend to pay?"

The guard's hand was on his gun.

"Cash. Bugsy's waiting outside with the dough. All in hundreds, okay?"

"I don't—"

Yashin winked. "Relax, I was only kidding. We've just come to look, haven't we, duke?" He slapped Hamilton on the shoulder.

The saleswoman's smile crimped. "Most amusing." She shrank from their presence like a sea anemone that has been touched.

In the street Hannah said: "Boy, you're really settling in. Wisecracking with the locals. You know something? Defection is a bargain and you're not trading."

A group of black building workers drinking beer and eating sandwiches in a patio among the becalmed stores stared at them incuriously.

"Supposing I haven't got anything to trade?"

"Communications Directorate? Who are you kidding?"

She wore no make-up and her tan had altered her. Pale, there had been room for humour, dissertation; the tan had flattened her expression and, bronzed, she was no longer a Pole. But she had retained grief: her husband's death was a black veil over her judgement.

But she wasn't a threat: hostility bred hostility. Hamilton was the danger. Sympathy was his weapon, not his weakness, and I must never forget that, Yashin reminded himself.

Hamilton said: "Okay, so why don't we go home and have a beer and maybe watch some baseball."

* * *

There were storm warnings on the television that evening. Alone, Yashin walked the chambers and corridors of the mansion. Glimmers of distant lightning lit the portraits of ancestors, finding knowing eyes and angles of cunning not apparent by day. A cockroach scuttered, mosquitoes hung outside the windows. Some of the floors were marble but his footsteps didn't echo; noise, too, was a prisoner.

He opened the French windows in the lounge and stepped out into soup. The dentist drilling of night insects, palm fronds switching, thunder grumbling, Atlantic rollers hushing it all, animal movements in the undergrowth.

Yashin strolled round the pool, underwater lights baring lagoon-blue depths, to the shallow end. Sliding floor-to-ceiling windows separated the terrace from the mouth of the tunnel which was hung with paintings and furnished with cane chairs and tables and was used as a salon.

He drew the windows. The tunnel was in darkness. Yashin imagined it filled with black vapours. Lightning flashed weakly and for a moment Yashin thought he saw a figure outlined at the far end. But when he switched on the lights the exit was empty, a gun-barrel without a target.

*　　*　　*

Letz sat in a stateroom of a Broward 73 ft. motor yacht moored at a dock on the 165 miles of navigable waterway at Fort Lauderdale 40 miles south of Palm Beach and 22 miles north of Miami.

The yacht belonged to friends of the family but today Letz, in navy, brass-buttoned blazer and white ducks, was skipper. And beneath his langour he was tight with anger, the ghost of Yurchenko, 8,000 miles away in Moscow, beside him at the mahogany table.

Letz said: "Glad you could make it, Jack. Get yourself a drink."

Hamilton poured a beer. The storm had by-passed the coast but the atmosphere was still thundery. The yacht moved drowsily and the water made silver sounds against its hull. On the other side of the dock shaved lawns disappeared behind hibiscus, bougainvillea and umbrella trees.

"Sit down, you're making the place untidy." Letz rippled his blond-grey hair with the tips of his fingers. And, when Hamilton was seated on the other side of the table: "How's our friend?"

"Settling in," Hamilton said.

"Settling in? What kind of talk is that?"

"We're winning his confidence."

"Sure he's not winning yours?"

"There has to be trust between interrogator and subject. Without it you get either nothing or a pack of lies. This isn't

99

Star Chamber or third degree; Yashin isn't a criminal."

Hamilton sipped his beer and stared at a pelican perched on the deck-rail: the pelican stared back; it looked as though it had a beak full of fish.

"It all sounds very cosy. How long have you had Yashin now?" The question was rhetorical. "Nineteen days, nearly three weeks. And what have you got from him? Name, rank and number is what." Letz pulled at a button on his blazer embossed with an anchor. "What am I going to tell Langley, Jack?"

"How about the truth?"

"The President is due to leave for Moscow in two weeks. He wants to negotiate from a position of strength. He wants to be able to deal cards from the future. The future is space; Yashin is space. When is he going to give?"

"He isn't a traitor," Hamilton said. "He has integrity."

"Bullshit." Letz mixed champagne and orange juice in a tall glass. "He defected, didn't he? What sort of integrity is that?"

And when Hamilton didn't reply: "Well I'll tell you. Yashin came across because he was about to be arrested on charges of bribery and corruption. How's that for integrity?"

Lousy, Hamilton thought. He remembered defending a kid at school – the name came down the years, Stainaker – who was the target of a gang of bullies; one day the bullies turned on his defender and who was in there punching with both fists? Stainaker, that's who.

"How do you know?" he asked Letz.

"Moscow. Our guys in the embassy have been checking out Yashin. According to a contact in KGB Special Investigations he was going to be arrested as soon as he stepped into the mission in New York. Which is why he jumped out of the car between JFK and Manhattan," in case Hamilton had missed the point.

"Maybe he was framed." Hamilton thought he sounded like a husband making an excuse for an unfaithful wife.

"Jesus, you two really are buddy buddies, aren't you."

"He just doesn't seem the type to me. Criticise Mother Russia and he's at your throat."

"And what has that got to do with anything?" Letz

splashed ice into his Buck's Fizz. "He's never once hinted why he quit. Why not?"

For a very good reason, it occurred to Hamilton, if he had been framed. It would immediately be apparent that he was stalling until his name was cleared. If he was exonerated he would hot-foot it back to Russia, another Yurchenko.

The possibility didn't dismay Hamilton. He glanced at the pelican; it flew away on heavily-flapping wings.

Letz said: "Guilty or not, framed or not, it doesn't alter the fact that Yashin must have information of inestimable value in his possession."

When Letz's speech became tortuous, tread warily, the words were minefields. "Must?"

"He flew to Plesetsk just before leaving the Soviet Union."

"So? Plesetsk was one of his bases."

"He only flew there twice a year," Letz said. "A coincidence that he should fly there two days before defecting, isn't it?"

"Not necessarily." Hamilton didn't bother to elaborate. "So Yashin is a wanted criminal. He's defected to avoid getting busted. He's brought with him information of *inestimable value*. Then why the hell hasn't he parted with it?"

"You tell me, you're the interrogator." Letz must have realised that, if Yashin had been framed, he was playing for time. "But I tell you this: he's got to trade pretty soon."

"And if he doesn't?"

"What the hell's got into you, Jack? You're supposed to be the best interrogator in the States."

"Maybe that's why I'm doubtful about Yashin."

"Maybe you don't want him to betray his country?" Letz tugged at the brass button.

"That's ridiculous."

"I hope so." Letz stood up and paced the stateroom, touching nautical adornments with convincing familiarity. "Have you considered sodium aminate?"

"He's KGB: he knows how to fool drugs."

Letz adjusted a display of mariners' knots, turned abruptly and said: "Tell him this, that if he doesn't come across we'll hand him back to his own people."

A breeze, the breath of another lurking storm, sidled past

101

the yacht. Small waves slapped the hull.

"You'd do that?"

Letz sat down again, crossing his legs carefully and pulling at the thighs of his ducks to minimise creasing. "No. But if he doesn't co-operate within two days we'll have to kill him. We don't want another Yurchenko, do we?"

*　　　*　　　*

Later they adjourned to the Pier 66 Hotel.

In the lobby Letz said: "I'm in Room 308. You go ahead, I'll join you."

Catherine was in Room 308.

She said: "Did you listen to Letz?" She wore pale blue and her blonde hair was coiled; only a photographer was missing.

"Of course, he's my boss."

"You know what I mean. Are you going to do what he wants?"

"Do you know what he wants?"

She shook her head.

Threaten to hand him back to the KGB? Double-cross him?

But if I don't he's dead.

Catherine said: "So you'll co-operate? For us?" she added so softly that Hamilton barely heard her.

"I'll do what I think's best," he said.

CHAPTER 12

Yashin decided that it was time to concede a little.

Q: Why did you fly to Plesetsk two days before leaving Russia?

A: To finalise my affairs.

Q: You flew all that way to clear out your desk?

A: My computer. Don't you have those in the United States?

Q: So soon before flying to New York?

A: Everything happened very suddenly.

Q: Why?

A: That's the way it is in the Soviet Union. The bureaucrats like to manipulate you. It feeds their egos.

Q: We have bureaucrats here as well. And computers.

Listener No. 1: He couldn't resist that.

Listener No. 2: Establishing rapport.

Listener No. 1: Maybe one of these days he'll get some information.

Q: Your computer, what sort of programming?

A: Classified.

Q: Military application of space?

A: Of course. Plesetsk *is* a military launch site.

Q: Cosmos?

A: And *Salyut* and *Soyuz*. I also worked on *Mir*, the first permanently manned complex in space.

Q: Military?

A: *Mir* means peace.

Q: Beam weapons, lasers, CPB's . . .

A: Are you referring to defensive weapons?

Q: Just weapons, Comrade Yashin. Did you have access to classified information about them?

A: The Eighth Directorate deals with every aspect of space. Communications. It goes without saying.

Q: Why would you keep such information in a computer?

A: As an insurance policy?

Q: You had been contemplating defection for a long time?

A: Only since I was told I was being posted to New York.

Q: When was that?

A: Three months ago, a little more, a little less.

Q: Ample time in which to assemble a dossier on Soviet intentions in space?

A: Time enough.

Q: What was your brief in the United States?

A: No comment.

Listener No. 2: Admission by non-commitment.

Q: Bearing in mind that you have decided to defect, bearing in mind that you are seeking political asylum, will you help us?

A: With the contents of my . . . desk?

Q: What else? In the interests of *mir*. In space and therefore on earth?

A: I don't have much option, do I?

*   *   *

On a map of the United States the Sunshine State of Florida is a long-handled pistol, its barrel resting on the Gulf of Mexico.

William Spivak approached it warily, flying first to its trigger, Tallahassee, and then driving south in a rented Cutlass on Routes 10 and 441.

All he had was Florida. The contact had cut the connection before elaborating. In Orlando Tal parked the Cutlass and called New York.

*   *   *

At 25 mph the Black Fin pushed aside the brown water politely. Standing beside Hamilton at the wheel, Yashin watched the wake close upon itself. Ahead and behind the sportfishing boat, whip-muscled beneath its bimini tower, two guardian powerboats cut impatient swathes in the intracoastal.

On the east shoreline of the waterway, Lake Worth at this juncture, big houses standing on carpet lawns waited indolently for their owners, the Stars and Stripes fluttering in some of the gardens; on the west shore the first of the Palm Beach palaces, a green sprawl that Hamilton reckoned could fetch $20 million. Yashin admired one mansion in particular: Hamilton told him it was the boathouse.

"I don't envy any of it." Yashin leaned against the bimini steps. Had he by implication given the opposite impression. "I really don't. No one should have privilege on this scale."

"Zhukovka?"

"The exception, you know that. The dachas were built for ministers and geniuses."

"Palm Beach is an exception."

"But wealth isn't," Yashin said. "Nor is poverty."

"No Communism versus Capitalism. Not on a day like this." Hamilton's outstretched hand embraced the serene sky, the broad waters, dozing mansions and islands of tangled mango.

"I wasn't thinking purely in materialistic terms," Yashin said.

"Materialistic . . . Do you know what Communism is? Collective clichés. How about that? *Izvestia*, *Pravda* . . . . You've got the worst PR's in the world."

"We don't need PR's," Yashin said. "You do the job for us. Watergate . . . On rainy days they still watch it on video in the Kremlin."

"If Mikhail Gorbachev is to be believed," Hamilton said, "corruption isn't an unknown quantity in the Soviet Union."

Yashin glanced at Hamilton. Did he know about Lozak? Hamilton stared ahead, a water-smelling breeze ruffling his thinning hair. He looked about as nautical as a truck driver.

Ahead on the west bank Yashin saw a shining pink skyscraper. Another yacht with a blue and white hull was coasting parallel with Black Fin blotting out one of the guardian powerboats from view; the helmsman made no attempt to overtake.

"*Na levo*," Yashin said. "That isn't corruption, it's a way

105

of life." He waved to the other yachtsman but he didn't respond. "And yes we do have alcoholism and we do have queues and maybe we are walking documents but we don't sniff cocaine and we don't buy cheap out-of-date food from the stores after hours and we don't sleep on Skid Row. So what?"

"You don't have freedom," Hamilton said, increasing Black Fin's speed.

"Freedom! Collective clichés, that's Capitalism. What's so great about freedom anyway? Freedom to do what? Catch a train from New York to Chicago, watch a pornographic movie, buy a gun permit, work yourself into the coffin to pay for your children's education, crucify your politicians? What's so great about freedom?"

"It means you can speak your mind."

"You don't think Russians do? You should go to a bath-house sometime. And as for dissidents, I'll tell you something – they don't get any sympathy in the Soviet Union. Why should they? All they're doing is slipping a stiletto in Mother Russia's ribs. Dissidents," Yashin said, watching the blue and white yacht accelerate to keep up with the Black Fin, "are a western invention."

Hamilton increased the speed again. "Do you really believe all this?"

"It has to be said."

"Are you saying life in the Soviet Union isn't so different from life in the United States?"

"A delicate equation," Yashin replied. "You should know, you've seen both sides."

"I only saw Intourist Russia, the polished side of the coin – except when I went walking in Moscow. I didn't see the camps where they send you if you buck the system."

"They make chess pieces in them. Did you know that? Black and white. But nothing is black and white, is it?" Yashin waved again at the other helmsman; no response. "I haven't seen your penitentiaries. A little overcrowded, aren't they? Why don't you slow down? See if he slows down too."

Ahead a bridge slowly opened its jaws to allow a tall yacht to pass underneath. The Black Fin held back. The blue and white yacht named *Lady D* surged ahead. The helmsman waved.

Hamilton pointed at a twin-towered building lazing in Palm Beach. "Breakers Hotel. Magnificent, real old time. Lots of film stars have stayed there. And the President."

"In that order?"

"Maybe even Paulette Goddard," Hamilton said.

The jaws of the bridge shut behind them. Yashin said: "We aren't getting anywhere near the truth, you and I. You see we've been processed. If you want the truth ask a child. A kid who's bought a crudely-made rifle in Detsky Mir is just as happy as a kid who's been given a computer game bought in Worth Avenue."

"So those blacks you saw and the poor whites and the bums on Skid Row . . . They should be happy?"

"That's different: they've been robbed of their dignity. You know something? I'd be happier cutting slabs of milk in an *izba* in Siberia than I would be in a kitchen with a food processor and a fruit crusher and a refrigerator as big as a shed. Do you know what they use for a refrigerator in Siberia? The back yard."

"That's the trouble with you Russians, you're all macho. Wouldn't your wife have preferred an all-American kitchen?" Hamilton pointed. "That's Peanut Island. There's a coastguard station there. We're going to head out to the ocean through Lake Worth Inlet." He spun the wheel. "What is stupid, I guess, is that you and I have to fight because we've been processed. A young man in . . . Give me a small town in Siberia."

"Ysyakh. You can drink fermented mare's milk there."

" . . . in Ysyakh doesn't want to fight a young man in Miles City, Montana. Why should he? He's never even heard of it."

The Black Fin pushed through the inlet into the rippled Atlantic.

"Fear is the driving force behind Russia," Yashin said. "It's so big it's vulnerable. And we have been attacked throughout history."

"Bullshit. Part of the processing. Obsolete reasoning handed out by hacks afraid to admit that reality has passed them by. You mentioned truth just now. Truth is here in this boat. You and me." Hamilton, shading his eyes against the sunlight jostling on the water, smiled; almost shyly, Yashin thought.

"Then why," Yashin said, "are you trying to destroy me?"

*   *   *

Lady D was waiting for them half a mile offshore. And now the helmsman, loud hailer in hand, monk's fringe of white hair hedging sun-burned baldness, was garrulous. Through the hailer he shouted: "How about you guys making a race of it?"

Hamilton said: "The yacht club sport and he's been at the sauce."

"What speed can you do?" Yashin asked.

"With these outboards? Maybe fifty-five. With the tower fifty-three. Want us to give it a whirl?"

"Why not?" Yashin drank from a can of beer. "Has it occurred to you that it's easier to escape on the ocean than it is in the inland waterway?" he asked Hamilton.

"Who wants to escape? You?"

"Perhaps he does." Yashin pointed at the sport. "Perhaps he has a passenger. With a rifle."

"Come on Mikhail, not here. An assassin's gunning for you, not a pirate."

"They could have traced us by now. They did before."

"This isn't an unsafe house."

"They can trace me through you, through your wife's family." Fear escaped from the tunnels of Yashin's life and visited him.

Hamilton raised one thumb, revved the engine.

"At the count of three," shouted the sport. One finger, two fingers, three. The two boats ploughed the water, waves hitting each other's bows like whales. Hamilton smiled fiercely into the wind; *Lady D* began to fall behind.

Hamilton pointed at the shore. "The Kennedy pile. Nothing spectacular by PB standards. Maybe he's slowing down to take a look." He jerked his thumb at the other boat.

Suddenly *Lady D* rolled up her skirts and sprinted. Her wake rolled the Black Fin. The sport turned and raised both arms, fist clenched.

"Shit," said Hamilton. He creased a smile at Yashin. "But you enjoyed it?"

"No one shot me."

"We're alike, you and me."

"We question," Yashin said. "When are we going to leave the house?"

"When you co-operate."

"I might get shot tomorrow."

"It's a possibility," Hamilton said.

He stooped.

Yashin felt sad for him.

*   *   *

Cradled and silent, the cream telephone demanded attention, its muted summons more insistent than terminal shrilling.

Tal saw her sitting on the grass in Battery Park, petals of her skirt spread round her, accepting rejection as commonplace. Her plastic cup had tilted and wine had spilled onto the turf.

He touched the receiver, his hand seeking reassurance.

He walked to the window of the small motel in the town of Lake Worth. On the other side of the waterway Yashin was holed up in a mansion on South Ocean Boulevard.

The phone broke its silence.

Dobykin said: "Cipher?"

"Close by."

"Today?"

"The day after tomorrow."

Dobykin's anger flowed into the receiver. "I must insist—"

"The day after tomorrow," Tal said. "Thursday."

"Don't miss your connection this time."

"Your mother," Tal said and hung up.

He stood looking at the phone, hand-grimed around the receiver. Outside, the sky was floating with galleons of white cloud. Clouds were meant to be shared.

Share nothing! Was he losing his mind? She was a possessive bitch. Even at a distance she was that. The dumb reproach . . .

A water-closet gushed in an adjoining bathroom.

Birds perched like notes of music on the telephone wires spanning the parking lot.

Murmurs of childhood reached him. The buried, stammering years.

He picked up the receiver.

Her voice was warmth.

"It's m-me," he said.

CHAPTER 13

The hurricane season in the western Atlantic lasts from July to October, peaking in September. On this steamy Wednesday in July the hurricane that was to be named Anna, spawned over the North Atlantic, was little more than an embryo, a disturbance; but conditions, including a water surface temperature of more than 80 degrees Fahrenheit, were perfect for the development of her muscles. It would take her an indeterminate time to reach maturity; then she would rampage as a tropical storm for perhaps five days whipping herself into a final hurricane frenzy that would exhaust her after two or three days.

On the watered lawns of spongy grass around the mansion on South Ocean Boulevard there wasn't a breath of wind. Dragonflies hovered, butterflies flirted, the delicate stems of Australian pine striping the sparkle of the inland waterway were motionless.

Yashin, patrolling the grounds, felt as though he was walking under warm water, deep-fathomed predators lurking behind trees and bushes.

Why didn't Hamilton care if the KGB killed him? The answer came to him on slow-spinning eddies of logic – because if I don't talk then alive I am a dangerous embarrassment, a potential Yurchenko. And if the KGB can't find me? The eddies spun themselves into spikes. Then the CIA will do their job for them.

Yashin decided to make another call to Moscow. In his twin-bedded room, furnished with warm woods and smelling of cedar, Yashin distanced himself from the helicopter overhead, from the patrol boat loitering on the waterway, to the faraway ringing.

July. The hottest month in the Soviet Union. In Central Asia the temperature could reach 48 degrees Centigrade. In Moscow the great squares would be glazed with heat, *kvas* would be flowing, ice-cream melting; and soon the great trek to country, sea and river would be under way.

Yashin was a river man. "Our life blood," his father had told him, a ten-year-old on the deck of a white cruise ship taking them down the Volga past the Tartar capital, Kazan, and Lenin's birthplace, Ulyanovsk and Stalingrad, renamed Volgograd, where the Soviet Union had won the Great Patriotic War. "100,000 rivers, our arteries. . . ."

In fact his father had been a seaman with the Northern Fleet. Weathered and trim, he had served on an ice-breaker crunching its way from the Bering Straits to Murmansk until one melting May day he had fallen between his ship and an iceberg and Mikhail had grown into adolescence with a widow who never ceased to grieve.

The phone continued to ring. Where was Tuslov? Yashin saw him, grey curls shaved, strapped to a bed, hypodermic sliding into a swollen vein. Yashin wrenched himself back to summer.

On a day such as this his mother might have taken him fishing to one of his father's rivers. To a log camp where you could catch 5 kg but no more of trout, bream or snapping pike. And, if there was money in the bank, and a sturgeon had been held back from the exporters, they might eat spoonfuls of caviar, served with ice and lemon.

If . . . We are a nation of improvisors. Beachcombers on the shores of an intransigent system. But some of us get 48 days paid holiday and who gets that in New York? And we're poised to break free into space unless . . .

The voice in the receiver said: "Tuslov."

Yashin said: "What are the odds now?"

A breathing pause. Then: "Evens."

"But—"

"I can't speak now."

Click.

Life could be lost just as abruptly. Had the barrel of a pistol been boring into Tuslov's neck?

Yashin walked down the stairs to the lounge beside the pool. Ancestors, divested of moonlit cunning, gazed at him blandly, the creaking stairs their rheumatic knees.

Hannah Martin was watching television. A soap opera in which everyone, men and women, had been to the same hairdresser, cosmetic surgeon and elocutionist. No one seemed happy.

Hannah changed channels. Spots on the glassware, menstrual pain, rashes and headaches more excruciating than thumb-screws. Yashin hadn't made up his mind whether Americans were obsessed by health or ill health.

A newscast.

And Yashin was looking at his son.

*   *   *

Her naked face was now clothed with feeling, her voice belonged to her as, sitting upright on a sprawling sofa, she leaned across a void, touched his arm and said: "I'm sorry, it shouldn't happen like that."

"I was stupid to think it could happen any other way."

With the remote control he killed a used-car salesman.

The newscaster had been abrasively defensive. The network had been approached by Soviet television: it was in the interests of democracy that the American people should know that a top-ranking KGB officer was seeking asylum in their country. "Where we don't know, but we sincerely believe it is our duty to convey a message from a son to his father."

Anatoly had been standing in a park, Sokolniki, where Yashin had once taken him to play. His features, Yashin's high cheekbones and Galina beneath them, were tight but he looked well enough. A breeze teased his soft black hair.

His pleas had been flat and predictable. Yashin was a Hero of the Soviet Union; he had once been poised to help his country take its rightful place in space; he owed it to himself and the Soviet Union to return; there would be no recriminations – the authorities recognised that he was a victim of

113

American manipulation. "I, Anatoly, your only son, want you back." A pause; Anatoly's eyes changed focus as though he were being prompted. And then: "Do you remember the games we used to play here?" The camera panned to the pavilions, the residue of international trade fairs, and closed-up on them.

Yashin remembered. Bang you're dead. The Great Patriotic War, the game that would never pall. He remembered it in winter black and white. They changed roles, Red Army or Wehrmacht, according to the fortunes of war. Often at the end of the game Yashin carried a struggling, rosy-cheeked corpse to the cafeteria for a cup of hot chocolate.

Bang I'm dead if you don't return. No one else would understand.

Hannah walked round the room taking her questions with her. She was barefoot and her feet made rubbery sounds against the polished wood between the islands of rugs. She wore a skimped yellow beach dress; beneath it Yashin could see the angles of her hips.

That was often the way with grief. Trivia temporarily buried it, leaves falling on a new grave. Then, suddenly, a wind bared it. He hadn't wept until he had seen how small his father's coffin was.

She said: "I didn't understand it all, did I?"

"It doesn't matter," he said. "Where's Hamilton?"

"Out." She stood at the long windows smoothing her dress against her thighs. Dusk was settling thickly. The thunder that never seemed to reach them muttered in the distance; insects were tuning themselves; in the undergrowth racoons would be on the prowl. "This changes everything?" she asked.

"You're like Hamilton, you never give up."

"Tell me this." She turned, hands outstretched, cradling the question. "Would you have betrayed your country?"

The leaves blew away and he was carrying the corpse, struggling and giggling, to the cafeteria for life-saving hot chocolate.

"I'm a Russian," he said.

*   *   *

At four in the morning you blame yourself.

He need not have joined the KGB. But communications in space had seemed innocent enough. Don't delude yourself, you were joining the secret police and you knew it. If I hadn't, if I had applied for a teaching post, then Galina might not have left me. Given a secure home, Anatoly would not have developed into a rebel. If I had been a lecturer at Moscow University then I wouldn't be in the United States and the KGB wouldn't be at Anatoly's throat.

The knock on the door was so light that he wasn't sure whether he had heard it. He called out: "Who is it?" and the door opened and Hannah said: "May I come in?" but by that time she already was.

She slid into the bed beside him and put her arms around him. He felt her warmth. He slept.

*   *   *

By morning it was difficult not to know there was an important defector somewhere in the United States. Newspapers, radio and other TV networks had all picked up the story. The media resounded with "No comment." From the White House, the Soviet Embassy in Washington and the Mission in New York, the CIA, the Senate Intelligence Committee . . . The reticence or ignorance – as was suggested in some quarters – provoked considerable speculation. Where was the errant Russian so important that the Soviet Union had televised an appeal from his son? How long had he been in the United States? Why was American Intelligence keeping the defection a secret? And, paramountly: who is he? In the absence of an answer the memory of Yurchenko reigned.

*   *   *

The pelican sat on the outside looking in. Hamilton liked to think it was the same one that had observed him so cynically the last time he had met Letz in the stateroom of the yacht at Fort Lauderdale.

Letz, wearing ducks and a nautical T-shirt bearing a Parisian logo, raged urbanely. The President, the director of the CIA, the chairman of the Senate Intelligence Committee who was engaged in a personal feud with the director and

115

hadn't even been told about the defection, were all homocidal, he said.

Staring across the table at Hamilton with his honest blue eyes Letz said: "We're not making the running anymore, Jack. We can't keep a phantom under wraps any longer. We've got to name Yashin and we've got to say that he's come across with information that could change the balance of power and we've got to state categorically that he's defected of his own free will and there's no question of him redefecting." Tortuous; Letz was sweating. "What I'm saying is this, forget the psychological approach. Hit him today. Coercion, drugs, threats, the whole bit. Tell him this, 'If you don't come across then we're going to say you did and what's going to happen to your son then?' But tell him that if he does co-operate then we'll put out a statement saying that he didn't and let him go back to Moscow." Letz dropped soluble aspirin in a glass of water and watched it fizz. "Your future is at stake, Jack; mine too." He drank the solution with a grimace. "I'm counting on you; so is Catherine."

"How long do I have?" Hamilton asked.

"Till midnight."

"And if he co-operates?"

"He will be killed by a KGB assassin. I'm preparing a preemptive statement in which we say he was murdered *after* he talked. Think about it, Jack. If he still refuses to co-operate then he's a dangerous embarrassment." Letz picked his way around Yurchenko. "If he does co-operate then fine." Letz poured the last grains of aspirin down his throat. "But he's still a dangerous embarrassment."

This time the pelican didn't bother to fly away.

CHAPTER 14

Although it was a Thursday it felt like a Sunday. Hannah preparing Chicken Kiev, reciting from a cookery book: "One chicken breast per person, one egg, beaten, bread crumbs, lump of butter, pepper, salt . . ." His mother in the kitchen wearing gloves of flour; his father arriving home from the frozen sea, cheeks Arctic cold; the spring music of snow melting; the wooden fence of the small dacha, No. 138, near the Baku railroad south of Moscow, steaming in sudden sunshine; potatoes boiling with earthy fragrance; burning candles spitting away the hours of repose.

He and Hannah talked about everything except Anatoly. "What," she asked, reading his thoughts, "were your parents like?" She began to hammer the raw chicken breasts.

"He was small, as hard as winter, as kind as spring. But my mother ruled – he was away so much. She was handsome in a way you Americans would never understand. She was big and strong but behind her defences there were graces only a Russian could see."

"America, Russia. You don't give up either. Does it always have to be like that?" She flattened pink flesh.

"Not if we outlawed propaganda. Rewrote the school books. A child isn't born a capitalist or a communist or a racist."

"We?"

"The American and Russian leaders are meeting in a few days. Maybe they should discuss minds instead of missiles."

"Chance would be a fine thing," Hannah said. She stopped

117

hammering and faced him. She wore a pale blue housecoat; her expression was confused, values scattered by pity. The kitchen was so big that it isolated each of them. Yashin moved closer to her and sat with his back to the steel-bright humming refrigerator. Through the window, on the sliver of sand bordering the waterway, he could see a guard with a stomach far too big for a young man.

I have to escape. How?

She said: "You're in a very amenable frame of mind. Is America still the pits?"

"I'm becoming more tolerant."

She atttacked another chicken breast. "Why?"

"Lots of reasons. A large black lady in charge of a large shabby car. *Occupying* it. Publix and K Mart. You." He slipped that in but he wasn't sure whether she heard. "Wisecracks. Racoons. A woman with shining white hair, a Red Indian suntan, black trousers, shoes with striped heels and Walt Disney sunglasses."

"I missed her," Hannah said.

Tuslov was still his only hope. Would Anatoly come to any harm if he gave him a little longer? Evens!

"In Boca Raton. Climbing into a Cadillac outside the shopping mall. Does anyone ever walk in America?"

"They jog. Place lump of frozen butter on the hammered breasts, roll them up and pin with toothpicks. The butter isn't frozen."

"My mother's refrigerator was the backyard."

"What happened in summer?"

"The butter melted." Yashin opened the refrigerator, took out a can of beer. "Do you want to know what else I like about America?"

"Baseball?"

"Fat people and fit people. Slang – bet your ass. State troopers in stetsons. Good causes – missing children on milk cartons. Cars built to do 120 mph on highways with 55 limit. Gideon Bibles in motels. Fresh orange juice. Soap."

"You don't have soap in Russia?"

"Soap on television. *I Love Lucy* and finding God on Sundays. Robot newscasters – V. I. Lenin has the de-tails. Black kids. Burgerbars. Have a good day."

"Crime, drugs, gluttony?"

"Mikhail Yashin for the defence, Hannah Martin for the prosecution?"

"Dip in egg and breadcrumbs and fry in butter for nine minutes."

"Break the egg first," Yashin said. Whatever happened Lozak would still want him good and dead. "Do you know what I like best about Americans?"

"Surprise me."

"Their illusions. They all believe they're originals and yet they conform. The pitch of their voices, the forced assurance, jeans, moustaches, macho men, golden girls . . ."

"You're going to fit in really well."

She placed a chicken breast on his plate. He cut it. Butter spurted as Hamilton said from the doorway: "We have to talk."

*   *   *

From a West Palm Beach boatyard Tal rented a black inflatable dinghy with a Honda outboard.

The salesman, white-haired and sun-wrinkled, everything about him theatrically scruffy except his groomed moustache, said: "Spivak. What kind of a name is that? Central European? No offence – names are my hobby."

"It's American," Tal said.

"Okay, okay. But names are people, you know that? Everyone is affected by their name. Even Smith. No one ever believes Smith, you know that? And it gives 'em a complex. Now take my name."

"Is the tank full?"

"Sure it's full. Khripin. Russian. How about that?" He smoothed the wings of his white moustache. "Got any plastic?" when Tal produced a thin wad of new bills.

"Cash."

"I prefer cards."

"Forget it." Tal withdrew the money.

"Okay, okay, no offence." Khripin licked a finger and counted the bills. "Anyway it's out of season; high-rolling muggers wouldn't be seen dead here." He slid the bills into his wallet. "Fishing?"

"Maybe."

"You gotta have a reason to go boating."

"I like boating."

"You don't like fishing?" Khripin looked incredulous.

"I'll leave the inflatable here," Tal said. "Pick it up later."

"Everyone likes fishing," Khripin said.

"Fish don't," Tal said. He walked towards the Cutlass. "You know something?" he heard Khripin call out. "Your name should be Smith."

In a Miami gun store Tal, armed with a licence in the name of Spivak, bought a Hush Puppy pistol designed originally for killing guard dogs and manufactured in stainless steel for naval amphibious forces to avoid rusting.

The salesman, young with greased hair and a barber's rash, said: "You boat people?"

"Just give me the gun," Tal said.

"You know what I'm talking about? Cubans who came over here pretending to be political refugees? You know, Castro put them up to it? Gangsters all."

"I'm from New York," Tal said. "Give me the gun."

"Shower of bastards. Responsible for most of the crime around here. On the other hand big business for us." The salesman ran one finger across his larded hair.

"Know what I mean?"

Tal took some bills from his pocket.

"Visa? Diners, AE . . .?"

"Cash," Tal said. "What's your name?"

"Smith," the salesman said.

In another store Tal purchased night vision goggles, a water-proof holster for the pistol and a knife with a serrated blade that could cut through bone.

Later he drove along the A1A, slowing down as he approached the mansion where Yashin was staying. A big house was being built close to it, a skeleton of beams and rafters.

An old tan Camaro was parked among the trucks and beat-up limos standing on rutted concrete and sand. It had been groomed with love and it exuded power. A young construction worker with dusty hair was sitting beside it eating sandwiches and drinking beer from a can.

Tal pointed at the Camaro. "Yours?"

"Ain't for sale."

"For two nights?"

"What the hell you talking about"

"I want to borrow your car for two nights," Tal said, sitting on a freshly severed tree trunk. "All you have to do," he said, taking a wad of dollar bills from his trouser pocket, "is to leave it here."

"You crazy?"

"Two fifty a night," Tal said, peeling off bills.

"A heist? I'm legit, mister. I'm buying a plot of land on the St. Lucie River and I'm earning enough bucks to do just that. I don't want no trouble." He bit neatly into the sandwich.

"Plus a five hundred bonus."

"For what?"

"None of your business. A thousand dollars." Tal made a fan of the bills. "Okay?"

"A thousand bucks for doing nothing?" The dusty young man tipped beer down his throat. "You're on, mister."

Tal said: "Has anyone else approached you?"

"Two guys checked me out the other day. Licence, papers, ID, the whole thing. What the fuck's going on?"

"A thousand dollars is what's going on," Tal said. "Leave the keys under the front tyre, driver's side. And leave a pair of trousers, jeans maybe, and a shirt on the back seat."

"That—"

"—will be another hundred dollars. Here, take this." Tal handed him 500 dollars. "I'll leave another 600 down the back of the driving seat."

The young man said: "And they told me Santa Claus was a phoney."

*   *   *

Hamilton said: "I'm going to level with you."

"James Cagney, 1937."

"You don't have much time now. You don't have any time."

Hamilton kicked a Budweiser can planted on the ocean beach. It was 2 pm. Thunderheads loomed on the horizon; they reminded Yashin of an army in the Napoleonic War poised to attack. The water was flat and green, the beach deserted except for two guards, one behind, one in front.

"Tell me what you want," Yashin said.

"You know damn well what I want. Everything you know about the Soviet space programme."

Hamilton wore a dark grey suit; on the beach it was ridiculous; it disturbed Yashin; he couldn't imagine why.

"So you still want to destroy me? If I betray my country I've got nothing left."

"You should have thought about that when you defected."

A motor launch wheeled on the ocean 200 yards offshore; a grey sedan crawled on the A1A separating the beach from big old houses. There was no escape here. Where?

Hamilton said: "Letz told me to use drugs, threats . . ."

"What sort of threats?"

"I never wanted it to be like this." Hamilton picked up a smooth pebble and skimmed it across the water; two splashes and it sank.

"What threats?"

"If you come across we'll leak it to the Russians in Moscow that you wouldn't talk. That way Anatoly will be saved."

"And if I don't?"

"The Russians will be told that you talked. That way Anatoly will die."

Hamilton stared at the thunderheads. His jacket was open and Yashin could see his pistol snug in its holster.

Hamilton addressed the wide ocean and the tall clouds. "Either way, Letz wants you dead," he said.

*   *   *

It was the worst way to escape but it was the only way and it should have been obvious but it hadn't occurred to Yashin until he had walked with Hamilton on the beach. He had told Hamilton that he would visit him in his room at 3 pm by which time he would have made up his mind whether he was going to talk.

He called Tuslov once more. No reply.

2.55. Watched by the ancestors, he creaked up the stairs. A radio was playing down the corridor. Golden oldies, said an announcer. Through a window Yashin saw an airliner chalk a line to Moscow in the sky. He knocked on Hamilton's door.

Hamilton was sitting in his shirtsleeves at a rosewood desk. The room was Hamilton. A composed unit that had relapsed into disarray. The bed and the chairs were wearing his clothes; toilet requisites had spread from the marble bathroom to the dressing-table; kicked-off shoes lay stranded on the white carpet; a television flickered soundlessly, a black and white movie starring Cary Grant.

Hamilton pointed at the set. "*Suspicion*. Joan Fontaine. Beautiful. That sad smile, the way she raises one eyebrow. Sorry I couldn't arrange Paulette Goddard."

The shoulder holster containing his gun lay on the bed.

"Old movies are ghosts," Yashin said.

"Are we in business?" Hamilton pointed at a cassette recorder lying beside the pistol, a Smith & Wesson.

"We always were."

"Gambling is what we were in. Except I didn't know the stakes. Not to begin with. If Tuslov had cleared your name you would have won."

"Does anyone win?" So he had guessed about the Moscow calls.

Cary Grant was driving an open tourer at a perilous speed. Sitting beside him, Joan Fontaine looked scared to death.

Yashin sat on the bed. Hamilton's face was drained but curiously guileless. He was too wise to be in intelligence, Yashin thought. He had outdistanced cleverness; he looked back and saw a wasting game.

Hamilton said: "Even our wives."

"Our wives what?"

"The same . . ."

Yashin smelled whisky. He saw a silver hip-flask on the desk besides Hamilton's wallet.

He said: "No, you still have your wife."

"You still have your soul."

But not if I talk. Did Hamilton know his secret?

The door on Joan Fontaine's side of the tourer flew open. Was Cary Grant trying to push her out or pull her in? Pull, if Yashin knew Cary. How could anyone's hair be so glossily compact?

"So I'm asking you again," Hamilton said, "are we in

business? Because if not . . ."

"You're going to tell Moscow we are? You make it very complicated."

Cary Grant's hair was like boot polish.

"*They* make it very complicated. They're always around. have you noticed that? They say this, they say that . . . never we, you and me." Hamilton drank from the flask and handed it to Yashin.

Yashin took a small swig. "To what might have been," he said.

"To what should have been." Hamilton screwed the cap on the flask. "I liked Moscow." He stared out of the window.

"I might have liked New York."

Cary and Joan Fontaine were struggling on the top of a cliff. Then he was explaining some terrible misunderstanding, insisting that he couldn't return with her.

Yashin eased the pistol out of the holster and pointed it at the back of Hamilton's head. "Stand up," he said, "hands behind your neck."

Cary, at the wheel of the tourer, made a sweeping U-turn. Cary was returning.

Hamilton, at the wheel of the white Mustang, his own gun cradled by Yashin beneath a copy of the *Miami Herald* pointing at his spine, told the guard at the end of the drive leading onto the A1A that he would be back in an hour.

"You sure this is okay, Mr. Hamilton?" Sweat clung to his bald head like gelatine.

"I'm in charge, Jerry. Remember?"

"Sure, Mr. Hamilton, but, you know, we normally get advance warning."

"Don't let it worry you. Our friend wants to visit the Pink Poodle. Okay?"

"I guess so, Mr. Hamilton. Have one on me." He winked and with the tips of his fingers smeared the sweat on his baldness.

"What's the Pink Poodle?" Yashin asked from the back seat.

"A topless bar. Interested?"

Yashin consulted the map of Florida he had taken from the house. He told Hamilton to continue along the A1A, make a left at Lantana Bridge spanning the waterway, then a right on US 1, then another left down Lantana Road across Interstate 95.

"Spoken like a native," Hamilton said.

The jaws of the bridge had opened to let a tall-masted yacht pass underneath and they had to wait.

Hamilton half turned his head. "I guess it's about time I said, 'You won't get away with this.'"

"Why not? All I have to do is hide out, call the Soviet Embassy in Washington and tell them to come and pick me up."

Yashin checked Hamilton's wallet. A surfeit of ID, credit cards, 100 dollars in bills, a photograph of his wife posing beside a black Jaguar. Perhaps it would have been different for Hamilton if there had been children. In the Soviet Union when a husband left his wife and family in a cramped apartment they said: "Perhaps it would have been different if they hadn't had children." He tapped Hamilton on the shoulder and handed him the photograph.

The jaws of the bridge closed ponderously. The Mustang took off.

They passed a hospital, a shopping complex and a small airport. The housing thinned out and the smell of swamp found its way into the car.

Behind the anxiety possessing Yashin a smaller worry trailed. Why had everything been so easy? Wallet on the desk, gun on the bed.

He told Hamilton to drive down a side road bordering an abandoned building site. Beyond the shells of houses the bulldozed land was returning to its origins, fantails of palm, hickory, clumps of flowering grass sprouting from black earth and builders' sand.

Yashin ordered Hamilton out of the car. Paradoxically Hamilton had acquired serenity since his capture. His back was straighter; his eyes no longer searched ahead for answers – perhaps he had found them.

Yashin opened the trunk of the Mustang and took out a length of rope. The heat was wet; sweat streaked his yellow T-shirt. Hamilton looked impossibly cool, white shirt plucked by a private breeze.

Yashin wagged the gun. "Over there," pointing at a leaning metal hut being devoured by rust. A smiling snake ringed in black and white slithered across their path.

"Now what?" Hamilton asked when they reached the hut. "Put down the gun and tie me up? Try and tie me up with one hand? It's not as easy as it is on the screen in the Metropole on Sverdlov Square." He folded a smile. "And then what are you going to do? Call the Soviet Embassy in Washington, the Mission in New York? Every line will be tapped."

Yashin prodded the Smith & Wesson at Hamilton. "I'm going to Cuba," he said. "Now sit down and tie your ankles. Tight."

"On Sundays," Hamilton said, making knots in the rope, "I used to visit the bird market on Kalitnikovskaya Street. Pigeon's feathers falling among the snowflakes. And a couple of miles away the two belfries of the Old Believers. Maybe that's what we should have been, Mikhail Mikhailovitch, old believers. Maybe that's what we are."

"Lie face down," Yashin said. The walls of the hut were closing on him. In one corner lay a mattress sprouting with straw, an empty wine bottle and a mouldering, open-thighed girlie magazine.

He knelt beside Hamilton and tied his ankles to his wrists, giving the rope as much play as possible. He stood up. "Write and keep me up to date with the Mets," he said and was gone.

*   *   *

There were so many imponderables, not the least of which was driving an automatic. Yashin had always imagined it would be easier than a manual but he found it impossible to co-ordinate brake and gas pedal. His erratic progress unnerved him.

He turned onto US 95. The breadth of the lanes disorientated him; cars drilled past him; exits beckoned; the zip of rubber on road expanded in his skull. He stalled at a red light. The driver of an old, shark-faced limo drove past tapping the side of his head with one finger. And it wasn't until he was approaching Fort Lauderdale that he realised that you drive an automatic with one foot.

Yashin grinned. There was hope. Then the state troopers

stopped him.

He pulled onto the shoulder and switched off the engine. He looked for the handle to wind down the window. A fawn-uniformed trooper stared at him impassively. The windows were automatic too. He pressed the button. Not automatic when the engine is switched off. He turned the key, pressed the button; the trooper's face was surprisingly close.

The trooper said: "You've been driving kind of strangely." He pushed the brim of his stetson with one finger; he was blond and tanned and looked as though he doubled as a lifeguard. "Furthermore you aren't wearing a seat belt. Mind telling me your licence number?"

"I forget. I just bought this car."

The trooper's hand strayed to his gun holster. "Okay, out you get. Nice and easy." He stood away from the door. "And now your driving licence and some other ID," as Yashin stepped out of the Mustang.

Yashin handed him an identity card. The trooper examined it and said to his partner who was leaning against their car: "Hey, Don, we got a spook." His partner who looked like a tennis player Yashin had seen on television came closer.

"A spook who doesn't wear a belt? Drives like he was stoned? Show us more ID, mister." He stretched out a freckled hand.

"You don't have the right . . ."

"Shut the fuck up," said the second trooper, "and give me the wallet." The first trooper drew his gun while his partner read: "John Duval Hamilton, born . . . How old are you, mister?"

"Thirty-eight."

"Not according to this you ain't. Address?"

"Does it matter?"

"It matters."

Hamilton's pistol was in the glove compartment of the Mustang. Yashin backed towards the open door. The first trooper levelled his gun. "Stay right there." He edged round Yashin, opened the glove compartment. Taking out the gun, he said: "I've been in the force four years and I've never found a glove in a glove compartment."

CHAPTER 15

The sky to the west was yellow, the air still and rich; the waterway between the strip of wealth and the mainland was silk.

Tal, planning in his motel room, found he was thinking in slow motion, as though the pending storm had curdled his reasoning. He sat on a chair beside the window and stared into the parking lot where a lone palm tree with a starved trunk stood motionless.

He touched his face; his fingertips found a stranger's features; he pressed the stranger's cheekbones, the line of the jaw; he found character which no one else saw; except, perhaps, the girl.

What was happening? He was thirty-four years old and he had killed one man for every year of his life and he had never been bothered by awareness of himself.

He closed his eyes tight and he was in an apartment in Warsaw gazing through the telescopic sights of a Mosin-Nagant at a CIA agent named Hammond who had penetrated the SB. That had been the last killing he had carried out and the preparations had been incisive and uncomplicated. Professional. He pulled the trigger, Hammond died. He opened his eyes, touched his forehead and lips: they still belonged to a stranger.

And the stranger was making mistakes: he shouldn't have called the girl. Worse, he had told her he was in Lake Worth. Why? To share a confidence, establish remote-control intimacy? Sharing . . . until now a unconsidered luxury. Lake

Worth. Had the sharing reached her in the small house in Brooklyn?

Abruptly Tal snatched his fingers from the stranger's face and picked up the *West Palm Beach Post*. The main stories were Anna, the storm that looked as though it might spin into a hurricane, and the defector hiding somewhere in the United States, identity still unknown. But, according to wire service reports, identification was imminent. Pictures of the defector's son taken from American television had been transmitted to Moscow; reporters were showing them to university students – the young man had been a Muscovite, well spoken – and youth leaders. But Tal knew that the journalists would be dogged by the 10th Department of the Second Chief Directorate of the KGB responsible through an army of interpreters, servants, *Novosti* watchdogs and UPDK *helpers*, for surveillance of the foreign press, TV and radio. As soon as they approached young people they would be molested, accused of provocative behaviour, threatened with expulsion. No, identification would come from the American authorities harassed by a remorseless media. Maybe tomorrow. By which time Yashin would be dead.

The phone rang, a death rattle. Dobykin said: "I'm calling from outside the Mission. Are you clean?"

Tal said he was.

"Postpone Cipher."

"Authority?"

"Moscow. The Center."

"Why?"

"In case Yashin escapes and comes back now he's seen his son on television."

"Who says he's seen him?"

"It's a possibility. Anyway he'll read about it."

"The Americans won't let him near a newspaper."

"Maybe, maybe not. But if he comes back we fly him to the Soviet Union and liquidate him there. No complications, no mess."

"I don't make a mess," Tal said.

"You don't hit the target," Dobykin said.

"How long is the postponement?"

"Forty-eight hours. Meanwhile expect a visitor. Kiselev,"

he said when Tal didn't ask who.

"I don't need assistants."

"You're not getting one: Kiselev is taking over."

"Who says so?"

"I do."

"Authority?" Tal squeezed hatred from his voice; it was weakness.

"I have it. That's all that matters."

Tal said: "Not according to Simenov," and hung up. Simenov had said: "If you get any shit from Dobykin call me." He had given Tal a private number.

Tal called it.

When Simenov answered he asked: "On or off?"

Simenov said in his rusty voice that it was on.

Tal cradled the receiver. So it was Lozak.

He sat very still for a moment. Then he went into the pygmy bathroom, yellow tiles bordered with mould, and looked at his face in the mirror. It was still nothing, pale and symmetrical, a page on which nothing had been written, but it seemed to Tal that now his eyes were looking out, not in; they narrowed slightly, acknowledging the scrutiny, and hairlines of amusement appeared at the corners. Soon people would be noticing him. Tal tilted his head so that his face was covered by a plague of dark blemishes from the mirror. Yashin, he decided, would be his last hit.

He dressed in brown slacks and cream shirt and packed pistol, ammunition, field-glasses, goggles, knife and frogman's belt into a Delta flight bag and covered them with soiled clothing.

When he left the motel the afternoon was beginning to search for evening. He parked the Cutlass behind a restaurant-bar, the Banana Boat, across the water from the mansion. The restaurant was more nautical than a yacht. He sat on the deck overlooking brown water; a waitress with sleek, tanned legs and a welcome-aboard smile took his order, Pepsi.

When she brought the drink she asked if he was a stranger in the area and when he said he was seemed genuinely interested in where he came from. New York, he said – that covered the world. Not only was she noticing him, she might even remember him.

He said he was in real estate.

He sipped his drink and stared across the water. The mansion was shy behind Australian pine. The yellow sky had now deepened to apricot. The air was as still as deep water.

A middle-aged couple sat at the table next to him and began to argue with practised venom. "At least Wyndham knew how to treat a lady." "What lady was that?" "Me, you asshole."

They retired into neutral corners while the waitress with the smile took their orders. As she headed inside she raised her eyes to Tal; pigs, her eyebrows said. He imagined her telling police: "Sure, I remember him. New Yorker, kind of funny accent, Pepsi . . . stammered . . ."

Had he?

"Wyndham was generous, too. Used to buy me flowers."

"Did his neighbours check the flowers in their gardens?"

"You really are a sonofabitch . . ."

"What kind of name is Wyndham anyway?"

A patrol boat from the sheriff's department cruised past. An aircraft searched the sky for emergent stars. The day seeped to the west but the heat stayed.

"What's in a name? He was a gentleman, is all."

"He was a pansy," the man said, wiping beer foam from his lips.

The waitress asked Tal if he wanted another drink. He shook his head but she didn't go away.

"What part of New York?" she asked.

"Brooklyn," Tal said.

"I got a sister living there. Cute but kind of crazy. You interested in animals?"

Again Tal shook his head but still she lingered. "Take a look at this. My sister sent it from a New York newspaper." She took a clipping from her purse; her fingernails were painted frost-pink.

KEEP YOUR PET FOREVER. The advertisement described how pets could be eternalised "virtually intact" with freeze-drying. The process included shampooing, grooming "and much more." ALL ANIMALS, DOMESTIC AND EXOTIC PETS. (Small dogs, Cats, Monkeys, Birds,

Reptiles and many more . . .)

"Isn't that hysterical?" the waitress said. "They'll be preserving corpses next."

Tal paid her and gave her a dollar tip and smiled at her and she smiled back. Then he drove to the boatyard and parked the Cutlass on a plot littered with broken oars, rudders and coils of frayed rope.

The outboard started at the first pull. He nosed the dinghy out of the marina and headed south. The broad Atlantic beach and the road where it bordered the mansion would be crawling with guards but the waterway shore with its small licks of sand, tangled vegetation and hidden reaches was vulnerable.

Darkness settled. Night birds called. Yachts hurried home. In the distance strands of lightning linked the night with the land. Tal scanned the far shore with the night-vision field-glasses. One guard was standing on the private jetty; a small yacht was anchored 50 metres offshore.

Tal stripped off shirt, shoes and trousers and opened the flight bag. He fastened the belt round his waist above black boxer shorts and fastened the pistol and knife onto it. He stuffed his discarded clothes into the bag which he had weighted with two bricks. He dropped it overboard; it floated for a moment then sank.

He idled the dinghy towards the shore 200 metres north of the mansion. He cut the engine and waited. There was no movement on the anchored yacht. He slid two paddles into the locks and rowed gently towards the yacht, modest by local standards but streamlined for speed. It was called *Blonde*.

He looked through a porthole. A squatly-built man with long arms was coming out of the head zipping his fly. He paused, then went into the cabin, picked up a bottle of Jim Beam and poured himself a shot. Tal tied the dinghy to the rope ladder hanging from the hull and climbed onto *Blonde*.

A cough, a belch, a gurgle of liquid – another Jim Beam. Tal waited beside the hatch, silenced Hush Puppy in his hand. He regretted that he would have to kill this man drinking whisky. Did he have a wife and kids? Or a girl who loved him despite his lack of grace. What humanised him was his inefficiency. He shouldn't have gone to the head, shouldn't have succumbed to the bottle. Tal understood mistakes now. And I'm making another, personalising a hit.

He tightened his grip on the butt of the pistol. Only the Americans could manufacture a gun designed to kill guard dogs. What did they do with the dogs when they had shot them? *Eternalise* them with freeze drying?

Blonde swayed gently in the wake of a homeward-bound yacht. The stillness of the air a steamy window on which you could write your name with the tip of one finger.

The guard began to climb the steps leading from the cabin to the deck. Tal could just make out a bald patch. He pressed himself against the yacht's bodywork.

The guard's bald patch was level with his own hip. One silenced shot, one obstacle removed. Why did he have to wear that small skull cap of hairless skin? And now the barrel of the Hush Puppy was in Tal's hand and when the guard was higher on the steps, turning and seeing Tal and going for his own gun, Tal hit him with the butt behind the ear and the guard fell down the steps and lay still on the floor of the cabin.

You should be dead you stupid, bald bastard, Tal thought as he bound and gagged the guard with nylon rope. Another mistake? Whatever happened he would kill Yashin; Yashin was a traitor, a legitimate target.

In the dinghy Tal put on the night-vision goggles. He could still see the guard on the jetty pacing up and down the boardwalk. He slid into the water, buried his face, kicked once and submerged. He swam strongly; he had never possessed an aptitude for sport but by application he had built muscle. The water was shallow; after a few strokes his feet found sand and slime. Gently he broke the surface. The guard stood with his back to him, legs astride. Tal swam a few more strokes; stones and weed touched his chest; he knelt; the water was too shallow to hide him; presumably it was deeper by the jetty.

He swam out underwater to make another approach. The water was thick and tepid. His lungs were inflated balloons; his chest ached and colours smeared his eyes despite the darkness. He raised his head and gulped air. The guard, young with a belly bulge, had turned; he seemed to be looking directly at him; he scratched his chest and turned away.

133

Tal reached the jetty in twelve more underwater strokes. He was underneath the guard. He could see racoons on the matted shoreline.

He stayed motionless. Originally he intended to kill any guard in his way. But it was better, surely, to leave them alone, unaware. The guard walked to the end of the boardwalk and stared across the still water. Tal made his way under the jetty to a rim of sand. He looked back; the guard was still staring across the water looking for an elite force of Spetsnaz to come furrowing through the water, AKS-74's blazing.

Tal slipped through the Australian pine and sea grape. The racoons fled. The mansion lay ahead beyond a paved barbecue area. The swimming pool to the right was a bare, illuminated aquarium. He assumed that guards between the waterway and the Atlantic beach would be thin on the ground and those on the ocean beach would be anticipating attack from the sea or from the A1A that passed over the tunnel.

Gun in hand, he skirted the lawns. For two nights, aiming the field-glasses through a slot in the trees, he had seen Yashin at this time in the evening sitting on the terrace at the far end of the pool. The blades of gamma grass were sharp under Tal's feet. Big trees with hanging roots loomed. From the mansion, above the drone of insects, he heard music, voices. He pushed his way through foliage until he reached the house that was being built next door. There was the Camaro.

He checked it. The keys were under the front, offside wheel; jeans and a shirt lay on the rear seat; he put them on and ran across the road onto the Atlantic beach. There were no waves but the ocean was invested with suppressed sound; the lights of boats moved far out like fireflies. Occasionally the darkness thickened into a patrolling figure.

Tal approached the tunnel patiently. It was framed by a glass-walled cabin, separated from the beach proper by wandering grass and fat-leaved succulents. A guard stood at one side of the cabin, arms folded across his chest.

In case the informant in Domestic Operations had decided to cheat, Tal had come an hour earlier than planned. If Yashin wasn't on the terrace he would go looking for him: the guards wouldn't anticipate an assassin inside their camp.

He was a body length from the guard. The mouth of the tunnel beckoned.

Two more sand-soft footsteps. He was behind the guard, a little to one side. This guard was just a silhouette; no bald patch, thank God, as Tal clamped an arm round his neck and thrust the barrel of the pistol into his temple. Now kill him but he hesitated and then he was on sand, over the guard's shoulder, and they were locked together and the gun was gone and the guard was a wall of muscle.

Tal forced one hand down to his belt, found the handle of the knife. The guard rammed his knees into his testicles. Pain lanced; vomit rose. They grunted at each other. He saw the guard's mouth open to shout; he rammed sand in it. Choking, the guard released the barrel grip of his arms. The knife slid easily into his back. Up, down, the serrated blade bit through rib bone. Tal withdrew the knife and pulled the body into the undergrowth.

He stared into the tunnel, the artery leading to Yashin's heart.

CHAPTER 16

Letz arrived at the mansion at 5 pm, half an hour after Yashin had been brought back by the state troopers astonished at the furore their capture had caused.

He led Hamilton across the spongy grass to the deserted tennis court. They sat on a bench watching phantoms at play.

Letz sat silently for a few moments composing his anger. Finally he asked: "So, how did it happen?"

"He fooled us, I guess." Hamilton searched his pockets for non-existent cigarettes.

"Fooled *you*." Letz rubbed the pepper-and-salt hairs on one tanned arm. "Or did you fool us?"

"What's that supposed to mean?" Hamilton saw himself stretching to serve, hustling to the net to volley; the picture had grown sepia with age.

"Did you give him the gun? Volunteer to lie down while he tied you up?"

"You should have me investigated." Hamilton, released from the abandoned building site after Yashin had told Hannah Martin where he was, felt curiously elated. "Maybe I just didn't want to destroy the guy."

"You're admitting culpability?" Letz made pebbles of his syllables.

Hamilton wanted to say that he admitted birthright; that he was as American as Yashin was Russian; that Jefferson had penned it all.

Instead he said: "I admit negligence." He saw himself leap and smash; his backhand had always been his weakness.

"If the state troopers hadn't stopped Yashin he would be on his way to the Soviet Embassy by now and the media would have another ball. Another CIA foul-up, another triumph for Soviet PR."

Hamilton said: "There's more at stake than that."

"He defected, for Christ's sake." Letz's skin had lost its sheen; his navy shirt was sweat-damp under the arms. "He was a valid subject for penetrative interrogation."

"He didn't defect, he escaped."

"There's a difference?" Letz folded his arms, pushing out his biceps with his fists. "I'll tell you what Yashin did, he outsmarted us. Accepted our offer of free board and lodging while he waited for an accomplice in the Soviet Union to clear him. And he never had the slightest intention of collaborating."

"Nor would I," Hamilton said, "if I had escaped to Russia."

"You and Yashin, you're twins?"

"Not unalike," Hamilton said. "Like you and Dobykin."

"What are you preaching, Jack?"

"Hope," Hamilton said.

"You're suspended," Letz said. "As from now." He stood up, swished an invisible tennis racket. "Shall I tell Catherine or will you?"

"Does it matter?"

"She would have enjoyed Paris," Letz remarked. "You realise you've condemned Yashin to death?"

"I thought you'd done that already."

"You signed the certificate. Very soon the world will know that the defector was Mikhail Mikhailovitch Yashin, Hero of the Soviet Union, murdered by a KGB assassin *after* he had revealed the secrets of the Soviet space programme. No more Yurchenkos," Letz added softly.

Hamilton stared at the empty court. Who had he been playing? Catherine, victorious, smiled into the camera, then, as he walked towards the net, turned away.

* * *

Hamilton telephoned Catherine who had returned to the house at Baltimore. "I've just been fired," he said.

A pause; he thought he heard the beat of her heart; he remembered it close to his; how fragile her ribs had seemed beneath small tender breasts.

"Why?" she said at last.

"Because I helped someone to escape."

"What sort of a someone?" Another breathing pause. Then: "I know, someone with ideals. A fool like you."

"A fool like me," he said.

"A beautiful fool. But one I don't understand." Her voice frayed. "Goodbye, John. Paris would have been nice."

Click. Whether you smashed down the receiver or pressed the handset with one finger that was all the person on the other end of the line heard. Click.

*   *   *

Yashin, sitting handcuffed in a stiff-backed chair in his bedroom said: "I want to speak to Moscow."

"After what you just did?" Letz circled the chair. "You've got to be kidding."

"If I speak to Moscow I'll trade."

He no longer had any choice: if he talked the CIA had promised they would tell Moscow he hadn't and Anatoly might be reprieved. Yashin's hand strayed to the scar tissue under his shirt. He had no illusions about his own future: whatever he did the CIA would kill him.

Letz sat in front of him, perching his chin on fisted hands. "No tricks?"

"No tricks."

"Okay, so this is what we do. First we get the hell out of here. The local press will get the address from the cops and by tomorrow the whole world will know that you were hiding out on South Ocean Boulevard, Florida. In fact I'm surprised your people haven't found you already. Your identity will also be common knowledge, ferreted in Moscow or leaked in Washington or both."

"Where will we go? Another *safe* house?" Yashin lifted his hands; the handcuffs were surprisingly light.

"Langley maybe."

"With a KGB sleeper there?"

"Don't worry," Letz said, blue eyes searching Yashin's

138

face for deceit, "we'll think of somewhere. West coast maybe. We'll take off this evening."

"After I've spoken to Moscow," Yashin said. "After you've taken these off," offering his wrists to Letz.

Letz looked at them doubtfully.

"Leave me some dignity," Yashin said. "You're taking everything else."

"Okay." Letz's smile shared trust. "Anyway there's no escape from this place anymore. Not since you pulled a Houdini. I'm surprised Hamilton didn't drive the car," he said casually.

"Hamilton's the best man you've got."

"His wife's a bitch." Letz unlocked the handcuffs. "Okay, make the call."

"Alone." Yashin said.

"Why not? There's a guard outside the window."

The phone rang distantly lighting a frame of Moscow. A queue, air sparkling with frost, the warm animal smell of Durov's menagerie. Bears, wolves, badgers, even a giraffe performing. And Anatoly gripping his arm, making a unit of them.

The phone continued to ring.

Another frame. The resin-smelling dacha on a hot summer evening. Radio Moscow's call sign " . . . If you only know how dear evenings near Moscow are to me." Anatoly on the porch making a model spaceship; Galina yawning with boredom.

The echo had returned. Tuslov said: "Hallo, hallo . . ."

"It's me, Mikhail, Mikhail . . . Where, where . . . How, how . . ."

Answers dipping and wheeling in space like wounded birds.

In duplicate, through shared knowledge and implication, tortuously and agonisingly, Yashin learned that Tuslov believed he was poised to break Lozak. How long? He couldn't say. Patience, patience . . . And Anatoly? Anatoly was okay, Tuslov said. So far. "Call again soon, soon . . ."

So there was still hope. And time. Somehow he had to stretch the hours; thread them with elastic.

He walked down the stairs with Letz to the table on the

139

terrace in front of the tunnel leading to the ocean beach where Hannah Martin was already drinking a vodka and cranberry juice.

*   *   *

Half-way down the darkened tunnel Tal paused: Yashin had just come into view. One shot and I could be out of the tunnel on the beachside and into the Camaro, part of the normal traffic passing along the A1A. Yashin sat down beside Letz, opposite the girl. To ensure total accuracy Tal needed to get a little closer. He inched forward.

*   *   *

"Okay," Letz said, "we leave in half an hour." He sipped a Black Label on the rocks; his blazer and slacks looked as though they had been delivered direct and untouched from the cleaners. "Are you ready?" to Hannah.

Yashin said: "Where's Hamilton?"

Letz looked at him candidly. "He quit, Mikhail. I'm sure I don't have to tell you why. I'm taking over," he added.

"Where are we going?"

"West. Arrangements are in hand." Letz reached out and touched a small gun on the table. A stun gun, he had told Yashin, capable of discharging a 50,000-volt charge and incapacitating a victim for three minutes. "A defensive weapon but of course they get into the wrong hands."

"Yours?"

Letz laughed and said: "*Touché*," humour scalped from his voice.

Hannah Martin said to Yashin: "You're really going to trade?" and Yashin, remembering the sleep that had come to him in her arms, felt ashamed, and Letz said irritably: "That was always the idea, Hannah. Don't you have some packing to finish?"

"I'm packed," Hannah said and Yashin wanted to ask her: "Don't you understand any more?"

"So what are we waiting for?" she asked.

"Transport," Letz said. "Not the Mustang. Anything but that."

Hannah stood up, stretched, emanating common sense and

reproof. What would she have done if it had been her son? "Why's the light switched off in the tunnel?" she asked. "It's spooky." An elongated salon to some, a gun-barrel to Yashin. He felt the walls squeezing the darkness, remembered the figure he thought he had seen, lit by a flash of lightning.

Hannah flipped the light-switch.

The thick explosion of a silenced gun poured out of the tunnel. The bullet hit Letz knocking him to the ground.

Hannah grabbed the stun-gun. Fifty-thousand volts leapt down the tunnel towards the figure lying on the floor among the cane furniture. Yashin dropped as the gunman fired the second shot. The bullet grazed pictures on one wall.

Hannah flipped the switch again. The darkness pulsed with threats. She grabbed Yashin's arm. "Down, down," she was saying, pulling him at the same time.

Another muffled explosion. Momentarily the tunnel was a torch. The bullet sang high over the pool punching out a window in the mansion.

Running footsteps. Shouting.

Yashin was running with Hannah, along the terrace, past the deep illuminated blue of the pool, through foliage to the gravel drive leading. to the road. The Mustang waited patiently.

"Get in the back," she shouted.

A man's voice: "Hey, what the fuck!"

Hannah thrust the key into the ignition; the engine fired. Another shot, breaking glass, a scream. The Mustang's tyres fired gravel.

Hannah shouted to Yashin: "Keep down."

Yashin, on the floor, pulled a travelling rug over himself.

As Hannah slowed at the end of the drive a guard shouted: "Hey, Miss Martin, what the hell's going on?"

"You'd better get down there," Hannah called out. "I'm going for help," and before he could ask what sort of help, had pressed the gas pedal. Tyres protesting, the Mustang swung onto the A1A and headed in the direction of Palm Beach.

*   *   *

Tal lay on the floor of the darkened tunnel for a second, thirty seconds . . . His body was a live wire; he saw it in cartoon zig-zags of current. His skull was full of light and jumbled pain. He had no idea what had hit him, only that, whatever it was, it had swotted his aim. He held onto a chair and began to climb it but it fell and he fell with it. Chords of pain strummed his brain. He saw a blurred figure at the end of the tunnel. Reaching . . . for . . . the . . . light . . . He aimed the Hush Puppy. The explosion was as dull as a punch. A scream, the figure disappeared. Tal turned on his knees and began to crawl towards the ocean mouth of the tunnel. His knees tingled. He saw another figure outlined indistinctly at the beach exit. He raised the pistol, lowered it as the figure blurted past him in the darkness. Then he was in the glass cabin, then in the warm, sea-smelling outdoors. He clawed at impressions and tried to mould them into thoughts. Faintly, he heard tyres squealing; nothing passed on the road heading south. If it was Yashin in the tyre-squealing car then he was heading north towards Palm Beach. Whatever, I have to get away. Limbs shuddering, he staggered towards the Camaro.

*   *   *

The Mustang galloped north, waterway to the left, ocean to the right. Lights from the servants' quarters of brooding houses quivered on quiet waters. The speed limit was as low as 25 mph in some places; the Mustang bore into the night at sixty. Yashin noticed a limousine from the Sheriff's Department parked in a driveway; the driver of an oncoming car squawked his horn on a curve.

Hannah said: "We'll cross onto the mainland and head inland." Yashin decided to ask her later why they were heading anywhere.

Above the throb of the Mustang's engine Yashin heard a snarl. He glanced behind. A pair of headlights was peering at them, orbs growing larger; he tapped Hannah on the shoulder. "We've got company." Hannah accelerated, took a left against the lights, sending an oncoming Volkswagen beetle onto the grass verge.

The orbs stayed behind them, larger still.

Ahead Lantana bridge spanning the waterway. Red stop

142

lights shone brightly, the barrier blocking the road was down, the jaws of the bridge were beginning to open to allow a tall ship to pass.

Behind the Mustang the two headlamps glared.

As Yashin crouched, a bullet punctured a frost-crusted hole in the rear window.

"Hold on," Hannah shouted.

Yashin peered over the back of the front seat. The hood of the Mustang swept aside the barrier. The jaws of the bridge were gaping wider, the jaws of a ponderous crocodile, the mouth between them full of water.

He gripped the seat. The Mustang stumbled in its gallop. Then they were flying. Beneath them water.

They landed on the opposite jaw, bounced, picked up speed down the steepening incline.

Hannah said: "Is he still behind?"

Yashin looked back. There were no inquisitive orbs of light.

The wounded Mustang cantered inland.

*   *   *

Tal, still charged with electricity, spun the Camaro into a U-turn on the other jaw, negotiated the barrier crowded with gesticulating drivers who had left their cars, and turned left on the A1A as a police car, roof lamp flashing, siren bellowing, approached from the right.

He continued north, crossing the waterway at the bridge at Lake Worth. He parked the Camaro in a side street, stowed the gun and knife in the toolbox in the trunk and made his way to the motel.

That was twice! He would quit when he got back to Moscow. But first Yashin.

He removed the motel keys from beneath the brick where he had hidden them, climbed the steps to the first-floor balcony and went into his room where Deborah Klein was waiting for him.

CHAPTER 17

His emotions confused him. Not just their contradictions: the fact that they existed at all.

He shut the door and said: "How the hell did you get here?"

She answered in Russian. "I checked out all the motels in Lake Worth. I'll go if you want me to."

She wore a yellow blouse and a pleated skirt which did nothing to taper the thick contours of her body; her hair had been rinsed lighter and styled in a cascade of curls; the birthmark on her cheek burned.

She sat on one of the beds looking at him calmly; he wanted to slap expression into her face.

He persevered with English. "You're lying."

"The name?" sticking with Russian. "That was easy. First I rang around asking if anyone of the name of Lvov had checked in. When I got nowhere I rang round again and described you. This was the third motel I tried."

"And you found Spivak." Tal paced the room. So now she knew both his pseudonymns but not his real name. Or did she? "Who let you into my room?"

"The receptionist; it cost me five dollars." She took a pack of cigarettes from her handbag and lit one; she hadn't smoked before; he took it from her and crushed it in an ashtray. "Not in a bedroom." And now he was speaking in Russian.

"Don't tell me what to do." Now she was speaking in English. She lit a crumpled cigarette and blew small puffs of smoke from her mouth as though glad to get rid of them.

"It doesn't suit you," he said.

"It doesn't suit anyone." She made a concertina of the cigarette in the ashtray. "Why did you come here?"

He lay on the other bed and, placing his hands behind his neck, locking his fingers, tried to compose answers.

Insects chafed in the parking lot. The manhunt for Yashin and his would-be assassin would be spreading across Florida like a stain. He remembered reading about stun guns, cited in a Soviet magazine as further proof of America's obsession with crime. One of his arms jerked involuntarily; he imagined sparks inside it.

"There are restrictions on Russians' movements in the United States. You know that. So we assume false identities. It's done all the time."

"Are you a spy?"

They were sharing a common language now, English. He was formulating a reply when she said: "You don't have to answer that, I understand. Everyone in the Soviet Mission at the United Nations is involved in intelligence. That's why Washington is cutting your staff."

"All diplomats are expected to report items of interest to their intelligence organizations," Tal said carefully. "Americans in Moscow do it all the time." He stared at the ceiling.

"I understand, I really do. Nothing you've said surprises me. But you haven't answered my question."

"I'm in trouble." He surprised himself. "They want to send me back to Moscow."

He heard her breathing quicken. He turned his head. She was trying to wipe the shock from her face with the tips of her fingers.

She said: "You should have come to me; I would have helped you."

"They would have found us." Unease, unidentified, pushed at his lies. "They knew about us."

"You told them?"

"We have to account for our movements."

"Associating with a Russian spy . . . You could have gotten me into trouble." Her hand uncovered the trace of a smile. "I would have been important." She reached out and touched his arm. "What are we going to do?"

145

"We?"

"I can still help you. What sort of trouble were you in? Why did they want to send you back to Russia?" Her fingers pressed his arm. "You needn't answer any of those questions. But tell me this, why don't you want to go back?"

He knew what she wanted him to say but he had locked away such words years ago. Her eagerness to believe irritated him. The unease persisted.

He said: "They think I'm a double agent. If I went back they'd kill me."

Disappointed, she said: "You can apply for political asylum."

"I'm not a traitor. I want to clear my name."

Which was presumably what Yashin was trying to do.

"How?"

"I have friends working on my behalf in Moscow. And in New York."

"Meanwhile?"

"Keep moving. "

The dinghy . . . the boatyard . . . the Banana Boat . . . the motel . . . It wouldn't take them long.

"I was just leaving," he told her.

"This minute?"

He began to pack.

"They can't have traced you here."

"They could have traced you." This was the stranger speaking, lying to both of them. "Come on," the stranger said, "let's get out of here."

She waited in the parking lot while he picked up the tool kit from the Camaro, and took a cab to the Banana Boat. He stowed the pistol and knife in the tackle bag beside the fishing rods shielding the Mannlicher-Carcano in the trunk of the Cutlass.

From the Banana Boat he called a car rental company on Lake Worth Road. A laconic voice agreed to open up for an extra 20 dollars and rent him a Regal.

He picked her up in the Cutlass, dumped it on Lake Worth Road, transferred the contents of the trunk to the Regal and took off. He reckoned he had driven more makes of cars in America than the manufacturers had ever produced in the

146

Soviet Union.

"Where are we going?" she asked as they turned south onto the Florida Turnpike, headlights of the maroon Regal searching the darkness.

"Anywhere," telling himself that it was resourceful to travel with the girl because the police would be looking for a man travelling by himself and knowing that this was still the stranger speaking. Had she believed anything he had told her? Wanted to believe, probably, and that was the next best thing.

They were flashed down at a roadblock by an exit to Pompano Beach. One policeman questioned them while his partner in a black and white bearing the legend *To Protect and Serve* talked into a handset.

Where were they from? Where were they heading? Why had they rented a car in Lake Worth if they had set out from New York?

"We flew to West Palm Beach International independently," Deborah Klein said. "We met in Lake Worth. Bill was on a fishing trip. Now . . . well things are kind of different. You know, we want to travel around together . . ."

"I know," the cop said. "I'm going to take a look in the trunk."

Tal handed him the key to the trunk where the rifle lay beneath the rods, pistol and knife in the tackle bag. He heard the cop rummaging around; he should have kept the Hush Puppy inside the car; mistakes were becoming the norm.

The policeman came back with the keys. "You should head for the Keys. Great fishing down there." Were all American policemen fishermen? "ID?"

Deborah showed him her United Nations pass. The cop was impressed. William Spivak, wages clerk from Jersey City, impressed him less. He waved them on.

"*Bill* on a fishing trip," Tal said. "That was smart."

"You checked into the motel as William Spivak."

Perhaps she was an asset; perhaps he had been resourceful. He hoped she wasn't too smart. The unease that had been worrying him took shape. She knew about Lvov and Spivak: if she found about about Tal he would have to kill her.

She settled herself comfortably in the passenger seat and relaxed, hands clasped on her pleated skirt.

Ten miles further south he left the turnpike on Route 84, then headed north on Route 27 into sugar country.

*   *   *

Hannah cut the engine, doused the lights. Walls eight foot high rose on either side of the car.

"Sugar cane," Hannah told Yashin. "Stretches for miles."

She lowered her window. The air was warm and damp and sweet. Although the night was still the cane breathed with its own life. Water trickled; night birds struck chords of loneliness in the darkness.

"We can't check in anywhere, they'd trace us," Hannah said.

Yashin stored questions he had to ask her. He concentrated on Tuslov. Tuslov was hope. Tuslov was time. How long? Twenty-four hours, forty-eight . . .

Hannah said: "We'll stay here for the rest of the night: every patrol car in Florida will be looking for a Mustang with a smashed hood."

She adjusted her seat so that it lay flush with the back seat. She lay back. He adjusted his seat and he was beside her. He pulled the travelling rug over them. Her eyes looked at him steadily from the shadow that was her face. He kissed her lips and reached for her.

Half clothed, they loved.

*   *   *

Later he asked: "Why did you of all people help me to escape?" and she told him: "My people were going to kill you just as your people killed my husband," and he asked her if that was all and she said no there was much more, if she was in America and he was in Russia and they both looked at a bright night sky they would see the same star. Their sharing filled the car.

In the greening dawn they reached for each other again.

*   *   *

And still Anna's vanguards taunted Florida. Skeins of light-

148

ning and balls of thunder skirting the still and breathless land.

The new light showed Yashin another Florida. Lush cane, more dense than corn, stretched high and wide to the horizon; canals cut it into green squares and triangles; a line of palms led the way to an old corrugated-iron warehouse leaning against a new sugar refinery; the black soil was as rich as a banquet; this, Yashin thought, was the land of plenty.

He kissed her.

"Why did you hate me so?" he asked.

"I despised you," she said.

"Why did you stop?"

"Because you were a phoney: you never intended to defect."

"And now?"

"We've got to keep you alive."

"For the KGB or the CIA? They both want to kill me."

"How about the forces of justice? We haven't seen too many of them."

"They're very timid," Yashin said.

Hannah drove the Mustang behind a live oak spreading its bows over the cane; then they walked to the highway to hitch a lift to Okeechobee.

"They will have sealed off all escape routes north," Yashin said. "Eventually we'll have to head south." To Cuba, he thought.

The driver of a small truck taking punished furniture to a camping site beside Lake Okeechobee gave them a lift. He was old, a country-wise philosopher; there were many such old men in Siberia. Liver-spotted hands light on the wheel, rheumy eyes a little vague on the open road, he told Yashin and Hannah, squeezed in the cabin beside him, what Florida was not.

Yashin, trying to find a way to extend the time before he would have to give himself up, half listened.

What Florida was not was condominiums, Disneyworld, the John F. Kennedy Space Center, shopping malls, roaring highways, shuffle-board, factory-fast Key lime pie and Miami.

Yashin stared across the tall green plains of sugar cane. Beards of Spanish moss hung from oak trees, from telegraph poles even. In the exterior driving mirror he noticed a maroon Regal poised to overtake.

Yashin half-heard Hannah ask: "What *is* Florida then?"

Florida was cinder-block houses and clumps of palmetto, pastures of peanuts, sweet potatoes and tobacco, oranges and grapefruit, and red-eye gravy, king-sized milk shakes and corn dogs, the walrus faces of manatee on the St. Lucie River and, to the south, deep peaceful swamp.

"And alligators," Hannah said.

"Sure, 'gators. Once they stayed home. Then developers drained swamps, turned rivers into trenches and dug their own ditches. Old 'gator takes one look at these ditches and paddles down 'em and finds himself in a trailer park and snaps up a pussy cat or puppy dog for dinner. Ain't old 'gator's fault, it's the ditch-diggers."

Just how close was Tuslov to denouncing Lozak?

The maroon Regal drew level with the truck. A girl in the front passenger seat was touching the shoulder of the man at the wheel, pointing ahead.

"That's Bell Glade," the driver said. "Capital of sugar country. Got its roots in dirt, black gold. Lake's three miles away, full of bluegill, bass, catfish."

If I can gain Tuslov 72 hours . . . three full days before they get really tough with Anatoly. What had they done to him to force him to make the appeal on TV? Yashin gazed at an old black man sitting on a rocking chair on the verandah of a green frame guest house, bottle of beer in one hand. A swarm of dragonflies flew past. The Regal swung into the lane ahead of the truck.

They skirted the lake beside the embankment built to contain its brimming water. Past fishing camps, Curry's Flea Market. Treasure Island. There was no sight of the Regal. The driver dumped the furniture at the camp and drove them to the small town of Okeechobee north of the lake. Yashin asked him to drop them at the railroad station.

Then, like a chess player surfacing from prolonged analysis, Yashin found his move. He said to Hannah: "I've got to call New York."

*   *   *

Dobykin said: "Where the hell are you?" His growl broke with emotion.

"America."

"Don't try and be—"

"Call Moscow and find out how Anatoly is. I'll call you back tomorrow."

Yashin heard a peppermint crunch on the other end of the line. He would be gesticulating, dashing off scrawled notes.

Dobykin said: "Your son is all right. You saw him on television?"

"Just do what I say."

"You're in Florida, right?"

"Was."

In the phone booth outside the station Yashin heard a train approaching.

Dobykin said: "Can I tell the Center anything?"

"Tell them I haven't talked."

"Is that all?"

The train was braking.

"Tell them that if Anatoly's okay – and I want proof – I'll come back."

"You'll have to escape first."

Dobykin didn't know? Yashin frowned at the receiver. The train was panting at the station. "Don't worry, I'll come across. I'll call you tomorrow, same time."

Still frowning, Yashin made his way to the station.

*   *   *

Hannah was waiting outside.

"Come on," she said, "they don't hang around."

Yashin took her arm. "We're not going anywhere by train; they'll be watching every station including this one."

"But—"

"Come on."

On Route 441 they thumbed a lift from a young man with long ginger hair wearing dungarees driving a rusting station wagon loaded with snap-brimmed hats made from plastic straw. He was as dour as the truck driver had been garrulous.

At Yeehaw Junction he volunteered the information that he wasn't taking the turnpike because it cost money. Yashin

151

picked up one of the hats and put it on, brim tipped over his forehead. "Can I buy it?"

"Suit yourself."

Yashin handed him a five dollar bill from the money he had taken from Hamilton's wallet.

"Ain't worth that."

"Keep the change," Yashin said. "Come back on the turnpike."

He slid down in the seat between Hannah and the driver. Police were stopping some cars. Not rusting station wagons loaded with fairground hats.

The driver dropped them in Orlando. The city was warm and spacious and watered with lakes. Yashin led Hannah to a department store.

"We're tourists," he said. "Make yourself look like one."

He bought grey lightweight slacks, a red T-shirt stamped FLORIDA THE SUNSHINE STATE and an Instamatic and film. He still wore the hat; in shape it wasn't unlike an FBI hat.

Hannah met him at a drinks dispenser in the store. She was wearing a pink hat like a drooping flower, plain white T-shirt and faded blue jeans; she carried a raffia bag embroidered with oranges.

In another store Yashin bought a pair of plain-glass spectacles. "Fugitives," he remembered Tuslov telling him, "always wear shades."

"Is there much call for these?" Hannah asked the blue-rinse shop assistant.

"Sure. Lots of guys and girls want to look studious. Have a good day, professor," she said to Yashin as they walked out.

"Disneyworld?" Hannah asked when they were on the street.

"Kennedy Space Center," Yashin said. "Where else?"

CHAPTER 18

Mikhail Mikhailovitch Yashin.

The name dropped in Moscow. Why was debatable – Kremlin decisions always were – but the most plausible theory was that the Politburo, realising that Washington was poised under pressure to release the name, had authorised a leak to pre-empt the Americans. A microchip of gamesmanship.

The recipient of the drop, leaked by a journalist on *Novosti*, a press agency with KGB links, was the bureau chief of an American wire service. Within minutes Mikhail Mikhailovitch Yashin had been telexed to New York; within an equally short space of time the name had been blitzed all over the world.

Florida journalists reacted swiftly. The road blocks . . . police surveillance at airports, railroad and bus stations . . . the incident at Lantana when a rogue car had blasted through a barrier and just beaten the opening jaws of a drawbridge . . . The police chief in the state capital, Tallahassee, could not comment on the identity of the fugitive, nor could spokesmen in Miami, Jacksonville, Tampa, St. Petersburg . . . it had to be Yashin.

The media descended on the Sunshine State – *In God We Trust* – from Washington, New York, Chicago, Los Angeles, San Francisco, Philadelphia, Boston, Baltimore, Houston, Atlanta . . . from Toronto, Vancouver, Montreal and Mexico City . . . foreign journalists based in the United States joined the rush . . . the world was in Florida.

153

By the afternoon of the Friday, local time, Mikhail Mikhailovitch Yashin had shouldered most other news off the front pages of the newspapers and become the lead item on television and radio newscasts. Some stories linked the manhunt with Hurricane Anna.

*   *   *

Letz, wounded arm in a sling, pointed with a ruler at the map of Florida hanging on the wall of the living-room of the mansion. "It's a trap," he said. "A beautiful trap." He reminded Hamilton of a ham actor playing a gallant commander in the Civil War.

Hamilton studied the map, jigsawed into counties in pastel blues and greens and pinks. He understood what Letz meant: excluding the panhandle, to the north-west, Florida was a poacher's bag hanging from America's belt: tie the bag tightly enough and Yashin was bagged.

But Florida was 447 miles long with 8,426 miles of tidal coastline and great seas of swamp including the 2,100 square miles of the Everglades. If he got lucky Yashin could play hopscotch here for weeks, jumping from one location to another; come to think of it that's what he had been playing all along, from Russia to America. And back?

Letz said: "So we're blocking all exits north to Georgia on the line of Interstate 10. And west to Alabama on the line of Route 319."

Hamilton said: "You can't stop every car on the highways; you'd bring Florida to a halt. Maybe they took a train after they dumped the Mustang in the sugarcane." He thought this extremely unlikely.

"So? We're covering every railroad station. And bus station. And port." Letz sought the bandaged gunshot wound high on his left arm with his free hand. "And every airport, Miami, Palm Beach, Lauderdale, Orlando, Daytona . . ."

"For every major airport," Hamilton said, "there are half a dozen strips."

"They're all covered," Letz said, wincing. "What I don't understand is why the bitch took off with him."

154

"Simple. She knew you were going to kill him. She's a liaison officer, not a murderess."

"And she was getting laid," Letz said. "I always figured she was unstable. Langley should never have employed her just because the KGB killed her husband."

Hamilton said: "How are you going to cover all the coastline?"

"US coastguards," Letz said, sitting in an easy chair as though his wounded arm had dragged him there.

"Coastguards? You've got to be kidding. Seventy percent of all marijuana and cocaine smuggled into the States comes through Florida. Maybe 12 billion dollars worth a year. Not a great advertisement for coastguards, is it."

"That's Drug Enforcement," Letz said. "And a lot of the junk comes by air. From Colombia. The 'glades are littered with crashed planes."

Letz stood up again, activated the computer brought from Miami and made the connection to the communications centre at Langley where the manhunt was being co-ordinated. Green letters and figures danced. Four sightings so far. Two in Miami, one in Fort Myers and one from a truck driver in Okeechobee.

"Now the media have projected it we'll be inundated with sightings," Letz said, words spinning into tortuous eddies.

Hamilton looked at the map. Miami, Fort Myers, Okeechobee – a triangle. "The first three, cops?"

"And all negative," Letz said, as more letters quivered on the screen. "But they're still checking out Okeechobee."

"Close to the plantation where the Mustang was found."

"A railroad station, too." Letz switched off the computer.

"He wouldn't be that stupid," Hamilton said.

"Did I detect a note of hope?"

"Will you kill the girl too?"

Letz gave the question a few moments' thought. Then he said: "We're trying to recoup, right? Convert a disaster into a triumph. To do that we have to claim that Yashin unfolded the Soviet space programme for us and we have to liquidate him in case he does a Yurchenko, makes contact with the Soviets and blows it. The killing will have another plus too: a ruthless murder by a KGB assassin dispatched to administer retribution."

Hamilton said: "I asked about the girl."

"Look at it this way. If she's capable of helping Yashin escape she's capable of telling the media that we killed him." Letz flexed the fingers of the hand protruding from the sling. "You're probably wondering why I summoned you here."

"I did think I was suspended."

"From the interrogation. But you may still be able to help."

Hamilton waited. He thought Letz could make slings fashionable.

Letz went on: "You know Yashin as well as anyone."

"Not as well as Hannah Martin."

Letz ignored him. "Empathy, that's the word. You were very close, you got into his mind. And you're very alike . . . What would you do if you were Yashin?"

"Yashin's a pilot," Hamilton said. "I'd get myself a small plane, at gunpoint if necessary. You can't shoot down every pilot flying by the seat of his pants."

"Which way would you fly?" Letz asked..

"North," Hamilton said.

Half an hour later he drove south.

*　　　*　　　*

Tal said: "I'm sorry."

The pause hung on the line between Florida and New York.

Finally Dobykin said: "About what?"

"I called Moscow. You were right. Cipher is postponed. But I have a proposition to put to you. Are you clean?"

Dobykin said he was.

A small boy stopped outside the phone booth beside a roadsign pointing to the Magic Kingdom of Disneyworld, stuck his thumb in his ears and waggled his fingers. His companion, a little girl, exhaled a pink balloon of bubble gum.

"Have you heard from Cipher?"

A longer pause punctuated by crackling on the line. Then: "We heard. Why?"

"You can't pick him up. Anyone who leaves the Embassy

or Mission will be followed. Put him in contact with me and I'll bring him back."

The bubble gum burst and pink confection deflated above the girl's lips; it reminded Tal of Deborah Klein's birthmark.

Dobykin said: "I don't know."

"I told you, I spoke to Moscow."

"Who in Moscow?"

"Simenov."

Coaches filled with children and their guardians sped past on their way to the Magic Kingdom and Epcot. The boy stuck out his tongue.

Dobykin said: "Call me back in an hour."

Tal cradled the phone. It was his second call in half an hour. The first had been to Simenov in Moscow. He had told him: "Instruct Dobykin to co-operate; that way I stand a better chance of finding Cipher."

To kill him.

Tal left the phone booth, thumbed his nose at the two children and returned to the Regal where Deborah Klein was waiting for him.

* * *

The bus tour was greeted at Kennedy Space Center on the Atlantic coast 42 miles from Orlando by an *astronaut* in a baggy white space suit.

"You," Hannah whispered to Yashin.

"Me. Grounded."

She squeezed his arm.

The high-rise rockets planted on the lawns were awesome and forlorn. Silver, white and black, they were burned-out cases; flag ships of the space age that had become instant relics.

Inside the Center Yashin gazed at the Gemini 9 flown by Thomas Stafford and Eugene Cernan in June, '66. Its original crew, Elliott See and Charles Bassett were killed when their jet fighter crashed at the McDonnell works at St. Louis a few yards from the spacecraft.

Yashin was back in Tyuratam. He smelled burning. Ice filled his skull. Hannah said: "Are you okay?" He closed his eyes and told his heart to beat blood back into his brain; he was supposed to be inconspicuous! He bit into flesh inside his mouth, tasted blood, felt warmth flowing into his head. He opened his eyes. "I'm okay," he said.

The tour reached the Apollo which, in July, 1975, had docked with Russian Soyuz 19. The handshake in space between Stafford and Cosmonaut No. 11 Alexei Leonov . . . Idealists had seen it as a symbol, peace in space.

A woman in tight pink shorts standing beside him was munching popcorn. How absurd that a former Soviet cosmonaut sent to America to penetrate its space programme should be standing next to a woman feeding her face with popcorn close to the launch pad for the space shuttles.

In the souvenir shop Yashin said to Hannah: "Have you heard anyone from the north on our tour? I wouldn't know Boston from Seattle."

"The couple in front of us on the bus. Chicago, I think."

"Someone with a car," Yashin said, "without Florida plates."

"Leave it with me," Hannah said.

Yashin watched two crew-cut men in lightweight grey suits circulating among the visitors. They stopped beneath a sign that read: *Smile. This store is monitored by a closed circuit television system.* They didn't smile. Yashin turned and bought a model rocket with Hamilton's money. He felt the cameras trained on him, saw himself on a screen.

Hannah said: "I'd like you to meet Mr. and Mrs. Theobald."

"Pleased to meet you," Yashin said.

"My pleasure," said Mr. Theobald.

Mr. Theobald wore rimless spectacles and a gentle smile; he looked like Harry Truman. Mrs. Theobald's smile was more forgiving; she was small and sturdy with tightly-curled white hair that reminded Yashin of watch-springs.

She said: "Your wife tells me you want to go south but you haven't got a car. Just fancy, no car." Her smile forgave them. "We're heading south and we'd be very happy for you to come along with us."

"And maybe share the cost of the gas," Mr. Theobald said.

"That's very kind of you," Yashin said, glancing at the two men in grey suits. "But—"

"Don't think anything of it. We left the car in Orlando; we figured it was easier to take the tour."

"Split the cost down the middle," Mr. Theobald said.

Outside Yashin bought a copy of the *Daytona Evening News* from a vending machine. His face stared at him from the front page.

* * *

Not an exact likeness. The face was too long; the tightness and Slavic angles that regarded him in the shaving mirror every morning, missing. An identikit.

He dropped the paper in a litter basket.

Two miles south of Orlando on the Florida Turnpike Mr. Theobald filled up with gas. "That'll be ten bucks," he said over his shoulder.

As they drove out of the filling station two policemen peered into the station wagon.

Mrs. Theobald smiled at them. "Just doing their duty," she said to Yashin and Hannah when they were back on the highway.

"Wonder who they're looking for," Mr. Theobald said.

"Drug pushers," Mrs. Theobald said. "If I had my way I'd shoot the lot of them."

They stopped outside a white frame Baptist church. A notice, black on white, stated: BELIEVE IN THE LORD JESUS CHRIST AND THOU SHALT BE SAVED.

"Shall we go in?" Mrs. Theobald asked.

Mr. Theobald stopped the station wagon. They all went inside. The nave smelled of scented wood and holiness.

Mr. and Mrs. Theobald prayed, smiling.

As the station wagon cruised past scrub oak, palmetto and mango, Mrs. Theobald said: "You folks fond of nature?"

Hannah said they were.

"Fancy accompanying us to the Everglades? We've promised ourselves a visit ever since we got married. And that's a long time." She touched Mr. Theobald's cheek. "Forty years this August. You see Mr. Theobald's just retired. A printer. One of the old school, pushed out by computers. Thank the good Lord." She turned and crinkled her eyes. "Now we can be together all the time. We're thinking of buying a condo in

159

Florida," she confided.

"If we can afford it," Mr. Theobald said.

"On the west coast," Mrs. Theobald said. "Fancy you folks living in New York and not owning a car. But you're not New York born and bred, are you Mr . . . ."

"Moszuk. Polish. My parents come to America from Lublin during the last war." He almost said the Great Patriotic War.

"The poor, long-suffering Poles," Mrs. Theobald said.

"More cops," Mr. Theobald said, pointing out of the window. "More than just drugs. Let's find out what's going on." He switched on the car radio.

It was tuned to an FM channel. A man's voice intoned: "O generation of vipers, who hath warned you to flee from the wrath to come?"

"Saint Matthew," Mrs. Theobald said. "Chapter three, verse seven. Leave it on, Harry.'

* * *

A hundred and fifty miles further south Hamilton pulled off the highway and bought a pack of cigarettes. The first few drags made him feel dizzy. When he had recovered he continued south, heading for Key West, the southernmost tip of the continental US, ninety miles from Cuba.

CHAPTER 19

It was late afternoon on the Friday when Mr. Theobald swung the station wagon onto Route 267 at Homestead, thirty miles south west of Miami, and headed into the Everglades.

He parked the wagon at the Royal Palm visitors' centre and the four of them walked round the Anhinga Trail, a mile-long walkway. More than a million acres of swamp breathed and grunted around them. Prairies of sword-edged saw grass, hummocks of cabbage palm and dwarf cypress, mahogany, mango, swamp apple and strangler fig, spider lilies and orchids, roseate spoonbills and purple gallinules, Florida panthers, marsh rabbits and turtles, coral snakes and diamondbacks, alligators and mosquitoes. And through it the Shark River slough fifty miles wide, six inches deep, easing its way towards Florida Bay to the south.

The mosquitoes coveted Mrs. Theobald, clinging like tufts of black hair to her arms, homing upon her sturdy neck above her pale blue print frock. She bore their attentions gamely, whimpering only occasionally, while Mr. Theobald searched for alligators through the viewfinder of his Japanese camera.

Yashin and Hannah dawdled fifty yards behind them. Hannah leaned on the wooden rail of the walkway and said: "I've got this friend who owns a house in Key West; she said it's mine whenever I want it."

Yashin sensed that she had been debating the announcement for a long time, just as he had been debating whether to disclose Cuba – she was American, her husband had been killed by the KGB, she could still betray him.

161

"And," Hannah went on, "it is the jumping off point for Cuba." She smiled sadly; a baby, black and orange alligator grinned at them from a pool of brown water.

"I've bought time," he said. "There's still a chance."

She ran the tips of her fingers down his cheek. "Do you shave twice a day?"

"In the air force I tried shaving the night before morning parade but it didn't work; a sergeant used to rub cotton wool on your face and if any of it stuck to the bristles you were charged." He pointed at the busy figures of the Theobalds. "We'll stay with them until we get to Miami because they're the best cover we've got. Then we'll rent a car and head for Key West."

They were joined by a young ranger with a priest's face who said: "You're looking at the largest subtropical wilderness in North America. That's the way the guide books put it. Any place you can't buy a burger is a wilderness. Fact is there's more life here than Miami."

"What brought you here?" Hannah asked.

"Beats the hell out of Detroit. And I got involved. Man is the enemy here, taking the Everglades blood – water. We're fighting to survive. Like a lot of the inhabitants. Herons, ibis . . . Man hunted them for their plumes; that's why we're here."

The ranger made Yashin feel he was part of the ecosystem.

The ranger said: "But you came the wrong time of year. Mosquitoes eat you alive. And there's a hurricane on its way. My guess is Anna's going to hit this time tomorrow."

Which opened up a vista for Yashin. He told Hannah about it on the putting green of the small, flaking motel on Espanola Way on the sandbar, once swamp, that is Miami Beach. The motel was at the southern extremity, remote from the luxurious piles to the north.

"Most people leave things too late. So tomorrow the highway linking the keys will be jammed with traffic trying to beat Anna to the mainland. And cars going the other way to pick up families, batten down the hatches . . . The police won't stop anyone; if they did there'd be a riot."

His golf ball rolled three times round the No 3 hole on the balding green and stayed on the lip. Hannah holed in one.

"If the ranger was right," she said.

"You heard the radio in the room."

"It wasn't definite."

"The ranger was. I'd back him, close to nature."

Yashin took three to down the ball on the fourth, Hannah two.

Yashin said: "But it's only a matter of time before someone recognises me."

"Keep that hat on. And those glasses. Who would suspect that a Russian fugitive would be putting – badly at that – on an apology for a green on South Miami Beach? With his wife," she added, holing the fifth in one. And, retrieving the ball: "I know how you can get to Cuba."

As children dived splay-legged in the small pool, as dusk settled heavily, she told him about Alpha 66. Years ago, in the 60s, the CIA had trained anti-Castro Cubans in Florida after the abortive Bay of Pigs invasion of Cuba in April '61. The legacy was a group of Cubans who still plotted Fidel Castro's overthrow. They claimed a membership of 6,000 and they camped 25 miles from Miami off Highway 41. "Back the way we've just come," Hannah said.

"Why would they help me?"

"Money," Hannah said. "For their cause. No questions asked." She took three shots on the sixth, a disaster; Yashin took four.

"You seem to know a lot about Alpha 66."

"Alpha for beginning, sixty-six for the original membership." Hannah crouched professionally over her iron. "Don't forget who I work for. I've had dealings with them."

"Interpreter?"

"Liaison."

"They'll think I'm CIA."

"Hopefully. They infiltrate Cuba by sea from Key West. You could go with a group. Or by yourself in one of their boats."

"I haven't got enough money to pay them."

"I have. A thousand down, a thousand on delivery. I'll drive out to the camp now."

"Not by yourself," Yashin said. "They're looking for you too."

"But you're the one, the identikit." The ball rolled sweetly into the hole on the seventh. "I'll be back in a couple of hours. Stay in your room while I'm away.

She handed him her iron and walked briskly across the greens of her recent triumphs. A star appeared in the sky glittering precociously. Yashin watched her until she disappeared behind a hedge holed like children's knitting. How was she going to get to Alpha 66's camp. Or was she making for a telephone booth to call Letz? Tell him that Yurchenko's successor was in Room 28 in a motel on Miami Beach? He could make a break for it now, lose himself in this daunting mongrel city of Miami, half American, half Hispanic. But he had rediscovered trust. He laid her iron on the grass and hit the ball firmly with his own; it sped into the eighth in one. He left the irons in the cabana beside the pool and went up to Room 28.

* * *

The Theobalds knocked on the door at 9 pm. Yashin who had been lying on his bed, eyes closed, midway between Moscow and Miami, let them in.

Mrs. Theobald was agog with an article she had just read about Miami and its parent, Dade County. "Ninety thousand Cuban boat people live here. Marielitos – because they set sail from Mariel in 1980. They kill each other with handguns all the time."

"So do a lot of Americans," Yashin said. Russians preferred kitchen knives and blunt instruments.

"Capital city of crime," Mrs. Theobald breathed.

"And drugs," Mr. Theobald said. "A kilogram of cocaine costs $60,000."

"The Hispanics are taking over," Mrs. Theobald said, sitting down and fanning herself with her straw hat. "The Anglos are leaving. Thank the Lord we're settling on the west coast."

"Sarasota," Mr. Theobald said. "It's cheaper than other resorts."

"How about coming with us tomorrow, Mr. Moszuk?" Mrs. Theobald said. "Hey, what's your first name? You never told us." She surveyed the room over the rim of the hat.

"Where's Mrs. Moszuk?"

"Gone for a stroll," Yashin said.

"She must be crazy. You let her?"

"She's a strong-willed girl."

"How about tomorrow?"

"Why not?"

"And if we find somewhere you can spend vacations with us."

"That would be great," Yashin said.

At the door Mr. Theobald smiled gently and said: "You know you look quite different without your glasses."

*   *   *

When Hannah returned she had been away nearly four hours. She spun her sunhat across the room, lay on the other bed, kicked off her shoes and massaged her feet together.

Why had she taken so long?

She told him she had found the camp. About fifty Cubans uniformed with beards, shades and cigars practising unarmed combat and firing GAU-5 assault rifles on a range.

"And?"

"They agreed to take you."

"Who agreed?"

"One of the leaders. Don't worry, it's genuine."

"What took you so long?" He rubbed the bridge of his nose where the glasses had rested.

"I had to wait for the guy in charge. He had taken a group on a survival course in the swamp."

"Supposing they recognise me. If they're anti-Castro they're anti-Russian. They won't want to help a Russian outwit the CIA and return to Moscow."

"Why should they care? You're not going to blow their plans; everyone knows they sail to Cuba from Key West. They don't care about one KGB agent returning to the roost."

She leaned on one elbow and gazed at him; she had changed in the past few weeks; fashion model and farmer's daughter had linked arms and departed; doubt had touched her with innocent beauty, fatigue had sculptured hollows of grace; he saw her as a teenager emerging from a bathroom,

165

towel-draped and damp-haired, staring at a young man lying on a bed and the young man was himself.

She said: "I rented a car and I didn't call anyone." She reached across the void between them. "Now shall we go to bed?"

He took her hand. "We've got to go. Theobald saw my face naked."

* * *

By the end of the day Yashin had become Snowbird, the name given by the 1½ million residents of Greater Miami to the denizens of the north seeking their sun.

At 10 pm Tal, poised in Orlando to move in any direction, called the Miami emergency number, 911, from a phone booth and was put through to the Snowbird extension.

Tal told the cop who took the call that he had seen Yashin.

"Where you speaking from, sir?"

If Tal had been Yashin he would have headed south; north was too predictable, exits easy to monitor. He flashed a torch on a map of Florida. "Fort Lauderdale," he said. "How does that tie in with other sightings?"

"Could be good. Depends – we just had a good identification from a motel on South Miami Beach. Best yet . . . Was the guy you saw alone?"

"He had a girl with him."

The cop's voice tightened, young, sniffing promotion. "Can you describe them both, Snowbird first."

"Like the identikit." Tal viewed Yashin through telescopic sights. "But more taut, more Slavic."

"Slavic, huh? Yeah, that figures." Tal imagined him writing Slavic with a splintered ballpoint. "Eyeglasses?"

If you say so, Tal thought. "Glasses, yes. Does that correspond with the information from Miami Beach?"

"Sure does. The guy who called us said he'd been wearing glasses all day, then he caught him without them."

"All day?"

"Sure, the caller had been driving them around. Figured they were a couple of tourists. He asked if there was any reward involved."

"Where did he pick them up?"

166

"Orlando," the cop said. "What did the girl look like?"

Tal described Hannah Martin.

"You've got 'em. What time was this?" The cop's anxiety filled the receiver.

"What time did you get the call from Miami Beach?"

"Half an hour ago. But Snowbird could have been there a lot longer."

"Which motel?"

"I don't think—"

"My wife and kids are in a motel on Miami Beach. I'm worried. You want the time, you give me the motel."

The cop gave it to him. "The time?"

Tal hung up.

*   *   *

The police cars had assembled outside the motel and two uniformed officers were standing at reception when the rented Escort took off from the parking lot and turned into Collins Avenue. The driver wore a neat-brimmed hat and glasses.

A police car took off, siren braying, roof light flashing. Half a mile down Collins it cut in front of the Escort; two cops approached, guns in hands.

The driver turned. No glasses. Hat tipped back unsteadily on short curly hair. She wound down the window, smiled and said: "Sorry, guys, is it that rear light again?"

*   *   *

What Florida was not, Yashin remembered, was Miami. But what was Miami?

Miami was a kaleidoscope of threats. Sugar-cube, night-black highrise, crowded him. Police cars whooped, Spanish voices beguiled, palm trees whispered, stars pried from slits in the cloud.

As he delved into downtown Miami, striding out, almost running, the city – fount of tourism, finance and crime – squeezed him.

He saw Hannah waiting outside La Tasca Restaurant on W. Flagler, the rendezvous they had selected from the Florida guide in the motel room. He wanted to cling to her.

167

Together they penetrated Little Havana. Latin American music and exuberance in exile broke open the night.

They sat at a sidewalk cafe and ordered *perros calientes*, hot dogs, and *cafe cubano*.

He held her hand tightly; the threats receded.

She told him that the police who stopped her in the Escort hadn't been told that the Soviet fugitive's accomplice was CIA: the last thing Langley wanted to broadcast was that one of their own was aiding and abetting a defector trying to redefect. The cops, Hannah said, had been deeply impressed by her credentials.

"The hat, the glasses?"

"No glasses by the time they reached the car. An easy mistake to make. Yashin is supposed to be holed up in the motel, a car takes off at speed with a driver at the wheel wearing the sort of hat described by Theobald – you anticipate glasses and you see them." Hannah took them from her purse and placed them on the table.

A teenage waiter wearing black trousers, tight and stained, and a white shirt with theatrical sleeves served them with the flourish of a bullfighter. The sidewalk was a procession.

"The hat had them worried," Hannah said. "But you don't interfere with CIA. And I got away fast. What about you?"

"Just as we planned, no hat, no glasses. I walked out of the room and across the putting green while the police were concentrating on the getaway car. I caught a taxi across the causeway over Biscayne Bay." He daubed his hot dog with mustard and bit into it discovering that he was famished.

Hannah said: "We can't use the Escort anymore, the cops will have reported it by now. And we can't hire a car, they'll be watching every rental company in town. We'll have to buy one. Or steal one."

"Steal one and the licence number will be in the computer as soon as it's reported missing."

"I haven't much ready cash left," Hannah said. "I'll have to go to American Express in the morning."

They were joined at the table by a skinny man wearing a crumpled white suit and a grieving moustache. "*Buenos tardes*," he said. He lit a punished cigar and began to read a

168

Spanish-language newspaper. The waiter brought him, unsolicited, a glass of anis and a small jug of water. He poured water into the anis and, without interest, watched them cloud together.

Yashin, still starving, ordered two more hot dogs with French fries. A guitar-playing minstrel strolled past; girls flirted with their eyes; youths pranced.

The skinny man arranged his newspaper upright on the table, folded so that a backcloth of newsprint presented itself to pedestrians. Onto the table behind the screen he poured a pocketful of watches.

He held one up. "Fifty dollars. Special price, just for you . . ." Accented words spilled from his mouth. His face creased into smiles and the moustache was a stranger among them.

Hannah said: "It looks like a Rolex Oyster but it's got to be a fake."

"President Day-Date Chronometer," the Cuban said. "Fake." He stroked the moustache into a smile. "Forty bucks."

Hannah tapped her wrist. "I'll sell you mine."

"Thirty dollars. Last price."

Yashin said: "I want to buy a car."

The Cuban held the watch to his ear; satisfied with what he heard he slipped it into his pocket. The others followed. The pocket of the white jacket sagged with their weight.

An ancient shoeshine boy offered to polish Yashin's shoes. He let him go ahead. The strokes of the brush tickled his feet through the black leather.

Finally the Cuban said: "Pedro only sell watches."

"A thousand dollars," Hannah said.

Yashin thought he heard the watches ticking in the Cuban's pocket.

"And a watch?"

"And a watch."

"One thousand thirty dollars. You got cash?"

"In the morning."

The old shoeshine, face as seamed as cracking clay, brought lights to one of Yashin's shoes with a yellow cloth. "Good leather," he said. "Fine leather. I know leather."

He shouldn't be listening to us, Yashin thought. He paid him. The shoeshine stood up slowly as though his footstool was a torture rack and said: "I get you a car seven-fifty bucks."

The Cuban spoke fiercely in Spanish.

The shoeshine shrugged. "See you in jail," he said and walked away, stool pulling his body into a lopsided angle.

"A Chevy," the Cuban said. "A Nova."

"How old?" Hannah asked.

"Not young."

"Miles?"

"Maybe twice round the world. But she goes. In Cuba we know how to keep cars on the road."

"Okay," Yashin said, "it's a deal. Eleven in the morning. Where?"

"The parrot jungle," the Cuban said. He pulled his moustache back into mourning.

*   *   *

Tal said: "I have to go alone."

Her eyes regarded him from the dark depths behind the strobe lights and chips of spinning colour reflected from a ball of mirrors revolving from the ceiling, searching for truth. "Why?" Deborah Klein asked.

Did she know, guess? "Because they're looking for the two of us as an entity." He spoke in Russian.

"They always were."

"We were spotted leaving Lake Worth."

"How do you know?" A waitress, a moth-eaten bunny with spreading holes in her fishnet tights, served their drinks in the disco-bar on the southern extremities of Orlando.

"I have been in contact with the Mission. I have friends there. I told you. In the Mission and in Moscow."

"Then we have to get out fast."

"I have to get out."

Tal sipped his root beer. Lights glanced off her face. On a small stage three young men and a heavy-breasted blonde belted out assembly-line country and western.

If Yashin had swung south, Tal thought, he was aiming for Cuba. The last sighting had been a motel on South Miami

170

Beach but if I know my man he won't be there when the FBI/CIA call.

She said: "I can't see that anything's changed."

Except that now I have a definite sighting, he thought. Yashin was almost certainly heading to the tip of America's tail, Key West. I have one last chance to stop him dead in his tracks and this girl, wearing a halo of trust, will be a hindrance.

"Together we're a target, a composite picture," Tal said.

"Nothing's changed."

He wished she would stop repeating herself. She stared into her beer. Her hair had lost its salon bounce. "Okay," she said, "I'll fly back to New York."

"If you stay with me you could be shot."

"I don't care," she said, "as long as I'm with you."

"Then you'd better c-come along," he said.

"Of course one thing has changed – I know your real name."

Tal froze.

She tapped the newspaper folded on the table. "It's Yashin, isn't it?"

*   *   *

Yashin said: "The Soviet Union is a collection of moods."

"What mood is it now?" She pushed the contours of her body into his in the bed in the musty old hotel; their legs entwined; her hair smelled faintly of lemons.

"Cold," he said because, together, their bodies were so warm. He ran his hand down the slopes of her back. "Cold joins. Sky to land, rivers to shores, people to people. I flew to Yakutia in Siberia once on a training course. The coldest inhabited place in the world."

"Tell me about it," she said, lips at his throat so that he felt her voice.

"I saw a woman selling small blocks of frozen milk with sticks inside them like—"

"Popsicles."

"And the cold crackled inside your nostrils and trees exploded and your cheeks were bruised with frost and the taiga stretched blue to the Arctic . . . It was the nearest I ever

171

got to space," he said. "Sometimes the capital, Yakutsk, was covered in people mist – breath and steam from human bodies. It joined everyone, that mist. Workmen building in minus fifty with heated cement, kids in reindeer boots going to school, housewives beating the ice out of the washing on the line. People smiled at each other," Yashin said. "And they never talked politics."

"I went to Fairbanks once," Hannah said. "In Alaska. The snow was like grit and your breath froze and the side-streets were canals of ice and when you went into a sourdough's home the stove was burning and everyone smiled and no one talked politics."

"The people of Yakutsk should visit the people of Fairbanks. Exchange visits. Six months a year."

"You should visit Dallas," Hannah said. "They like communists there – for dinner."

"I'm not a communist, I'm a Russian."

She held him tightly and her breath was soft on his throat and the music from the street below, rippled by laughter, was first snow bringing peace and he lay beneath it, arms stretched wide, and then it was morning and immediately he made love to Hannah.

After breakfast, *churos* dusted with sugar, and black coffee, at a table where a craftsman from Padron Cigars extolled the virtues of hand-rolling, she visited American Express and bought new clothes while he waited in the hotel. Black trousers and white shirt, very Russian, for him; blue blouse and white slacks for her. This time she wore the spectacles.

As they left the breakfast room his face stared at him from a black-and-white TV. The cashier stared at them, the Courtesy Cab driver stared at them. A neurosis: the identikit could be anyone and the fact that he was travelling with Hannah hadn't reached the media yet. A black man sweeping the sidewalk stared at him.

The cab driver who had a wrinkled neck, wanted to talk. "Don't get much call for Parrot Jungle," he said. The wrinkles changed direction as he craned his neck to peer round a corner. "Coach traffic mostly and snowbirds with their own autos. Eleven miles south of US 1. What the hell you want to look at birds for? And why you staying at a tacky

172

hotel like that? You folks got class."

"Soaking up atmosphere," Hannah told him.

"Atmosphere my ass. City's jail's got more atmosphere. And, say, when you're through looking at them birds why don't I take you . . . You've gotta go to the Poodle Lounge in the Fountainebleau, right? Everyone has to take in the action there. You should see those blue rinses on the make, wow." He turned his head making ravines of the wrinkles. "How about it?"

"We're meeting someone at the Parrot Jungle," Hanna said.

"Jesus, what a place to meet. Strictly for the birds if you ask me."

The jungle was cypress and live oak. Flitting with bright plumage, studded with cynical eyes.

The first show in the geodesic dome had been 9.30. The next, 11. Yashin and Hannah sat beneath a cypress loaded with birds as thick as fruit.

Yashin opened the *Miami Herald* he had bought from a vending machine. The hunt was closing on Miami but there was no mention of the near-thing at the motel on South Miami Beach.

He said to Hannah: "I'll make two calls when we get to Key West. One to the mission, one to Moscow. If Tuslov hasn't come up with anything I have to quit. Tell the KGB to pick me up in Cuba."

"How long do we have?" she asked.

"Twenty-four hours. Whatever happens I have to get to Cuba because even if the KGB don't want to kill me anymore the CIA will."

"And me?"

A pink bird sailed past, wings making fleecy music. Children led parents past the bench.

She regarded him through the plain-glass spectacles; her hair had been combed at a different angle; her face was devoid of make-up; her eyes were deep and green.

"I don't know," he said.

"Don't say, 'We'll work something out.'"

"If I'm cleared—"

"You can't come back here. Letz will be waiting for you.

Supposing . . ." What? She didn't say. Instead she said: "What's the mood in Russia now?"

"Russia's one of fifteen republics. The Soviet Union is the world, more than a hundred languages. Now? Heat, like this. Samarkand, Tashkent, Moscow . . . The heat in Moscow is a pool waiting to be frozen by winter."

Ice cream, he thought. And a small boy's hand in his and a beautiful woman he could scarcely remember. Suddenly she had become indistinct, a face in a crowd.

Yashin, stripped of words, continued to stare at the front page of the *Herald*.

She said: "And they thought you were a genuine defector; they were crazy."

He said: "It's almost eleven. Time to see the show."

Macaws, cockatoos, parrots roller-skated, rode bicycles and solved mathematical problems.

A woman with thin hair and a nasal voice said to Yashin: "It's degrading; they should be in their natural habitat."

"They look as if they're enjoying themselves to me," Yashin said.

"How would you know?"

"They're laughing," Yashin said.

The Cuban said from behind them: "The car's outside. You got the cash?"

The Chevy was a pensioner. Tan, with liver spots of brown on its ancient skin, it looked as though it had suffered a stroke; its belly drooped, its hood gaped. "But she goes," the Cuban said, pushing his moustache into a smile. "Boy, does she go."

They tested it on Killian Drive. The engine howled with power. "Like I told you," the Cuban said, "in my country we know how to keep cars on the road."

Hannah gave him $1,030. The Cuban gave her a watch.

They picked up the US 1 again and headed towards the first of the keys linked to the mainland by road, Key Largo.

"The name of an old black-and-white movie," Yashin said. "A thriller."

CHAPTER 20

Saddlebunch, Pigeon, Snipe, Duck, Big Pine, Grassy, Sugarloaf, Vaca, Islamadora, Matecumbe, Tavernier, Plantation, Loggerhead . . . the 330 or so Florida Keys curling south-west for more than 100 miles into the Gulf of Mexico have been described as coral beads, jewels in a necklace, stepping stones to paradise . . .

The islands, thirty-two of them linked by the Overseas Highway, the US 1, which ends its journey from the Canadian border at Key West, are hemmed by soft beaches; Key deer found nowhere else in the world graze among the mangos on Big Pine; orchids bloom; osprey take to the skies over Lignumvitae Key where the heavy, hardwood Tree of Life grows; the warm seas swarm with fish – tarpon, barracuda, sergeant majors, snappers and bluestripe grunts – and the marinas are crowded with fishermen, arms outstretched.

But when a hurricane threatens the keys are vertebrae, the twitching tail of the United States. And off the shores of Long Key, so it is said, you can hear the cries of railroad workers washed into the ocean seventy years ago.

Hurricane Anna, spinning at 120 mph, clothed in cumulonimbus cloud eight miles high and generating enough energy in one day to sustain the US in electricity for more than two years, raised her skirts at 11.15 on the morning of the Saturday and headed for the Keys.

Hamilton, waiting for Yashin on the neck of US 1 where it enters Key West from Stock Island, heard about Anna on the radio in the CIA-issue Buick he had taken from the mansion on South Ocean Boulevard. It was black, the same model favoured by the Soviet Mission in New York.

Anna's eye, which had been wobbling, confusing predictions at the National Hurricane Center in Miami, had finally settled malevolently. And, said the newscaster, there was a distinct possibility that her ranking, four, extreme, would rise to five, catastrophic. Since 1900 there had been only two catastrophic hurricanes, 1935 and '69.

This century, according to the newscaster, hurricanes had killed 45,000 people in the Caribbean, the Gulf of Mexico and the Atlantic seaboard, 13,000 of them in the US. Most of the victims had been drowned by storm surges, barriers of water that climb from the sea into the area of low pressure in the eye of the storm and, fed by water carried on the winds, can top 25 feet. Much of the damage – 12 billion dollars' worth in the US since 1900 – had been caused by the hurricane's vanguards, sledgehammer winds and torrential rain.

But the greatest danger, warned the newscaster, was complacency. More than ten years ago it had been estimated that less than a quarter of the 40 million people living in endangered areas had been hit by a hurricane. "This time," the newscaster intoned, "it could be your turn."

He enumerated some of the century's worst hurricanes. David and Frederick in '79, Agnes in '72, Camile which killed 300 in '69, Betsy in '65, Donna in '60, which devastated Marathon, on Vaca Key, the second largest metropolis on the Keys . . . the Labour Day hurricane in '35 which, with winds reaching 200 mph, killed 408 and wrecked the railway built across the Keys by Florida's pet multi-millionaire Henry M. Flagler.

From the Buick, Hamilton watched traffic streaming towards the mainland on the highway built on the foundations of Flagler's railroad. Police with bullhorns tried to shepherd them; warnings and advice continued to pour from the radio – Anna was expected to hit an hour before dusk.

Hamilton switched off the radio. The sky was milky. When he and Catherine had spent a vacation in Key West three years ago, pretending for a week that they had taken out a new lease on their marriage, the sky had been infinite blue.

The sky, and the sun, had aided and abetted the pretence. So had Key West, an appendage of suspended time. White frame, sharp-roofed conch houses with shutters built by ships' carpenters . . . terraces aquarium-filled with green light behind idle palms . . . Audubon's birds . . . sunsets from Mallory dock spilling memories on the ocean . . . Hemingway's six-toed cats . . . all pickled in salt, and sweating air.

They had stayed in a small motel with a deep pool and a boardwalk reaching into the ocean where dawn and dusk anglers sat with the pelicans, and they had found casual moods that had bypassed them, and they had become tanned and indolent and often in public places they had touched each other. Among the strolling players in Duval Street, Cubans, Indians, pirates, fishermen, homosexuals and tourists; over a 99 cent breakfast in the Chit-Chat; on a glass-bottomed boat watching barracuda cruise among armadas of small bright fish patrolling the coral reef; on a seaplane flying over the Dry Tortugas.

And often, beach-warmed and aroused, they had made love in the afternoon in the motel room and they had wondered if she would become pregnant; then they had returned to the divides of Washington and she hadn't been pregnant.

We passed here on our way back, Hamilton remembered.

He watched a station wagon filled with dogs and driven by an old man in a yachting cap on its way to the mainland more than 100 miles away. Its engine coughed. One breakdown and the escape route, the only road threading the keys, would seize up. Drivers behind the station wagon played their horns; the driver of an ancient bus crammed with children spoke angrily with his hands. A few cars passed Hamilton in the opposite direction, heading for Key West.

A breeze sprung up. Foliage rustled. The sky was darker. Hamilton looked at his watch. If she stayed on course Anna would present her visiting card in seven hours; normally the Hurricane Center managed to give twelve daylight hours of notice but Anna had confounded them.

He switched on the radio again. The hurricane warnings had a new rasp of urgency about them. Sail your yachts into havens, drive your cars into shelter, batten down your planes,

177

board up your homes and get the hell out of it to the mainland.

A blue and white police car drew up beside Hamilton. A policeman leaned out of the window and said: "You figuring to get blown across the Gulf of Mexico?"

Hamilton displayed his ID.

"The Russian?"

Hamilton nodded.

The policeman said: "All we need," and drove away.

Hamilton switched off the radio. He had no idea what time Yashin would drive past, only that he would.

The fender-to-fender procession of mainland-bound traffic stopped; somewhere ahead a vehicle must have stalled. Bullhorn voices reached Hamilton on the strengthening breeze. A helicopter tilted above the highway. Horns brayed.

Hamilton had driven to Key West to warn Yashin that the CIA no longer wanted him to co-operate if they caught him: they wanted to kill him. But there were other things he wanted to say. That the two of them were never meant to fight.

This was the place to say such things, the end of America, but he didn't know if he would be able to find the words. Did anyone ever find the right words?

The traffic began to move again.

Hamilton lit a cigarette and began to cough.

*   *   *

When Tal had arrived at the motel on South Miami Beach in the early hours of Saturday morning the Russian snowbird had flown. One police officer stood outside watching visitors with martyred interest.

Tal who had left Deborah Klein in downtown Miami asked the night clerk, middle-aged with a boxer's nose and a boozer's eyes, about the excitement.

"You press?"

Tal said he was.

"Late, ain't you?"

"Different time zone; we have a later deadline."

"So what you want to know?"

"What the others wanted to know."

178

"Time's money," the night clerk said.

Tal gave him ten dollars. Yashin, it seemed, had walked out of the motel while the police chased a girl who had nothing to do with Yashin. Or so they thought at the time, said the night clerk, knowingly.

"She did know Yashin?"

"Judging by the shit the cop got on the phone."

"What room?"

"Twenty-eight. You wanna see it? You'll be the first; the cops finished in there maybe thirty minutes ago."

"I'd like to see it," Tal said.

"Ten from forty, the price of a double, leaves thirty bucks. Hey, you might get a bonus, a raise even."

Tal handed him another thirty dollars and the night clerk said: "They used to write about me in the papers when I was fighting."

Tal slid the key into the lock. The fingerprinted, photographed, dissected room was ready for occupation once more. A frayed, twin-bedded setpiece.

Tal lay on one bed, hands behind his head. He looked at the vacant bed. Had Yashin screwed the bitch here? Normally he never thought about sex – it had always ended in humiliation – but there was no norm any longer.

How had Yashin heard that the hunters were closing? A sighting through a slit in the curtains? A call from a bribed receptionist? Intuition?

I am Yashin. Why Miami? To get lost in a big city and meet contacts who aren't interested in catching or killing me, anti-communists who aren't pro-American either. Anti-Castro Cubans!

In 1980 when Castro had allowed political refugees, the boat people, to leave Cuba for America, he had taken the opportunity of emptying the jails of criminals. The KGB had also taken the opportunity through the Cuban intelligence, the DGI, of infiltrating agents into the US.

Two were still stationed in Miami.

Tal got up from the bed and went down the outside stairs. The night clerk was waiting beside his car with a middle-aged couple. "They identified Snowbird," he said. "Mr. and Mrs. Theobald. They've been giving lots of interviews."

"You people have a job to do," Mrs. Theobald said. She smiled forgivingly at Tal.

Mr. Theobald said: "Most of the other boys have been giving us twenty dollars."

"For church funds back home," Mrs. Theobald said.

"I'm an atheist," Tal said.

He climbed into the Regal and drove north. He stopped at the Doral-on-the-Ocean and called Dobykin's home number from the lobby. Dobykin's voice yawned with sleep as though he had taken a drug. Tal told him to call back from an outside phone.

No word on Yashin, Dobykin said heavily. But Center had decided to change tactics: when Yashin did make contact he would give himself up. Dobykin didn't elaborate. "Keep in touch," he said, urgency finally dispelling the residue of sleep.

"What about Kiselev?"

A pause. Then: "He was apprehended."

"Outside the limit?"

"One mile."

"Stupid. The FBI must have been on to him from the beginning." Tal thought about it. "More than stupid, irresponsible. The Americans will realise that someone has been brought in to kill Yashin."

Routinely the FBI fed every visiting Russian into their computers. They would have checked back when they realised that it wasn't Kiselev who had tried to kill Yashin on South Ocean Boulevard. Lvov would have surfaced immediately. Why wasn't he at the United Nations? Get Lvov.

Dobykin said: "I'm still not convinced that you can help."

"Simenov is."

"I suppose so." Whatever Dobykin had taken to make him sleep had dulled his venom.

Simenov was convinced because, at Lozak's behest, he wanted Yashin dead. Tal said: "As soon as Yashin tries to walk into the Embassy or the Mission or any residence he'll be picked up by the FBI. I'm the best you've got."

"I don't see—"

"No one's looking for me. Lvov maybe but not William Spivak, American citizen. So I shepherd Yashin back north. To Long Island. And with Yashin in the trunk drive straight through the gates at Glen Cove."

"But—"

"Call Simenov," Tal said.

"That won't be necessary."

Tal told Dobykin to get the contact addresses for the two KGB agents infiltrated into Miami with the Cuban refugees. He would call back in one hour, he said.

Two hours later he rang the bell outside a shabby town house shouldered by a club and a pornagraphic bookshop in the red light area on the periphery of Little Havana. It was 4 am.

The beat of frantic music pulsed from the depths of the club, all instruments except drums lost in transit. The silhouette of a man smoking a cigarette said: "Don't waste your time, man. All the action's here. You want a girl, mebbe two?" The cigarette lit his eyes. "A stud? You wanna stud, man?"

The door of the house opened on a chain. A woman's voice came round the aperture. "Who's that?"

Tal moved closer and whispered the password Dobykin had given him. "Santiago."

"A guy *an'* a chick?" the man in the doorway said.

The woman opened the door. She was middle-aged, blue-black hair grey at the roots, figure spreading beneath her dressing gown. She gestured up the stairs.

The man sitting at the table in the kitchen was less hospitable: he held a .45 Colt automatic in one hand, barrel pointing at Tal's chest.

He nodded at a chair on the other side of the table. "Sit down," he said. "Identify yourself." He spoke Russian.

His name was Lazishvili, a distant relative of the one-time godfather of Georgian crime. He had been planted in Cuba 15 years ago. Who could tell a Georgian from a Cuban? He had been activated in 1980 and had sailed to Key West in a fishing boat sardine-packed with refugees.

Tal told him who he was.

"ID?"

"Assassins don't identify themselves. I'm William Spivak, an American."

The Georgian said: "I'll have to kill William Spivak unless

181

he can prove he's someone else."

"Call Dobykin," Tal said.

The Georgian considered this. He was a man who measured everything, life even. His hair was Valentino slick, combed with grey. The hair at his chest above the V of his prison-grey dressing gown was white. One side of his face was prickled with stubble, the other was smooth as though long ago someone had tried to erase his good looks.

After a while he said: "Who is Dobykin?"

"You know who Dobykin is."

"I do?"

They stared at each other across the table. It was scrubbed bone clean; the whole kitchen was as clean as the street outside was soiled; a shelf extending along one wall was a parade ground of jars containing herbs.

The Georgian aimed his voice over Tal's shoulder. "Darya, bring a bottle."

His wife placed a bottle of Stolichnaya and two glasses on the table. With his free hand the Georgian poured two shots. He raised his glass. "To Mother Russia."

"I don't drink," Tal said.

"Then you're not Russian." The Georgian prodded the automatic at Tal.

"Call Dobykin."

"Drink." The Georgian refilled his own glass. Tal noticed that he had a blood spot in one eye.

"Get me some mineral water."

"Five seconds to drink. One . . ."

Tal had drunk vodka once in his teens. He had been disgustingly ill. He didn't doubt that he would have adapted but he hadn't wanted to: drinking was an assassin's private enemy.

"Call Dobykin and he will explain everything."

"Two . . ."

"Kill me and you're dead."

"Three . . ."

"Stupid."

"Four . . ."

Tal heard the Georgian's wife leave the room behind him. Curiously the centre of his tongue stung with anticipation. He picked up his glass. "To Mother Russia." He tossed back the vodka. It was like warm breath on his tongue. He felt it hit his stomach. It did nothing to him.

The Georgian's wife returned. The Georgian told her to bring mineral water, black bread, gherkins and two more glasses. He said to Tal: "Drunk like a true citizen of Kalaki."

"*Madlobt.*" Tal thanked him in Georgian acknowledging the familiar name Georgians gave to Tblisi.

"You're Georgian?"

"I spent a vacation there once," Tal said.

"An excellent choice. The Paris of the Soviet Union. Why did you lie just now about not drinking?"

"I didn't. Now telephone Dobykin."

The Georgian opened a bottle of Borzhomi mineral water.

"You can get anything in America," he said — and poured two more shots of vodka. He picked up his glass. "To Tblisi, the Warm City."

Tal reached for the mineral water but the Georgian stabbed the gun at him. "Fire water first, piss second."

Tal stared at the vodka. On Friday nights the streets of Moscow reeled with its blows.

He touched his cheekbones with his fingertips. The profile of the stranger. A stranger who boozed, went out with girls and made mistakes. One more shot? He tossed the vodka down his throat, washed it down with Borzhomi, broke a piece of black bread.

The Georgian did the same, and, still pointing the Colt at Tal's chest, said: 'Why should I believe you? You could be CIA, FBI; you could be anyone. The fact that you know Dobykin means nothing." The Georgian picked up a newspaper from the tiled floor. "For all I know you could be Yashin." Tal stared at the identikit picture; the Georgian was right, he could.

"Santiago?"

"Yashin could have found that out." The Georgian poured more vodka. "Supposing there is an assassin named Tal. Supposing he found Yashin. Supposing Yashin outsmarted him, killed him. That makes you Yashin," the Georgian said lifting his glass.

Tal picked up his glass without prompting. He sipped the

183

vodka this time, holding it on his tongue. It extinguished the prickling. It was warm in his throat. "If I were Yashin why would I come here?" Despite the gun he felt relaxed.

"Yashin is clever. Maybe he would pretend he's Tal to find sanctuary for a while, two KGB colleagues together. And at the same time pick my brains, to find out how to escape to Cuba. You could be anyone," the Georgian said. "I have many enemies," and to his wife: "Check him for wiring, take his gun."

Tal felt her breasts against his back. She took the Hush Puppy from its holster beneath the windcheater he had put on over his sweat shirt, ran her hands over his chest. "No wires," she told her husband.

Tal said: "I'm an assassin, I carry a gun." He tipped the rest of the vodka down his throat. He felt exaggeratedly sober which meant that he wasn't; he was pleased with his acumen.

The Georgian's wife sat down and poured herself a shot of vodka. She drank it and snapped a gherkin in half with surprisingly white teeth. She appraised him from brown, dark-ringed eyes.

The Georgian picked up the Hush Puppy with his free hand. He was double-fisted with guns. He said: "I've never seen a pistol like this before."

"It's for shooting dogs." The absurdity of the remark made Tal laugh.

The Georgian replenished their glasses. "Peace and good-will to all men."

They drank.

With a gun pointing at him Tal thought about Deborah Klein. Crazy.

He said to the Georgian: "What do I look like?" His tongue rolled the words like marbles.

The Georgian lowered the Colt fractionally. "So you don't drink."

"Tell me what I look like."

"Like the identikit."

"No really. What sort of man do you see?"

The blood spot in the Georgian's eye seemed to glow. "An innocent face," he said. He laid the automatic on the table, hand still on the butt. "Maybe I am drunk."

"Not you," his wife said. She snapped at the rest of the gherkin.

"Is that all?" Tal asked.

"It's difficult . . . a face from which bandages have just been unwrapped . . . I know about bandages . . ." He touched the smooth skin on his cheek.

His wife looked away; Tal wondered if she had been in any way responsible. Passionate, devious people, Georgians.

"No more vodka," as the Georgian filled his glass. It barely touched the sides of his throat.

"If you are Tal," the Georgian asked, "what do you want?"

Tal said he wanted to find out who Yashin would contact to reach Cuba.

"Which is just what you would say if you *are* Yashin."

"You . . . must . . . call . . . Dobykin . . ." Each word was inside a capsule.

The Georgian said to his wife: "Tie his hands and his ankles to the chair." When she had finished he said: "Very well, now I will call New York."

Tal closed his eyes; patterns swam like oil on water.

Voices. The Georgian's. "He's okay."

His wife's. "Dobykin identified him?"

"He said it was difficult. No outstanding features . . . He described Yashin instead. This man isn't Yashin. And Tal had called him in New York shortly before he came here."

"Spivak?"

"One of Tal's aliases."

Tal smiled. His wrists and ankles moved freely. He was in a bed; the sheets smelled clean. He was in a playground and he was playing football and he scored a goal and the rest of the team cheered.

*   *   *

Surfacing slowly, Tal was surprised to find that the vodka hadn't left an aftermath, none of the aching misery which hard-drinking acquaintances noisily endured as though the experience was a novelty to them.

He opened his eyes.

The light in the bedroom was gentle, the smell of the sheets

185

still fresh; he also smelled coffee. The Georgian's wife held a steaming mug in front of him. "How do you feel?"

Resting on one elbow, reaching for the mug, he told her he felt fine.

"Vodka's a clean drink," she said.

The Georgian said: "I've found out what you want to know."

Tal observed him through the steam rising from the coffee; he was sleekly groomed and shaved. "Cuba?" delighted with the clarity of his memory.

"Yashin made contact with Alpha 66. You know what that is?"

"One of the anti-Castro groups in Florida?"

"The Cubans in Miami are a close-knit society. It isn't difficult to get information."

Tal sipped his coffee; it was black and very sweet. "Key West?"

"That's where Alpha 66 sail from."

Tal glanced at his watch. Midday.

"How long does it take to drive to Key West?"

The Georgian spread his eloquent hands. "Today? Impossible to say: you're competing with a hurricane."

He handed Tal a handwritten sheet of paper. On it was the name of the Alpha 66 contact in Key West, the name of the Cuban-bound ship, the *Santa Lucia*.

When the Georgian's wife left the room Tal swung his legs out of bed and it wasn't until his feet touched the floor that he discovered that he was still drunk.

He drove with elaborate care to the Howard Johnson's on Biscayne Boulevard where he had left Deborah Klein. But the room was empty; nothing remained except a trace of her perfume.

CHAPTER 21

Cubans know how to keep cars on the road in Cuba, in America they aren't so handy – the geriatric Chevy began to cough five minutes from the Parrot Jungle. Yashin piloted it to a garage on US 1 near Goulds. There it dredged up a last cough and lapsed into silence, blue smoke rising from the hood.

A bespectacled mechanic who looked like a professor stared at the engine, pulling at the beginnings of his beard.

Yashin stood beside him. In his black trousers and white shirt he felt like a waiter. "Can you fix it?"

The mechanic shook his head. "Nope."

The forecourt was crowded with broken-down vehicles. The northbound lane of the highway was crammed with cars, coaches and small vans; southbound traffic was much lighter and faster. The sky was heavy; a foraging breeze blew from the ocean.

Hannah climbed out of the Chevy. "We've got to get back to the animals," she told the mechanic.

"Everybody's got a reason." He pointed at the other wounded autos. "How far you going?"

"Largo," Hannah said.

"Some people are trying to make Key West. Gotta be crazy." The mechanic took a spanner from the pocket of his dungarees. "I got three dogs, Dalmatians. Soon as Anna hits I'll bring 'em into the house." He plunged his hand into the smoking engine. "What kind of animals?"

"German shepherds," Hannah said.

187

"Good dogs with a bad name. Why? 'Cos they're big and they look like wolves."

He plunged both oil-grimed hands into the engine. "I wanted to be a vet. Instead I ended up with sick cars. Maybe one day . . ."

He straightened up. "Should get you to Largo. No further. You look after those shepherds, mind. Dogs need a lot of kindness when a storm hits."

Yashin glanced behind him as he steered the Chevy onto the highway. The mechanic was pulling at the straggle of hairs on his chin; Yashin hoped they would grow. He said to Hannah: "Animals?"

"The button on his dungarees. An animal sanctuary some place."

Yashin pressed his foot hard on the gas pedal. Forty miles an hour, no more. Drivers behind the Chevy sounded their horns. The Chevy whined, wheel bearings by the sound of it.

"Suppose we run into a road block," Hannah said.

Yashin tilted the plastic-straw hat onto the back of his head; he had debated whether to keep it on; in the end he had compromised – hat and no spectacles, half the description provided by the Theobalds. Hannah was wearing the glasses.

He said: "If the police try and stop evacuation traffic they'll be lynched."

"The CIA think you're more important than a hurricane."

"The local police won't." Yashin tapped the cracked dashboard. "Whoever heard of a fugitive escaping in a wreck like this? Whoever heard of a fugitive driving into a hurricane?"

He switched on the radio. Dead as the fuel gauge. He turned the Chevy into a gentle bend; the steering wheel that had been responsive on Killian Drive was a sponge.

On the opposite lane a small van had broken down. A Greyhound bus was trying to squeeze past it. Gasoline fumes poured into the Chevy. Yashin tried to wind up the window; the handle rotated impotently.

A white sports car snarled past, its driver brandishing a fist.

They reached the tip of mainland Florida. More than a hundred miles and forty-two bridges from Key West. A corruption Hannah told him, of the Spanish *Cayo Hueso*,

Bone Key, because of the bones of Indians found there. In 1860 the richest city in the United States, in 1935 after a hurricane destroyed the railroad, bankrupt.

But Yashin wasn't interested in what had transpired a hundred miles away and fifty years ago. A hundred yards away police had set up a road block.

*   *   *

The police had stopped an Escort. "Blue, like the one I rented," Hannah told him. At the wheel sat a man wearing spectacles; beside him a girl wearing a pink sun hat. The couple were gesticulating; one of the police officers had drawn his gun.

Between the Chevy and the roadblock drivers played their horns; some climbed out of their cars to shout at the cops.

A man wearing a brown blazer and a wig approached the police on foot. You could feel his anger from the Chevy. His wig remained motionless despite the strengthening breeze. The policeman with the gun waved him back; the man with the wig took no notice.

One of the intervening cars edged forward pushing at the fender of the automobile in front of it. Then all the autos began to inch forward, an inexorable cavalcade.

The second policeman held up his hands in defeat. He strode into the middle of the highway and guided the procession past the Escort. As each car passed him he stared inside it.

"Stare right back," Yashin told Hannah.

Three cars separated them from the policeman.

Two.

The policeman's face was at the window, sweat-bearded and furious.

Yashin spread his hands sympathetically. Hannah stared and smiled. The cop swept them past with one big hand.

They crossed the bridge onto Key Largo.

*   *   *

Tal left Miami as Yashin and Hannah Martin drove through the road block, two hours behind them in the congested traffic. He calculated it would take him six hours to reach Key

189

West. 6.30, the time the hurricane was expected to strike.

Sometimes as he drove he forgot he was alone and opened his mouth to speak. At such times he wanted to stretch out his hand and touch her.

Why had she gone? Because I made it plain I didn't want her, that was why. Because I left her alone. She had left at midday, according to the bell captain. That must have been the time limit she had given him. *But I have to go alone.*

Never had a car been so empty. Fear stirred inside the stranger at the wheel. Where was she now? On a plane bound for New York? He would dump the car in Key West and fly back to her.

But first I have to kill Yashin.

Her birthmark burned on his cheek.

*　　　*　　　*

On the approaches to Key West Hamilton lit another cigarette. The inside of the black Buick smelled like an ashtray.

*　　　*　　　*

The Chevy made steady progress through Key Largo. "Long Key," Hannah translated from a guide she had bought at the garage.

Through mango, palmetto and Caribbean pine they glimpsed the sea, Gulf of Mexico to the right, Atlantic to the left. The turquoise water was tufted with small waves; the breeze which was growing wings blew paper and plastic across the road; watery clouds approached from the east.

The northbound lane was clogged with traffic; southbound thinning as drivers peeled off to batten and barricade and evacuate their families.

Hannah charted the Chevy's progress by the green mile markers which began with No. 126 near Florida City and ended with zero in Key West.

"Butternut and Bottle Keys to the right," Hannah read. "Porpoises and baby sharks."

The mile markers led them through Tavernier, Plantation, Upper Matecumbe, Islamadora – "Purple isle, named after the snail shells that coloured it when the Spanish

190

discovered it."

They passed the Matecumbe Methodist United Church, Barnett Bank, blacks vacating shacks which a hurricane-force wind would scatter across the sea and thumbing lifts, Bud and May's Fishing marina, Papa Joe's, pelicans on poles . . .

Police on motorcycles urged forward traffic that needed no urging.

A roadsign cautioned: YOU'RE HERE NOW SO WHAT'S YOUR HURRY?

"How long can a hurricane last?" Hannah asked. "How long before you can sail for Cuba?"

Yashin who as a trained cosmonaut had studied meteorology said: "Anything up to two weeks. It depends on conditions. More likely to be a week at this time of year. Anna's probably got two or three more days' life left in her."

"What will you do when you reach Cuba?" Her eyes behind the plain-glass lenses were the colour of the ocean.

"I've got to call the mission first, convince them I'm still giving myself up. And call Moscow to find out if Lozak's been nailed."

"If you're cleared—"

"Then I still have to go to Cuba. To give myself up if Lozak's still in the clear; to escape from the CIA if he isn't."

If Hannah had been in contact with Letz in Miami, Yashin thought, the police at the roadblock would have stopped them. The logic warmed him.

Red flags striped diagonally with white snapped outside dive shops, Lady Cyana, Holiday Isle, Buddy's . . . Insects splattered against the windshield.

"So we can have a couple of days together in Key West," Hannah said.

"Battened down to our beds."

"According to the radio in Miami the hurricane will probably hit the middle keys. That's where Donna struck in 1960. She wrecked Marathon."

"Hurricanes," Yashin said, "are unpredictable. If they run into dry air rotating in the other direction they change direction. The eyewall is the danger area. Wind and rain screaming around the eye."

"You make them sound live. Monsters. Cyclops."

191

"They beome monsters. They start as nothing. Wet air streaming off a land mass, Africa in this case. The air rises from the warm sea, more takes its place, and you get rain clouds." Yashin remembered the lecturer at Moscow University, a myopic old man who made weather breathe. "The clouds spin with the rotation of the earth, pick up speed around a centre of low pressure and dredge up more water. A storm develops, then a hurricane maybe 400 kilometres wide."

"Why did you learn about weather to explore space?" Hannah asked.

"Launches can be affected by weather conditions." A grating roar from the exhaust drowned the Chevy's whine. "We learned a lot about a lot of things. We didn't know what we were to find up there. We still don't. People talk about infinity but there's no such thing; it's a word invented to describe what we don't understand, Man trying to adapt space to his own dimensions. Measurements, the enemy of truth. Light years, six million million miles, the distance light travels in one year. Absurd, isn't it, measuring space with values introduced to assess this pinhead planet of ours. What we have to do is re-think our judgement; as far as space is concerned we're Neanderthal Man."

Hannah said: "Do you know what we see when we look at the farthest star?" and when Yashin shook his head:"Ourselves, earth."

"Better than most theories," Yashin said. "Do you know what we need in space?" and when she shook her head: "A poet."

When they reached Marathon on Vaca Key, the second largest town on the Keys, the southbound traffic thinned dramatically, fanning out to marinas and waterside homes and the airstrip.

Yashin said: "If they're going to catch us it will be between here and Key West. How far is it?"

Hannah pointed at a marker. "Fifty miles."

Yashin stared ahead. Traffic fading . . . police waiting . . . an automobile destined for the scrapheap . . .

He glanced at the clock on the dash. It was 6.10, it had been 6.10 since they had set out from the Parrot Jungle. He looked at his wristwatch. Eight minutes past two.

The next keys, Hannah said, were Hog and Knight. From Knight the Seven Mile Bridge stretched 35,800 feet to Little Conch.

"So once we get on that bridge we're trapped?"

She studied the guide map. "There's a very small key after Knight. Pigeon. The Institute of Marine Science."

Yashin pressed the gas pedal. The Chevy blew noisily through the fractured exhaust. "That's where we're going," Yashin said.

As their speed slowed to 20 mph a motorcycle cop drew up beside them and shouted through the open window: "You're gonna have to get that heap off the road."

"Only a few miles more," Yashin shouted back. "Pigeon Key."

"You folks from the Institute?"

"Just joined."

"You picked a helluva time." The motorcycle roared away.

The Chevy crawled along the edge of the highway.

"Why are we going to Pigeon Key?" Hannah asked.

"To steal a car," Yashin told her.

*   *   *

Tal debated whether to stop the Regal and telephone New York. Even if she hadn't got back he could leave a message; it would make the car feel less empty.

He stopped at a phone booth in Key Largo. Sweat trickled down his chest inside the blue T-shirt he had bought along with a pair of jeans in Miami.

He made the connection, heard the phone ringing in Brooklyn.

The wind blew a sheet of newspaper into the phone booth. For as little as 2,480 dollars down, he read, he could be the landlord of an occupied, rent-earning co-op home.

He noticed a girl leaning against the Regal. Her hair was tight-curled and uncombed and she was round-shouldered as though she was defending her small breasts bra-less beneath a soiled sweat shirt stamped CONCH REPUBLIC.

She waved to him.

An old man's voice spoke in his ear. "Klein speaking."

"Is Deborah there?"

The voice was fretful. "No, she ain't. Gone south someplace. You from the UN? Two guys called already and I told 'em I didn't know where the hell she was. She ought to have more consideration . . ."

Tal said he wasn't from he UN, he was a friend.

"What kind of a friend?" as though it was unusual for Deborah Klein to have any.

"Just a friend. Can you give her a message?"

"Just told you, she ain't here. Left me to look after her mother single-handed. I tell you, mister, kids of today don't know the meaning of gratitude."

"She'll be back soon," Tal said. "Just tell her I called."

"Tell her who called?"

"Just say I telephoned from Miami and I'll call again when I get back to New York."

"You gotta have a name, mister."

"She knows it."

"She was acting kind of strange before she left. You know anything about that?"

"Strange in what way, Mr. Klein?"

"She kept singing."

The girl said: "Got room for one?"

Singing!

"Get in," he said.

Another mistake?

*　　　*　　　*

Hamilton wound down the window of the Buick and watched the cigarette smoke pour out.

Most people, he supposed, would interpret his actions as treasonable. If trying to stop a man who had once enjoyed integrity from being destroyed was treason then, sure, he was guilty. What would Catherine's verdict have been? he wondered.

He switched on the radio, station US 1 on 105 FM. "As Hurricane Anna threatens the Keys the hunt continues for Soviet defector Mikhail Yashin. According to informed sources in Washington" – Letz, Hamilton thought – "he may also be fleeing from KGB agents seeking retribution. Latest reports have Yashin driving north after a stake-out in a South Miami Beach motel . . ."

Which wasn't surprising as Hamilton, using assumed names, had twice called Miami with false sightings. He glanced in the driving mirror; the wandering lines in his face had found direction.

*   *   *

"You don't talk a lot," said the girl who talked all the time. "What do you do?"

Kill people.

"I'm a wages clerk," William Spivak said.

"In Key West?"

"I've got a time-share there." He had read about time-shares in the *Sentinel-Star* in Orlando.

"You should be heading inland," the girl said. She slipped a wafer of gum into her mouth and began to chew.

"So should you."

"I don't give a shit where I go," she said.

"You should."

"Why?" She chewed vigorously. "Just tell me why. Wherever you go you get screwed. I was living with this guy in Miami. Said he wanted to get married. Woke yesterday and he'd gone. So had my money." Her small breasts trembled beneath her soiled sweat shirt.

"You were lucky."

"Huh."

"Wouldn't want to marry a thief, would you?"

"Hey, a philosopher. My name's Peggy," the girl said.

"Bill."

He wondered if Deborah Klein was home yet.

A truck had spilled a load of oranges on the road. The tyres of the Regal squashed them. Zap, zap. A cardboard box flew across the highway shedding feathers. Palm trees swayed. The wind nudged the car.

The girl said: "I'd rather shack up with a thief than a holy Joe. Stealing ain't so bad. Not if you're hungry. Who makes laws anyway? People who don't have to break 'em, that's who." She glanced at Tal. "You don't look like you stepped

195

out of line in your whole life."

"I stepped out a couple of times," Tal said.

"You stole candy from a store?"

"Money from my mother's purse to buy candy."

"Wow," the girl exclaimed, "a real gangster. But you're not violent. I'm a good judge of character. Everyone tells me."

"You're right," Tal said. "I don't like violence."

"Not even killing insects?"

"I swotted a fly once."

"Murderer!" She wound down the window and flicked the pellet of pink gum onto the road.

A fat blob of rain hit the windshield and scattered into the shape of a spider.

*   *   *

Yashin swung the Chevy off the highway at Pigeon Key. The Institute of Marine Science lay below on the islet. To the left the Atlantic jostled with foaming waves, to the right the Gulf was calmer, green and waiting. Thunder rumbled; on the horizon lightning stitched sky to ocean. Rain hit the car in shotgun bursts. Ahead the 65-foot high Seven Mile Bridge, beaded with traffic heading for the mainland, reached for Little Conch Key. Birds flew west beneath leaking clouds.

The Institute looked as cosy as a farm. The Chevy coughed, the engine stopped, Yashin smelled burning rubber. He pressed the clutch and the Chevy coasted downhill. It stopped beside a lawn. There were no cars in sight; the buildings looked empty.

Hannah said: "We could stay here."

"And be drowned."

Waves slapped the banks of the key tossing spray into the air.

They left the Chevy and walked round the side of the Institute. A small truck was parked beside a packing case bearing the words MARINE SPECIMENS HANDLE WITH CARE.

Yashin climbed into the cabin; it smelled of diesel and

iodine. Maps, stale candy, a half-eaten apple, a packet of tissues, an oily rag and a St. Christopher key ring were scattered around. No keys.

He said to Hannah: "Did the CIA teach you how to start vehicles without keys?"

"They only taught me how to seduce Russian spies."

Yashin grabbed the wires beneath the ignition. He had only a vague idea of what to do. "If it was a spaceship I'd be okay," he said. He connected two wires, touched them with the wire from the starting motor. Nothing. Maybe the battery was flat. The noise of the waves was louder. He tried another two wires; they were as lifeless as numbed fingers. He swore eloquently in Russian.

Hannah shouted up to him: "My father used to hit the hood with a wrench."

"Get a wrench," Yashin shouted back.

She picked up a stick. "Okay, try again."

Yashin linked three more wires. Hannah struck the hood with the stick. The starting engine caught. The engine fired. Blue smoke gushed from the exhaust. Hannah climbed into the cabin beside Yashin. He made a U-turn and drove the truck up the ramp to the highway.

The bridge seemed too fragile to take the weight of vehicles heading north. The wind sighed in its limbs, the cries of the railroad workers washed out to sea . . .

Police stopped the truck over Moser Channel.

The motor-cycle cop saluted. "You guys know what you're doing?"

"Specimens," Hannah said, leaning across Yashin. "They'd be dead by the time we got them to Miami."

Traffic was piling up behind them. A bald man behind the wheel of a Cadillac shouted to the policeman "Save your speeding tickets for Anna."

Yashin glanced at the motor-cycle. The identikit was stuck on the tank. Someone had pencilled eyeglasses on it.

The cop peered at Yashin and Hannah. "You new at the Institute?"

"Started today," Yashin said. "Some baptism."

"Yeah, well . . ."

The Cadillac moved forward. Horns brayed. "Okay," the

197

cop said. "Take care." He waved them on.

An hour later they drove onto Key West followed by a black Buick.

CHAPTER 22

Now the wind was pushing the car and the rain was bouncing on the hood and streaming up the windshield. Tal switched the wipers onto fast; they conducted the girl as she talked. Tal decided that she talked to fill silences with words; silences had once bothered him when his lips and his tongue were struggling to make words; later when he no longer cared he had allowed silences to become caves and other people's voices had echoed in them, tinny and uncertain.

He said: "You don't have to talk, you know."

She stopped. Raindrops drummed, tyres hissed, wipers swished.

"You see," Tal went on, "you don't have to speak to communicate. Not all the time. We can share this" – he pointed at the heavy ocean – "without putting it into words. It's a pity people think they have to talk all the time."

"You're something else," she said after a while.

Self-consciousness and shyness. What a contribution they must have made to history. Americans disguised them with assertion; Russians bandaged them with suspicion. How many people drank to oil their tongues?

He wanted to stop the car and try the Brooklyn number again.

He said: "Why Key West?"

"Why not?" And then: "I'm a Conch, a native. See?" She tapped the motif on her sweat shirt. "Descendants of Bahamians who settled in the Keys. And I've got no place else to go," she said.

199

"You've got a family in Key West?"

"Everybody's family in Key West," she said. "And I can always hustle."

"Hustle?"

"Screw around."

Ahead a silver sports car swung out from the oncoming traffic to overtake a compact driven by a man so small that he peered over the wheel like a tortoise; it hit a green limousine in front of Tal. Tal braked. The Regal skidded into a series of serpentine curves; then it leapt into a bed of palmettos. The wheels splashed into water, the engine stalled. Tal turned the ignition key and engaged first gear; the wheels sprayed water but the Regal didn't move. He said to the girl: "You'll have to hitch another lift."

"No way. I'm staying with you. As long as we don't talk." She smiled; he noticed that one of her front teeth was chipped.

"No one's going to help us."

"Then we'll have to help ourselves."

The sharp-bladed palmettos lay at the foot of an incline. Rainwater trickled down it feeding the spongy soil. Tal unlocked the trunk and took a knife from the tackle bag containing the pistol. He checked the rods: the rifle was still there.

He began to cut palmettos. The leaves cut his fingers; blood greased the handle of the knife. Where was Yashin? In Key West probably. But he wouldn't be able to sail until the hurricane passed.

A squall of rain blew across the highway drenching him. The highway resounded with anger as traffic built up behind the crashed cars. A police car arrived, roof light flashing. Bullhorn voices boomed.

Tal took a bucket from the trunk, scooped gravel from firm ground beside the palmettos and poured it into the hollows gouged by the rear wheels. The girl was ripping the carpets from the car. He thrust the palmettos under the tyres; he placed the carpet over the protruding fronds.

He told her to engage reverse and let up the clutch gently. "And pray," he said. He went to the front of the car, leaned against the hood and pushed.

The engine fired. The girl's face was tight with worry. The wheels spat out palmettos and gravel. She cut the engine.

"You didn't pray hard enough," he said.

"I used to pray a lot."

"What happened?"

"The prayers never got answered."

"Maybe God was biding his time."

Tal rammed more gravel into the gouges and covered it with palmettos. The girl emptied her purse, ripped it in two and with the handle of the knife, wedged the halves under the tyres. She placed the carpet over the palmettos and forced the frayed edge under the portions of her purse. A bullhorn voice exhorted people to push. The green limousine reared over the lip of the highway and bounced into the palmettos.

Tal against the hood of the Regal. The girl behind the wheel. Engine firing. Into reverse. Wheels spinning. Two halves of a purse regurgitated. Regal inching back . . .

"Just biding his time," Tal said as they drove away from Key Largo.

"Do you pray?"

They passed a white wooden church.

"Everyone should pray," Tal said.

"You didn't answer the question. Did you pray as a kid?"

To whom? Lenin?

*   *   *

Hannah took over the wheel of the truck after they crossed Cow Key Channel Bridge into Key West. She drove along North Roosevelt Boulevard skirting the Gulf past the obligatory motels, Holiday, Quality, Ramada . . . past chain stores, the yacht club, Garrison Bight docks . . .

Hannah said: "I've been here once before. This takes us to the old town at the other end of the island, the real Key West."

The rain blowing across the island briefly spent itself. Yashin wound down his window. He smelled jungle scents. Bougainvillea, frangipani, poinciana and hibiscus daubed the countryside between resort concrete.

He asked her if she had come here with her husband.

"After he died." She swung the truck past two sodden

201

cyclists. "That's when this girlfriend of mine offered me the house.

It occurred to Yashin that she never elaborated about her husband. Even the details of his death were vague. Perhaps he was still alive, his death a masquerade to strengthen her CIA front – hostility towards a defector followed by sympathy. And a sharing of secrets. But I've told her nothing. And she *is* helping me to escape.

He said: "You never speak about your husband."

"Should I?"

"It's natural."

"Premature death natural?"

"How did we kill him?"

"Please," she said.

"Poison? A shoot-out?"

"What's got into you?" she asked.

"I don't know. The hurricane maybe." He stared across the docks; the water was knifed with small waves. He glanced behind him and saw Hamilton.

He looked at Hannah. She was frowning, biting her bottom lip. He said: "Take a look in your driving mirror." He watched carefully. She narrowed her eyes; the shock seemed genuine.

She said: "How the hell did he pick us up?"

Yashin remembered. *I'm going to Cuba*. Key West was Alpha 66's outlet to Cuba; Hamilton would have known that. There was only one road from the mainland to Key West. Easy. Or had Hannah kept in touch with him?

He said: "Lose him."

"In a truck?"

"Do your best."

Part of him hoped she would fail.

Roosevelt Boulevard became Truman Avenue. Hadn't he seen a Kennedy Drive? Where was Nixon? Hannah drove into the past. Wooden conch houses, white, green and gracious, stood shuttered and silent. Palm trees switched their fronds. The wet streets were printed with windswept pink and white petals. A rat ran in front of the truck. The Buick stayed behind them.

They came to the ocean. The waves were climbing. Spray

stretched for the clouds. Painted on a buoy were the words SOUTHERNMOST POINT CONTINENTAL U.S.A. KEY WEST, FL. On the quay beside an arrow: 90 MILES TO CUBA.

Hannah made a screeching U-turn. The Buick passed in the opposite direction. Hamilton waved frantically STOP. Hannah accelerated. But Hamilton had nothing to worry about: he could follow the truck until it ran out of fuel. What did he want?

Hannah drove north, turned sharply right. The Buick skidded, tilted; Hannah spun the wheel; the truck straightened up. An arrowed road-sign pointed to the city cemetery. A hearse was crossing a T-junction.

Yashin said: "Put your foot down."

"I'll hit the hearse."

"And kill the dead?"

"The hearse won't be alone."

"You've got room."

"But—"

"Now!"

Yashin glimpsed startled, funeral faces in the front of the hearse. It accelerated. The truck clipped it stirring the coffin. The Lincoln behind the hearse stopped in the middle of the crossing as the truck took off towards the centre of the old city.

The Buick also stopped.

Hannah drove through a confusion of streets becalmed in green light. Whitehead Street containing Hemingway's gloomy old colonial house; Duval, the main drag, Fast Buck Freddies store, Sloppy Joe's where Hemingway drank, boutiques and bars and Mallory Dock where crowds gathered to watch the sun go down.

"Too much white clapboard," Hannah said. "I'm lost." She stopped the truck.

"You must have an address."

She produced a map and pencilled a cross off Simonton Street. Despite the threat of the hurricane neither the dock nor the streets were deserted. Indians, Spaniards, British, Cubans, Bahamians . . . wreckers, smugglers, pirates, fishermen . . . What was a storm?

"A mixed race," Yashin said, pointing at a man in need of a shave wearing a red dress with a flared skirt.

"A foreigner," Hannah said.

Yashin showed the map to a man with a soft beard and dreaming eyes selling conch shells. "Over there someplace." He waved a languid hand. "You want to smoke some shit, man?"

A German who had arrived on a cruise ship from Miami directed them to the cross on the map.

It was a rundown conch house leaning towards a Spanish laurel. The white clapboard was stained with banners of green mould, moss grew between the boards on the porch. The house reminded Yashin of a telephone that never rang.

"The key's across the street," Hannah said. "You stay here, out of sight."

She returned with a rusty key. The door opened with a stage-prop creak. Powdered wood fell from its frame. Most conch houses, pickled in saline air, built from pine that hardened with age, had withstood hurricanes for more than a hundred years. Yashin suspected this one was reaching the end of its tenure.

The living-room was a tableau. Rocking chairs, a mahogany desk bearing a half-burned red candle in a brass candlestick, a quill pen and a pewter inkwell, rich, threadbare rugs on polished floorboards, a stag's head and pictures of Commodore David Porter, commander of the Anti-Piratical West Indian Squadron and John James Audubon, the birdwatcher, on the walls, a leather armchair that sighed when you sat in it and a green-marble coffee table. There was no trace of dust as though a ghostly maidservant had been in attendance.

"When did you last come here?" Yashin asked Hannah.

"Five years ago. Maybe six."

"It looks as if it's been prepared for us."

"The woman across the street keeps it clean."

"Doesn't your *friend* ever come here?"

"Why the emphasis?"

"I don't know." Fatigue settled like gauze. "I don't know." The house was a museum; he was a waxwork. "Is there a 'phone?"

She shook her head: a visitor had slipped a kopek in a slot and animated them. What now? Upstairs with jerky, marionette movements? The stairs creaked too. The bedroom smelled of lavender. He lay down on the four-poster.

"What's the time?" he asked.

"Four."

"Wake me in an hour. I must phone . . ."

"So soon?" He detected wistfulness, a chord from a Russian folk song.

He felt the warmth of her body beside him. An arm round his waist. The smell of lavender was stronger.

He closed his eyes. The kopek ran out.

*   *   *

Hamilton spread a map of Key West on a table on the terrace of the Chit-Chat restaurant where he had once bought 99 cent breakfasts for Catherine and himself.

It shouldn't be difficult to trace the Marine Institute truck. The island was only $3\frac{1}{2}$ miles long, $1\frac{1}{2}$ miles wide, and he doubted whether Yashin would book into one of the big motels to the east where he could be traced easily; he was more likely to find a guest house in the old town or one of the smaller motels in the Simonton Street–South Street area. That compressed the search area to a quarter of the island, and in that quarter the streets, with a few deviations, were geometric. And although bravado ruled, the streets weren't nearly as crowded as he remembered them.

He sipped black coffee. Sweat dripped down his cheeks onto the table. He wished he could take off the jacket of his grey suit but the pistol was still in the shoulder holster; when he got back to the Buick he would put it in the glove compartment.

A middle-aged man wearing a ginger hairpiece joined him. "Do you mind?" he asked after he had sat down.

"It's a free country."

The newcomer ordered toast and tea and, touching the hairpiece with the tips of his fingers, said: "You look kinda down in the mouth. You heard the one about the guy at the Olympic Games who saw this other guy carrying a pole?"

Hamilton said he hadn't. He decided to start with the

rectangle of streets, Fort, Angela, Amelia, Emma, Thomas, adjoining the US Naval Base.

"He said, 'Excuse me, pal, are you a pole-vaulter?'"

Then work his way east. The truck wouldn't be parked outside wherever Yashin and Hannah Martin were staying. But they would be in that area. What were Hannah's motives in helping Yashin? Love? If so he felt sorry for her: whatever the future held for Yashin there was no place in it for her.

" . . . and the guy carrying the pole said, 'No, I'm German, but how did you know my name?'"

The newcomer laughed. The freckles on his face danced. He checked the hairpiece again. "Gettit? You know, pole-vaulter . . . the guy carrying the pole thought he was asking if he was Polish."

He would also call Letz to check out developments; find out if they had realised at Langley that Yashin was travelling south, not north.

" . . . and he thought this other guy was calling him by his first name. Vaulter, Walter . . . gettit?"

Hamilton stood up.

"Hey, you left your sense of humour in the closet?"

"You should be on television," Hamilton said. "Great material."

"You mean that?"

"Sure. Here, allow me." Hamilton picked up the two bills. "For entertainment value."

"I got a lot more jokes."

"Tell them to Merv Griffin," Hamilton said.

"He's retired."

"I know," Hamilton said. Wait till Anna gets at that hairpiece, he thought.

As he turned off Duval he switched on the car radio. Anna was still on course for the Keys, still due to hit just before dusk. But, warned the forecaster, her stormtroops – rampaging winds, rain and surge-waves – would precede the eyewall. Drivers who hadn't yet reached the mainland should leave the Overseas Highway.

At 4.30 Hamilton began his sweep.

By 4.45 he began to wonder if he was losing his mind: he had seen two Ernest Hemingways, one on Duval near Sloppy

Joe's, another striding down Angela Street towards Duval, both grey-bearded and paunchy.

Then he saw a poster. HEMINGWAY DAYS FESTIVAL. It included a billfish tournament, a Hemingway quiz on the radio, A Night On The Town With Papa, an arm-wrestling contest – and a look-alike competition.

As if a mere storm could keep Papa off the streets.

*　　*　　*

Yashin woke just before five. Hannah was lying beside him, looking at him. The line beside her mouth had straightened.

"Two days," she said. "At least we have that."

"If Anna doesn't blow this shack out to sea."

"Do you have hurricanes in Russia?" she asked.

"Somewhere, at some time, we have everything. You see we are a world; the West should realise that." Yashin touched the line beside her mouth. "When the wind is freezing flesh in Yakutsk the sun is peeling skin in Samarkand. In Moscow we pretend to hate the cold; the truth is we worship it. First snow, nothing compares with it. Light the colour of pearl in your bedroom, snowflakes peering in the window, the calm that you can hear . . ."

"I can hear it now," Hannah said.

"And on the street *babushkas* touch your cheek if they see frostbite taking hold and in Gorky Park you can hear the song of skates on the paths and sometimes you can see the golden domes of the Kremlin floating in the falling snow and when you get home everything melts into one feeling. It's good to be tired in Moscow in the winter," Yashin said.

Wind blew down the streets outside playing a dirge in the slatted shutters.

"Could you live in America?" Hannah asked.

"A Russian is never happy away from home. He might lust after your luxuries but all he really wants to do is take them home, show them off."

"But you like what you've seen?"

"I'd seen it all before," Yashin said. "In black-and-white movies, only I didn't believe what I saw. I love black-and-white movies," he said, swinging his legs off the bed. "Does that answer your question?"

"What do you like best?"

He grinned at her. "Chutzpah."

Downstairs a clock chimed five. "I have to go," he said.

"Take this." She handed him the stun gun. It was called a Taser and it looked like a flashlight and, according to Hannah, it fired darts trailing wires and stunned a victim with 50,000 volts of battery-powered electricity. It immobilised temporarily and was effective up to 15 feet. "The cops love them," Hannah said.

Yashin bent and kissed her.

"Take care," she said.

She curled her body and on the lilac-coloured, lavender-smelling coverlet she looked smaller than she really was.

Yashin creaked down the stairs.

One of the rocking chairs was swaying gently. A draught from a crack in a window reached him; he stepped between the draught and the chair; the chair stopped rocking.

He opened the door and walked out of the house.

Garbage spun down the wet street; beer cans rolled in the gutter; the air smelled of the sea. Yashin leaned into the wind and pushed his way towards the Post Office on Simonton Street. The wind snatched a woman's hat and tossed it into the air. Yashin remembered a childhood joke. How do you tell a country girl from a town girl? In a high wind – the country girl clutches her skirts, the town girl her hat. The hatless woman laughed; so did the men watching. They wore cut-offs and sweat shirts and sandals and they were intensely carefree. Macho man was abroad this dangerous evening.

Yashin telephoned New York from a phone booth. Across the street a young couple were boarding up the windows of their house. Yashin was put straight through to Dobykin. Dobykin gave him another number to call in five minutes.

Yashin walked with the wind. Why had Dobykin sounded so complacent? A police car cruised past, bullhorn voice advising people to take cover. Yashin returned to the phone booth and telephoned the number Dobykin had given him.

"So, Comrade Yashin, where are you?"

"Virginia," Yashin said.

"Not far from Washington then."

"Not far."

"Is that wind I can hear?"

"I don't know what you can hear," Yashin said.

"Sounds like a prelude to a hurricane. According to the newspapers a hurricane is about to hit the Keys."

Yashin didn't reply.

"Are you there, comrade?"

"I'm here."

"In Key West?"

"In Virginia."

"Not according to our Georgian friend in Miami."

"I was going to Cuba to give myself up."

"A devious route, comrade."

"A devious game, comrade."

"Why not the direct route?"

"Isn't that obvious? The CIA want me as much as you do."

"Why did you lie just now?"

"There's always the risk of a leak."

Yashin heard Dobykin bite into a peppermint; it put gravel in his voice. He said: "Cancel your passage to Cuba."

"From Cuba I can fly to Moscow."

"We have a man in Key West," Dobykin said. "His name is Tal. He will bring you back to New York."

"Cuba," Yashin said.

"You see there's been a change of plan: if you don't give yourself up your son will be executed."

Rain spattered the phone booth. Yashin tasted blood.

"Are you there, comrade?"

"I'm here."

"Give me the address where you're staying."

Yashin gave it to him.

* * *

Hamilton telephoned Letz from a phone booth near the Old Lighthouse Museum.

Letz asked: "Where are you, Key West?" and when Hamilton hesitated: "Don't give me any crap: you knew where Yashin was heading."

"I did?"

"The Buick was seen crossing from the mainland into Key Largo."

Hamilton said: "That doesn't mean Yashin is on the Keys."

"I said no crap. Yashin was sold a beat-up old Chevy in Miami. What he didn't know was the Chevy was stolen. Clever, I guess . . . Yashin wouldn't suspect a heap like that . . . Anyway the owner reported it stolen and the number was fed into the computer."

"And?" Hamilton tried to adjust.

"A scientist at the Institute of Marine Biology somewhere along the Keys returned to pick up a truck after the headquarters had been evacuated. And guess what he found? No prizes . . . No truck, one beat-up old Chevy. And cops en route from the Institute to Key West report having seen the truck . . ."

"Okay," Hamilton said, "so I'm in Key West."

The hectoring tone left Letz's voice. He said: "You're probably the only guy in the Company who can get anywhere near Yashin. You know, you have this understanding."

"You want me to set him up."

"I just spoke to Catherine," Letz said. "She said there's still a chance you two can get it together."

The lie hovered on the line. "I'll think about it," Hamilton said.

"You do that. One other thing – we picked up Kiselev, the resident assassin, outside limits."

"Then who . . ."

"We believe the hit man is a diplomat named Nicolai Lvov who flew to New York from Moscow just after Yashin defected."

"Description?"

"Nondescript judging by the photograph taken at Kennedy. Medium height, in his thirties, pale hair, pale face, no distinguishing features . . ."

"Everyone has distinguishing features," Hamilton said.

"A nonentity. Maybe that's his strength . . . He hasn't showed at the UN for a few day."

"Any leads?"

"According to one of our own guys at the UN he struck up a friendship with a girl working there. We're checking her out. And Jack . . ." Letz's voice was creamed. " . . . Keep in touch. As soon as you make contact with Yashin call me. Okay?"

Hamilton said it was okay.

He cradled the receiver. Yashin, Hannah Martin, a Moscow assassin, me, all in Key West. He had walked past the truck bearing the words MARINE INSTITUTE OF BIOLOGY before it registered. He retraced his footsteps.

* * *

Yashin opened the door of the conch house with the rusty key. Hannah was waiting for him in the living room.

He told her what Dobykin had said and he told her: "In a way it's a relief. Now I have no choice."

CHAPTER 23

From a distance the first surge wave was a hillock of crested water slightly higher than its fellows. Tal took little heed of it. He was through Marathon, approaching Seven Mile Bridge. Despite police and radio warnings traffic in the opposite direction was still thick.

The road ahead of the Regal was clear. Tal accelerated. He felt as though he was driving along an endless jetty, ocean on one side, Gulf on the other. Terns stood guarding their nests on the embankment.

The girl said: "Hey, look."

The wave had reared. It was about half a mile away. It reminded Tal of a line of hooded snakes poised to strike.

"We've got to get off the road," Tal said.

But there was nowhere to go.

He pushed his foot down on the gas pedal, sounded his horn at a Blazer in front of him and swerved round it. The girl remained calm. She said: "Don't worry, everything happens to me and nothing happens to me."

"Strap yourself in," Tal told her. He braked, changed down, turned the Regal across the road so that it was facing the wave. Behind him drivers blew their horns; then they copied him. But the traffic on the oncoming lane was too congested for escape.

Inside the throat of the wave Tal saw fish, coral, sponges, seaweed. As it moved majestically forward it climbed. When it hit it was towering above the highway.

Then it swallowed the Regal and he and the girl were

212

encompassed by green light, squeezed by it. Tal felt the weight of the wave and its strength. It pushed the car backwards, buckled the roof. Tal's ears roared, his chest ached. He touched the girl's arm; she turned towards him and her face was still serene.

The wave had brought the ocean with it. They were imprisoned in water. Debris swirled past the windows. A baby peered through the windshield. The girl screamed. Tal shouted: "It's a doll." The doll, bright-cheeked and yellow-haired, swam away.

The wave went on forever.

Jets of water sprayed them from the edges of the window. Tal found that he was gripping the steering wheel. The car shifted again. He pulled hard on the handbrake. If ever there was a futile gesture that was it.

He was grateful for the presence of the girl in the car. He pretended she was Deborah Klein. He wished she had left a note. If I get out of the wave the first thing I will do is call New York.

The windshield burst inwards and water gushed over them. They raised outstretched hands to ward it off. Tal opened his mouth to shout, what he didn't know. His mouth was full of water; he felt it in his stomach and his lungs.

He breathed – air. He opened his eyes. The ocean was in front of him, sky above. The girl tried to speak. Water poured from her mouth. She coughed, more water. Finally she made it: "I told you, everything happens, nothing happens."

Cars were sprawled over the highway. Doors opening. Screaming. Streaming windows made photographs of children's faces. Starting engines whined. A Pekinese escaped and splashed through the water running off the highway; a pink-faced man wearing suede shoes chased it and scooped it into his arms. A few cars began to move.

Tal turned the ignition key. The engine fired first time. He depressed the clutch pedal protruding from the water on the floor, engaged first and turned the car towards Key West.

The girl touched his arm and pointed. A police car was sinking in the water on the Gulf side of the highway.

Tal glanced at his watch. Five-thirty. He wanted to be in Key West before dusk. He stopped the Regal and climbed

213

out.

A bubble burst where the car had been. Tal strode through warm water. Suddenly the sea-bed dropped away. He swam. Small bubbles fizzed ahead of him. What they had to do in the car below was open the windows: only then would the doors open against the pressure of water.

He dived. The water was mud-brown. He searched for the car without success and surfaced, lungs pleading for air. The surface of the water bobbed with other rescuers. Tal breathed deeply and waved at the girl standing beside the Regal. What the hell was he doing? Atoning for those he had killed? For the man he was going to kill? All he knew was that he couldn't have driven away with Deborah Klein beside him.

He dived again. The face of a policeman stared at him from behind the windshield of the blue and white car. Blood ran from a wound on his forehead. Water had risen to his waist. Tal tried a door. It wouldn't move. He mimed opening a door. The policeman stared at him. As far as Tal could make out he was the only occupant. He pulled the door again. Nothing. The policeman blinked. Tal surfaced, pointed downwards to the other swimmers. He sucked down air; his ears, eyes and chest ached. He dived again.

Again he pulled the handle of the door but the pressure of water was too great. He knocked on the window with ponderous blows. The policeman stared at him. Tal made circular motions with one hand, indicating the point where the door-handle was. The policeman blinked. Blood ran between his eyes. The water inside the car rose.

Once more. Tal surfaced, then dived; he felt his feet kick the air. The policeman's face was masked with fear. Tal performed his mime again. The policeman stretched out one big hand. Tal rotated his hand. So did the policeman. The window inched down. Water poured in. Tal tugged the door; it opened. Like a good cop the policeman had fastened his seat belt. Tal sprang it as a bubble ballooned from the policeman's mouth, hit the roof and sidled out of the window. Tal slid his arms round the cop's chest and manhandled him out of the car. One kick and they would float to the surface; they stayed on the sea-bed. Tal had to breathe. Now, he kicked again. The cop struggled. Tal rammed his knee into his crotch. The cop's body slackened. I must breathe. Cold entered Tal's lungs . . .

Hands grabbed him, broke his lock on the cop's chest, pulled him to the surface. He blew air and water like a whale.

"You okay?"

"Okay."

Two other rescuers broke surface beside him with the cop and made for the shore. Tal followed. By the time he reached land one of them was giving mouth-to-mouth resuscitation.

Tal said: "Is he going to be all right?"

The cop blinked.

"You did a great job," someone said.

Tal nodded slowly.

The girl squeezed his arm. "Some hitch," she said.

He walked towards the Regal. Traffic was on the move again. He sat behind the wheel.

"You okay to drive?"

"I'm okay," he said.

Save one, kill one.

He started the engine and headed for Key West.

Five minutes later he stopped. Dripping, he went to a phone booth and telephoned Brooklyn.

Deborah's father said: "You again? What the hell's going on?"

"What the hell *is* going on?" Tal asked.

"Couple of guys who said they were CIA have just been round."

"What did they want?"

"What did you say your name was?"

"I didn't. Those two men, what did they want?"

"Bastards wanted to know who Deborah had been seeing. I told them none of their goddam business." He cleared his throat; his breathing sounded asthmatical. "Is your name Lvov?"

Tal stared at the receiver in his hand.

"Are you there?" breath wheezing.

The girl in the car waved; Tal waved back.

"I'm here."

"I asked you a question, goddammit."

"No," Tal said, "not Lvov." So, after Kiselev had been

215

picked up, they *had* checked out all recent Soviet arrivals. Lvov, UN, missing – easy. He said: "Is Deborah there?"

"No she ain't. But she's sure got some answering to do when she does show. What *is* your name, mister?"

"It doesn't matter. Just tell her I called."

"Tell her who called?"

"William."

"William who?"

"It doesn't matter."

"Where you calling from Mister Williams?"

"Washington," Tal said.

The girl said: "Does she still love you?"

"A business call," Tal said as the Regal picked up speed.

Cars and trucks incapacitated by the wave stood by the side of the road; men tinkered with their engines, families thumbed lifts. Debris was scattered across the highway. Further on, ambulance crews were tending to Anna's first victims; the faces of those beyond help were covered by blankets. Tal counted five dead. Anna, bruise-black and trailing tentacles of lightning, loomed.

The girl shivered. Her nipples budded her wet sweat shirt.

Tal said: "Do you have a place to go? You can't hustle during a hurricane."

"I'll find somewhere," she said.

Lightning fizzed, thunder cracked.

She said? "What about you? Do you have a place?"

"Any motel will do."

"Make sure it's anchored to the ground."

Rain bounced high on the road. Palm trees bowed.

She said: "Maybe you and me—"

He shook his head.

"Married?"

"No."

"A girl?"

"Yes," he said.

They drove into Key West just before dusk. He stopped outside a chain motel on North Roosevelt Boulevard on the Gulf side of the island. He opened the glove compartment and took out a hundred dollars.

"No charity."

"Take it."

She opened the door and climbed out. He stuck the bills through the window. "Don't worry, I'll collect."

"Promise?"

"I promise," he lied.

"What's my name?"

"Peggy," he said.

She took the bills from his hand. It was raining hard and he couldn't tell whether there were tears on her cheeks.

* * *

Hamilton consulted a map of Key West. With a felt-tipped pen he marked the point where he had found the Marine Institute truck. Then he drew a circle with a radius of half a mile around it. He climbed out of the Buick and knocked on the door of a framehouse surrounded by a white fence. The windows were shuttered, a board had been nailed across the door. The house echoed with emptiness.

He tried houses, stores, restaurants, a couple of guesthouses, one catering specifically for men. Some were deserted; no one had seen anyone answering Yashin or Hannah's descriptions.

He switched on the radio. A surge wave had caused "widespread damage" to the middle keys; although Key West hadn't been affected there was little hope that it would escape the hurricane's eyewall.

Hamilton continued his sweep. The rain-loaded wind began to gust. A sheet of metal sailed down the street, a guillotine looking for heads. The street was deserted except for one other man.

Ernest Hemingway said: "Better take cover, pal."

* * *

It was dark and the wind was tearing at the roots of Key West when Tal telephoned Dobykin from a guest house.

Dobykin said: "Cipher's come to his senses – he wants to come home."

"Where is he?"

Dobykin gave him an outside number. "Call this in five minutes."

217

When Tal called Dobykin gave him an address off Simonton Street in the heart of the old town of Key West. "He's waiting for you," Dobykin said.

But not waiting to be killed.

"I'll get him," Tal said.

"Don't forget, you're a shepherd, not an assassin."

Tal telephoned Simenov in Moscow. Then he walked into the night. Into a maelstrom. The wind pinned him against the wall, rain machine-gunned his face. He dug his head into the wind; it was a wall. He struggled across the parking lot, arms crossed across his chest. A branch of a tree swept past clawing his face. Thunder split his senses . . . Glass shattered. His car was parked behind a wall. He opened the door and slid behind the wheel.

He decided to wait till dawn, good shepherd that he was.

CHAPTER 24

The house was being stripped away from them. The wind tore lengths of timber from the outside walls, ripped the balustrade from the porch, tossed the shutters of one of the bedrooms into the street. Yashin, lying clothed on the bed, Hannah beside him, pictured them defenceless in the hurricane as the last remnant of the house disappeared into the night.

But it was the noise that shocked him most as the winds in the eyewall spun round the tranquil core. A howling lament dredged from the depths of the ocean.

Hannah lay close to him; from time to time she trembled. He stroked her hair and tried not to contemplate a future without her. Not that it would be prolonged: the KGB would perpetrate another Yurchenko, stage-manage a press conference in which he would accuse the CIA of abducting him. Then they would kill him.

Where was Tal? Trapped, presumably, by the hurricane. Would the Center in Moscow understand? As soon as the hurricane abated he would telephone the Mission again.

He told Hannah.

"Call Moscow too," she said. "You said you had no choice. You could be wrong."

The house shook as thunder and lightning rent the night.

She said: "Supposing you had been a bank teller and I had been a librarian."

"You wouldn't have hated me."

"I had to hate you to love you?"

219

"That's how it happened."

"Love is circumstance."

"Love is love," Yashin said.

Glass shattered in the adjoining bedroom and the wind entered the house. Yashin opened the connecting door. Glass from the window punched in by the hurricane lay in shards. The wind swept through the open door taking pictures and ornaments with it.

Yashin seized one side of a wardrobe and, helped by Hannah, manhandled it to the window. The wind thrust against it; Yashin pushed the bed against it, two chairs and a bookcase heavy with words. The wardrobe held.

Yashin peered through a slit between wardrobe and window. The street, bared by lightning, was a wind tunnel. Debris flew; trees and houses crouched.

He looked at his watch. 4.20 am. He heard a section of the roof go; water poured through the ceiling. He shut the door. They lay on the bed again. "Perhaps it should end like this," she said.

"When the Russian comes," Yashin said, "I'll go down, you stay here."

"I want the hurricane to last forever."

"There's no such thing as time," Yashin said. "There is only now."

"No such thing as after?"

"Only now." He kissed her.

The electric light went out. He kept his lips against hers.

* * *

By dawn Anna had spent some of her fury. A temporary lull according to the meteorologist on the radio who said the winds that had devastated many of the Keys had reached a sustained force of 150 mph with gusts of 175 mph.

A temporary lull was all Tal needed. He took the tackle bag containing the Hush Puppy from the trunk of the Regal and, map in the other hand, headed for the address Yashin had given Dobykin.

* * *

Yashin said: "I won't be long. Don't open the door to

anyone. And keep this." He handed her the gun and picked up a bunch of keys.

The street was littered with bins, branches, clapboard, glass. Houses sagged, windows gaped. A garden hut stood in the middle of the road, a beetle Volkswagen lay on its back. Further down the street a dinghy with an outboard that had been plucked free from its moorings and dropped where it lay. Beyond an uprooted live oak, windowless boutiques and gift stores stood naked.

Water ran in the gutters and still the wind blew pushing Yashin as he burrowed into it on his way to the phone booth. The booth wasn't there anymore, just the foundations.

He turned into the shambles that had been Duval Street. Traders and restauranteurs were sweeping water from their premises. Two bodies were laid on the sidewalk. He found a booth; there was a queue outside. He joined it. Gusts of rain bowled down the street.

Dobykin's voice was indistinct, muffled by the wind.

"Thank . . . you called . . "

Yashin shouted: "He hasn't arrived. The hurricane's delayed him. You've got to extend the deadline."

" . . . misunderstanding."

"I can't hear you."

The wind filled the receiver.

The man behind Yashin tapped him on the shoulder and said: "Hurry up, pal, we all got troubles."

The wind was finding its muscles again. A police car cruised past warning everyone to take shelter. A stand containing picture post cards, bowled across the street distributing sunsets.

Yashin heard "Lozak . . . "

He shouted again: "Speak up."

The tap on his shoulder was a punch. "Come on, pal, you had your ration."

The wind had changed tack. Dobykin's voice was loud in Yashin's ear. " . . . sensation in Moscow. Lozak's under arrest."

*   *   *

Hamilton got lucky on the third call of his dawn sweep. The

door of a frame house was swinging on its hinges and he shouted into the uncertain light beyond it. A middle-aged woman wearing a striped towel around her hair and smelling sweetly of rum appeared.

She said: "Know something? I don't give a goddam if the wind blows this heap into the Gulf." Her words swallowed each other.

Hamilton described Yashin and asked if she had seen anyone answering his description. "He could have been with a girl," Hamilton said. She smiled lopsidedly. Hamilton described Hannah Martin.

The woman laughed. "That's funny," she said wiping her eyes with the corner of the towel which was coming adrift.

"Funny?"

"Saw a girl like that yesterday but she was all alone. Like me." The woman began to sob. Hamilton asked where she had seen her. "Been alone for twenty years . . ." The towel fell off; her hair was sparse, turning grey. "Where? Here, of course. Where else? When do I go out?"

So it was true, your heart did leap. "What did she want?" Hamilton asked.

"What the hell do you think she wanted? The key to the house across the street is what she wanted. Why else would anyone visit me. Why are *you* calling?"

The door slammed in Hamilton's face and then swung open again; but the woman had vanished.

Hamilton stared at the house across the street. Someone was knocking at the door.

The wind screamed down the street.

*   *   *

There was no reason why Yashin shouldn't answer the door: he had agreed to give himself up. Just the same Tal held the pistol under the map.

Hannah Martin opened the door.

"Comrade Ilyina?"

She nodded, "Come in, Comrade Tal, I've been expecting you."

*   *   *

Yashin saw Hamilton from the end of the street.

He turned back into the wind. It tore at his white shirt and waiter's trousers, sculpted the flesh of his face against the bone, ballooned his mouth when he opened his lips. A tree snapped and toppled. Hanging cables flailed. A blizzard of poinciana blossom swept down the street.

Yashin, bent double, turned into the garden of another conch house and picked his way through debris. He leaned against a sheltered wall of the house, heard its bones creak. Glass shattered, a dog barked, a woman screamed.

It was possible that Hamilton's mission was friendly; impossible to risk it.

Yashin thrust his way into the mutilated garden at the rear. The house where Hannah Martin was waiting was four gardens away. No fences to obstruct him: the wind had seen to that.

At times he was on his hands and knees. Past hibiscus stripped of leaf and bloom. Pausing beneath the hanging roots of a banyan tree. Russians were superstitious about the banyan trees that grew in the south of the Soviet Union – don't stand under one for too long. Russians were superstitious about everything. Yashin moved on.

The wind tried to push him past the house. He cut across its path. Reached the back door. Tried two of the keys hanging from the ring. The third slotted home. He squeezed past the door, holding it so that the wind didn't snatch it from its hinges.

A short corridor lay ahead. To the right the kitchen. In front a door leading to the living room. Yashin heard voices. He stopped and listened.

*   *   *

"He's not here," Hannah said.

"Where is he?"

"Telephoning Dobykin."

Tal noticed that she was carrying a flashlight.

He said: "He's coming with me. You know that?"

"He guessed you were delayed by the hurricane. He was scared they'd hurt his son . . ."

Flashlight? It wasn't dark.

223

She said: "Have you always known about me?"

"Only since last night. I called Simenov in Moscow."

Wood creaked, snapped.

Tal said: "Why did you help him to escape?"

"You wouldn't understand."

"I might."

She raised the flashlight.

He remembered the electric charge in the tunnel.

He shot her in the hand with the Hush Puppy, a marksman's shot.

Yashin kicked open the door. He grabbed Hannah, held up one hand. "It's all over, I just called Dobykin."

"What's all over?" Tal aimed the pistol at Yashin's chest.

"I've been cleared."

Not by Simenov, Tal thought.

He began to squeeze the trigger. As the wind thrust aside the wall to one side of him, as a supporting beam fell on his shoulder. The bullet knocked the stag's head from the wall.

Yashin leapt at him but a rafter fell between them. Tal tried to pull the trigger again but his arm was numb. He crawled towards the front door. Another wall fell inwards. The clapboard was straw. The ceiling collapsed, the bedrooms and room fell majestically. The wind howled, the house died.

Tal made it to the front garden. He looked behind him. Yashin was pinned to the heaped wood of the porch by a fallen beam. Unarmed. Tal transferred the pistol to his left hand.

The first bullet thudded into the trunk of the Spanish laurel beside Tal. The second hit him in the left shoulder. He shifted his aim across the street; Hamilton was shooting from the side of a frame house.

Tal waited until he showed himself again. Blood flowed down his arm taking his strength with it. The pistol was heavy in his hand. So many mistakes . . .

Hamilton showed. Fell back as the bullet took him in the chest. Tal stood up and let the wind take him down the street.

*   *   *

Yashin dislodged the beam and ran across the street.

Hamilton lay on the grass beside the scattered remnants of

a children's tree house. His face was more serene than Yashin remembered it, as though the wind and rain had cleansed it of questions.

Yashin knelt beside him.

Hamilton said: "This scene never fails. Not a dry eye in the house."

"As long as it's in black and white."

"Starring?"

"Gary Cooper?"

"Miscast . . . always a hero. Bogart?"

"Okay, Bogart."

Hamilton closed his eyes.

As a child Yashin had always been irritated by members of the audience who got up from their seats before the film ended. He stayed beside Hamilton until he stopped breathing.

CHAPTER 25

She sat on a chair in the lobby of the hospital filled with hurricane victims overflowing from the wards. Her hand was covered by a blood-stained bandage, her arm in a sling; her face had been cut and bruised by falling timber.

Yashin sat opposite her. "Hallo comrade," he said.

"I couldn't tell you," Hannah said. "Not just before you were leaving."

"It was a lie right from the beginning," Yashin said. Everything was a lie. Everything."

"Not everything . . ."

"Tell me about it," he said.

"At first I despised you. Why not? You were a defector, you were betraying Russia."

"You guided Tal to the house in Vermont?"

"And to the mansion in Florida. I was their informant in Domestic Operations. I made it very easy for them. All they had to do was wait till I called."

"What went wrong?"

"You went wrong," Hannah said. She stared at the blood spreading on the bandage. "That night after your son had appeared on television. I asked if you could betray your country and you said: 'I'm a Russian,' and I knew I couldn't go through with it."

"That was a ghost in the tunnel?"

"He came early. I was going to help you escape. I *did* help you."

"Did you enjoy your work?" Yashin asked.

Somewhere in the hospital a woman was crying out; it sounded as though she was giving birth. The lobby was full of walking wounded. Exhausted nurses moved among them. Outside, the wind had dropped to a sigh; tears of rain ran down the windows.

She said: "I was planted a long time ago. In 1970 when I was 12. My two *guardians* escaped with me from Czechoslovakia two years after the Soviet invasion. They told American immigration that I had seen my parents gunned down by Soviet troops. I was good CIA material: I hated Russians."

"You spoke the language?"

"My parents were stationed in Prague but they weren't shot. They were Russian. KGB," she added looking away from him.

"Why Polish?"

"That was a CIA decision. From the top. A good Polack background was more plausible. More acceptable to the Letz's inside the Company who still distrust refugees from Hungary, Czechoslovakia . . ."

"What about your husband who was killed by the KGB?"

"No husband," she said. "You would have been the first."

"To make you appear genuine to defectors? Hostility followed by a softening." It gave Yashin no pleasure to remember that the possibility had occurred to him. "Get him into bed. Is that what they told you?"

"I love you," she said.

An old man, small inside loose-fitting, striped pyjamas was wheeled past on a stretcher. He was calling out a name. Mary. His voice was parchment.

Yashin said: "And all this time you've remained loyal to the Soviet Union?"

"I lived in the Soviet Union for ten years before my parents moved to Prague. Ten years . . . the ones that count."

"But you grew up with American kids."

"It takes capitalism to make a good communist." She smiled at him sadly. "And communism to make a good capitalist?"

"And your parents?"

"My father died five years ago. But my mother was still

227

useful to the KGB . . .Dobykin must have sensed that I was reluctant to set you up in Florida. When I called him from Palm Beach he hinted that something might happen to her if I didn't co-operate."

"You risked her life?"

Hannah said: "I called a friend in Moscow that night I visited Alpha 66 in Miami. My mother is dead."

"I'm sorry," Yashin said.

"She was old, sick . . ."

"Tell me one thing: if she had still been alive would you still have helped me to escape?"

"I don't know," Hannah Martin said.

The rain had stopped. The grey clouds were luminous.

She said softly: "Mikhail, we're both on the same side."

"What side is that?"

"Ours," she said.

He stared into the deep of her eyes and heard lies. The walls of the lobby began to close upon him.

He said: "Goodbye, Hannah," and walked out of the hospital into the calm after the storm.

*   *   *

The runway at Key West International Airport was clear half an hour after Anna had departed. Tal caught a Southern Express flight to Miami and an Eastern to New York.

From the airport he called Deborah Klein and told her that he wasn't Yashin.

And when he told her he wanted to see her, to explain, she said: "I don't care what you were, only what you are."

Tal made one more call from the airport. To the headquarters of the CIA at Langley, Virginia. He told Letz he wanted political asylum.

That evening he was driven with Deborah Klein to a safe house near Scranton, Pennsylvania. And that night he reached uncertainly for Deborah Klein who was lying in the bed beside him.

On a hill overlooking the house Kiselev stared through the telescopic sights of his rifle and waited.

*   *   *

Yashin stayed on shore until the sunset shoals of red-gold light had sunk in the ocean before he boarded the *Santa Lucia* at Key West Bight where the battered shrimping fleet was moored.

Standing on deck, he slid his hand inside his shirt and touched the patch of scar tissue hemmed by suture marks between the 5th and 7th ribs where he had concealed the micro-film of the computer print-outs from Plesetsk.

Once he had regarded the film as an insurance policy. So why hadn't he traded it? Yashin gazed into the stars where all the answers lay.

The *Santa Lucia* picked up speed. He watched the lights of Key West receding and for a moment it seemed to him that the island, and all the other stepping stones to the great land to the north, were being propelled away from him.

He turned and faced Cuba.

Then he went below. Hannah was waiting for him in the cabin.

A selection of bestsellers from Sphere

FICTION

THE PHYSICIAN	Noah Gordon	£3.99 □
INFIDELITIES	Freda Bright	£3.99 □
THE GREAT ALONE	Janet Dailey	£3.99 □
THE PANIC OF '89	Paul Erdman	£3.50 □
WHITE SUN, RED STAR	Robert Elegant	£3.50 □

FILM AND TV TIE-IN

BLACK FOREST CLINIC	Peter Heim	£2.99 □
INTIMATE CONTACT	Jacqueline Osborne	£2.50 □
BEST OF BRITISH	Maurice Sellar	£8.95 □
SEX WITH PAULA YATES	Paula Yates	£2.95 □
RAW DEAL	Walter Wager	£2.50 □

NON-FICTION

THE SACRED VIRGIN AND THE HOLY WHORE	Anthony Harris	£3.50 □
THE DARKNESS IS LIGHT ENOUGH	Chris Ferris	£4.50 □
TREVOR HOWARD: A GENTLEMAN AND A PLAYER	Vivienne Knight	£3.50 □
INVISIBLE ARMIES	Stephen Segaller	£4.99 □

All Sphere books are available at your local bookshop or newsagent, or can be ordered direct from the publisher. Just tick the titles you want and fill in the form below.

Name_____

Address_____

_____

Write to Sphere Books, Cash Sales Department, P.O. Box 11, Falmouth, Cornwall TR10 9EN

Please enclose a cheque or postal order to the value of the cover price plus:

UK: 60p for the first book, 25p for the second book and 15p for each additional book ordered to a maximum charge of £1.90.

OVERSEAS & EIRE: £1.25 for the first book, 75p for the second book and 28p for each subsequent title ordered.

BFPO: 60p for the first book, 25p for the second book plus 15p per copy for the next 7 books, thereafter 9p per book.

Sphere Books reserve the right to show new retail prices on covers which may differ from those previously advertised in the text elsewhere, and to increase postal rates in accordance with the P.O.

FROM THE SUPERSELLING AUTHOR OF THE
CRASH OF '79

THE PANIC OF '89

Paul Erdman

It's a world where sleep is wasted time, where digital
screens are constantly flashing the latest prices and only the
quickest lock into the lucrative main chance with a
predatory instinct as deadly as the eagle's eye on a silver
dollar. It's the whizz-kid world of international high finance
where profit and power are the only principles . . . and with
the money market on the brink of a massive collapse, the
heat is really on!

The Swiss, the Russians and the Latin Americans are
conspiring to bring the United States' economy to its knees.
A combination of ruthless financial machination, searing
political power-play and suicidal terrorism is threatening to
trigger the greatest economic catastrophe the world has ever
known. Across the globe the PANIC OF '89 is about to
begin . . .

Also by Paul Erdman in Sphere Books:
THE LAST DAYS OF AMERICA
THE CRASH OF '79

0 7221 3355 3   ADVENTURE THRILLER   £2.99

A top secret SBS mission during the Falklands
War soars into explosive action . . .

SPECIAL DELIVERANCE

ALEXANDER FULLERTON

In the war-torn, storm-swept South Atlantic, a small band of
highly-trained SBS experts embark on a vital secret mission: to
sabotage Argentina's stock of deadly Exocet missiles.

The dangers are unthinkable: the coastline is exposed and treacherous,
the missile base is surrounded by vast tracts of open land, they must
infiltrate and destroy without ever being detected. Some say it's
impossible . . . but no one underestimates the SBS's lethal capacity.

And one man, Andy MacEwan, an Anglo-Argentine civilian recruited to
the team as guide and interpreter, has more than the success of the
mission on his mind. His brother is a commander in the Argentine Navy
Air Force and there is no love lost between them . . .

*'Good rollicking stuff – full of tension and highly authentic on SBS
technique'*
TODAY

'The action passages are superb. He is in a class of his own'
OBSERVER

0 7221 3719 2   ADVENTURE THRILLER   £2.99